COINCIDENCE OF SPIES

Also by Brian Landers

Empires Apart: The Story of the American and Russian Empires

The Dylan Series:

Awakening of Spies
Coincidence of Spies
Exodus of Spies

COINCIDENCE OF SPIES

BRIAN LANDERS

Red Door

Published by RedDoor

www.reddoorpress.co.uk

© 2021 Brian Landers

ISBN 978-1-913062-44-6

A CIP catalogue record for this book is available from the British Library.

Cover design: Rawshock Design

Typesetting: Jen Parker, Fuzzy Flamingo
www.fuzzyflamingo.co.uk

Printed and bound in Denmark by Nørhaven

Dedicated to my wife Liz, co-author of Julia's chapter and champion of Olsztyn's chicken cutlets

PROLOGUE

MAY 1980

The street in Yaroslavl where the Turkish general, Samet Demirkan, was assassinated was wide but unremarkable.

There was an irony in the fact that the avenue had once been dedicated to Catherine the Great, the Russian empress who had devoted so much of her life to killing Turks. When the Bolsheviks came to power it had become Peasant Street. Today it bears the name of local hero Yuri Andropov who, for a mere fifteen months, was the country's leader, or to give him his correct title, General Secretary of the Central Committee of the Communist Party of the Soviet Union. That last name change had not yet taken place when Demirkan was murdered. Back in 1980 Leonid Brezhnev was still in the Kremlin and Yuri Andropov was chairman of the KGB.

I wondered how Andropov reacted when told that the Turkish military attaché had been shot dead on the streets of his own home town. Did he nod in quiet satisfaction at a job well done? Or did he scream at the three KGB minders who had been shepherding our group around without noticing the killer approach nor even noticing him depart? Would the three have dared to admit that they had been distracted by the tour guide's story about a train full of cats?

It was a story that appeared not to interest Demirkan, who was standing at the back of the group. I had looked around for my wife Julia and noticed him and the American, Ethan Jacobs, standing a little apart from the rest of us. Julia was standing in front of them.

Winter was officially over but the wind off the Volga was biting and the whole group were wrapped in their thickest clothes. The tour guide, who had introduced himself simply as Oleg and who was undoubtedly himself KGB, clearly did not enjoy showing a group of middle-ranking members of the Moscow diplomatic corps around his city. He seemed determined to provoke an argument.

The French cultural attaché refused to rise to the bait when the guide smugly related the story of the Russian princess Anna, favourite daughter of Yaroslav the Wise, who was sent to marry the French king in 1051. After signing the marriage documents in both Cyrillic and Latin script she was amazed to discover, said the guide, how backward were the nations of Europe. Her new husband, Henry I, was completely illiterate and could not even write his own name.

Only Ethan Jacobs seemed as keen to argue as the guide. He had recently arrived in Moscow and had an innocuous diplomatic title I have long forgotten. He was in fact the new chief of the CIA's Moscow Station and had all the fervour of a true Cold War warrior. Jacobs pushed his way through our little group as the guide started explaining how Soviet education had banished superstition, as exemplified by turning the nearby Church of Elijah the Prophet into a museum of atheism.

'Why, ' Jacobs demanded, 'don't you tell us about the magnificent old cathedral I'm told used to stand here in

Yaroslavl, right where the Volga and Kotorosl rivers join? Why did the Communists blow it up?'

The guide trotted out the Party line and then tried to deflect attention with a story about a train load of cats. It seemed that at the end of the Second World War the city of Leningrad was overrun with mice and rats. The inhabitants there had endured three years of siege during which they had been forced to eat all their cats. The patriotic citizens of Yaroslavl had therefore collected together all their own cats and sent them on a special train to Leningrad.

It was at that point, Julia recalled, that she heard a gentle cough behind her.

Turning around she looked directly into the eyes of Demirkan's killer, but she only realised that later. The man was off before Julia had time to do more than register the peculiarities of his face. Demirkan was falling and Julia thought the stranger had accidentally collided with him. She reached for the general, trying to help him keep on his feet, but his legs were buckling. He was too heavy for her to do anything but cushion his fall.

The killer's gun had been pressed deeply into his victim's fur-lined coat and had in any case been fitted with a silencer. It was a moment or two before Julia realised how badly Demirkan was injured. Not until his wife pushed her aside did she look down and see his blood on her hands. It was then that the full realisation came: Demirkan had been shot and not only had she seen the face of the man who had pulled the trigger but she was almost certainly the only one in the group who had.

An image imprinted itself on her mind. Thin face, narrow nose, almond-shaped eyes, high forehead with short almost black hair. Most strikingly two deep, dark vertical crevices below the eyes. From more of a distance they would have looked like two identical birthmarks on the weather-beaten cheeks. It was a face she would never forget, although we were both sure Julia would never see it again.

In that we were wrong. Eighteen months later, when she had returned to her desk at the Defence Intelligence Staff in London, she would indeed see the face again. It was the face of a man the British police believed, quite wrongly as it turned out, was an IRA terrorist.

I had left the DIS, the Defence Intelligence Staff, at the end of 1977 in circumstances that would be unthinkable today. The new Director General was 'rationalising' the organisation but when he called me in it was not my departure he wanted to talk about.

'Your wife will have to go, Mr Dylan,' General Fearmont announced without preamble. 'We can't have a husband and wife working together.'

'It's not been a problem before.'

'Well it is now. Many would consider it most improper that my predecessor had his niece working here at all, let alone with her husband. It certainly would not have been allowed in the Army. She will need to be reassigned as soon as possible.'

Had Julia been in the room I knew just what she would have said: she had joined the DIS before me, she was therefore the more senior and so if he wanted one of us to move on it should be me. It was a view I shared, partly because I had already decided that spending much longer working as a civilian analyst in this part of the Ministry of Defence was not for me.

'If one of us has to leave why should it be Julia?' I asked.

General Fearmont looked bemused. 'You have a career here. Don't you want that? The reports from your superiors have been excellent.'

'So have Julia's. What about her career here?'

It was clearly a possibility Fearmont had never considered. I wasn't really surprised. My generation were only just starting to come to terms with women wanting their own careers, for his generation a woman's career path was straightforward and ended in marriage and motherhood. Julia and I had married earlier that year and so, he assumed, she would soon be moving on whatever he proposed.

I didn't know Fearmont well. He had only been in post for a matter of weeks and for much of that time I had been away starting to learn Russian at the Foreign Office language school (absurdly closed in the name of 'efficiency' thirty years later). I didn't want to lose the opportunity of adding another language to my bow but the more I saw of the new DG the more I was determined to leave the DIS.

'I will talk to Julia and see what she thinks about giving up her post,' I said.

'Nothing to talk about,' responded Fearmont. 'She's an RAF officer, remember. She will go where she's posted. It's in your best interest, your wife's best interest and most importantly in the best interest of the Service.'

When I told Julia what General Fearmont was proposing she was predictably furious. She was outraged that Fearmont had chosen to discuss her future not with her directly but with me and she had no intention of being posted off to some remote RAF station. My wife had started to realise that she was not cut out for life in the RAF but she would resign at a time that suited her. I half expected her to storm into his office but she had other ideas.

'We'll see,' she responded and set about plotting. She

phoned her uncle. 'Thomas and I have a small problem,' she told him.

Admiral Lord Grimspound, Julia's uncle and General Fearmont's predecessor, was a popular figure in Intelligence circles, despite the occasional run-in with colleagues in the Secret Intelligence Service, MI6. He was what today would be described as a consummate networker. Back then he was merely known as a clubbable sort of chap. He enjoyed nothing more than coming up to London from his retirement home in Cornwall for lunch at The Reform with the Permanent Secretary of the Ministry of Defence, tea in a much more discreet club with someone high up in MI6 and dinner with former colleagues at somewhere like the In and Out, which in those days was still in its original premises in Piccadilly.

As a result of Lord Grimspound's endeavours General Fearmont soon found himself being reminded of the wider policy agenda within which the Defence Intelligence Staff operated: the need to improve cooperation between the DIS and MI6, the need to demonstrate a commitment to equal opportunities (where practical) for women, the need to keep close to the evolving situation in Eastern Europe. A plan emerged to which he reluctantly agreed.

The upshot was that I left the DIS and joined MI6, where I would finish my Russian course, have a three-week induction at Fort Monckton, the Service's training base in Hampshire, and then take up a position at our Embassy in Moscow. Julia would leave DIS headquarters immediately and after two months of what was termed 'furlough' be sent to increase the DIS contingent in the Moscow Embassy from two to three.

To some it might have seemed that Moscow was a plum

posting but in those days the city was unimaginably dreary. It was the worst of the Brezhnev era. After the glimmer of hope that had followed the period of so-called détente the Soviet Union had collapsed again into economic stagnation. Repression was not as bad as in Stalin's day but perestroika and glasnost were not even a glimmer in anyone's eye. The enormous GUM store on Red Square, which today is a mass of expensive boutiques and trendy coffee shops, was then floor upon floor of monotonous wooden counters with either no stock or overflowing with whatever useless commodity a state factory in some distant republic had decided to produce that month.

One of our local staff told me that she had spent a whole day dragging her young daughter from place to place trying to find a pair of school shoes that were the right size. In the end she had found a pair that would do, she said, although the left shoe was significantly smaller than the right. Shopping to Muscovites was very different to shopping back home.

I learned to see behind the Cold War slogans. I remembered university friends thinking they were being witty when they parroted the old aphorism that capitalism is the exploitation of man by man while communism is the exact opposite. To me it seemed simply that capitalism encourages us to buy what we don't need while communism stops people buying what they do need.

In the West the focus is on consumption and in the East it is on production. In London the shop assistant is there to sell, in Moscow, in those days, the shop assistant was there to distribute. Capitalist firms survive by producing what consumers can be persuaded to buy; they make a profit by using the minimum of resources. In Soviet Russia factory managers survived by hitting absurd targets; they did so by using every man, woman and machine available.

The result, as I was told at a US Embassy party, is that everyone in Russia may have a job but everyone in America has a television, an automobile and a McDonald's.

Embassy life proved claustrophobic and uninspiring. Julia and I as a married couple were novelties, even more so given Julia's RAF rank, but we were low down in the Embassy hierarchy. Although ostensibly I was a junior member of the press and public affairs team everyone knew that I was a spook and some kept their distance as a result. Others treated us as something of a joke.

We had not been in Moscow for long when the Embassy's 'cinema' screened the latest James Bond film, *The Spy Who Loved Me*, in which Roger Moore as Bond teamed up with a glamorous KGB major to find stolen submarine secrets. The film prompted great hilarity as my colleagues debated which was more improbable: a glamorous KGB officer or a dashingly handsome British spy. Julia and I had another cause to smile, we had actually met while investigating stolen submarine secrets.

The Russian authorities wanted us to live a quarantined existence, kept away from all contact with the population around us.

Our flat was inside a walled compound and when we went outside we were often followed, not particularly discreetly, by a dark-suited KGB minion. His role was less to observe us than to keep Russians away. We could drive around more or less freely but our distinctive diplomatic plates warned the general population not to get too close. We assumed that our flat was bugged and played games with those poor souls who must have spent hours listening to our banal conversations.

I used to leave Shostakovich's Symphony No. 13 playing when we went out. Shostakovich's commemoration of the massacre of tens of thousands of Jews by the Germans at Babi Yar had been premiered by the Moscow Philharmonic despite the vehement opposition of Khrushchev but had disappeared from the Philharmonic's repertoire after just three performances. Fortunately a recording had been smuggled to the West and I wondered what my KGB eavesdropper made of it: Babi Yar had been rewritten by the official Soviet historians as a massacre not of Jews but of Russian patriots.

'Give the man a break,' Julia would sometimes urge, replacing Shostakovich with the ubiquitous Abba.

'Knowing Me, Knowing You' playing repeatedly in a dingy bar in Sicily had become the soundtrack of our honeymoon; in Moscow, 'Take a Chance on Me' became the anthem of the early years of our marriage. Our anonymous eavesdropper probably preferred Julia's very worn copy of *Grease*: John Travolta and Olivia Newton-John endlessly celebrating glorious Summer Nights as we battled Moscow's freezing winters.

In terms of our work both Julia and I were kept busy by two events well away from Moscow. The invasion that was and the invasion that wasn't, at least for now.

The Russian invasion of Afghanistan suddenly put the Red Army back on the agenda in London and Washington. Any snippet of information was pored over, however inconsequential. Julia received an endless stream of requests for detail on Russian troop movements which she could not possibly obtain and which would have been much better directed at our Embassy in Kabul. I spent hours with journalists, Western not Russian of course, trying to pick their brains while they pretended not to know what I was doing and I pretended to drink as much as them.

The other matter exercising the minds of our masters in Whitehall was the possibility of the Red Army mounting a second invasion, this time in Europe. Since the Second World War Russian tanks had stood ready to suppress any signs of dissent in Eastern Europe. Workers' revolts in East Germany in 1953, Hungary in 1956 and Czechoslovakia in 1968 had been brutally crushed. As the 1970s drew to a close it looked as though Poland might be next on the list.

One report claimed that in the previous twelve months more than half the adult population of Poland had taken part in some form of political protest. Shipyard workers in the north and miners in the south brought the country to a halt. Dissidents like Jacek Kuroń and Adam Michnik had long played hide and seek with the Polish secret police, the SB, but their underground publications had only a tiny circulation in Poland and their names were more widely known abroad. But now men like Feliks Radlowski were starting to bring together the propaganda skills of the dissidents and the political muscle of the labour activists. Lech Walesa and Solidarity were becoming a real threat to the government.

In Moscow febrile rumours started to circulate. Some of my journalist contacts assured me that the Russian Politburo had refused their Polish comrades' desperate requests for military intervention while others were equally confident that the Politburo were threatening exactly such intervention which the Poles were desperate to fend off. Solid information about the Russian leadership's intentions was impossible to obtain. We were reduced to trying to track military movements by looking at the photos of military parades in local papers. London undoubtedly learned more from the Americans who passed over selected extracts of the intelligence gathered from their spy planes.

I decided that as I had originally been recruited as a linguist, and now had a pretty good grasp of Russian, my career might benefit if I spent my evenings learning Polish. Abba and Travolta made way for Mateusz and Weronika introducing themselves and urging me to repeat phrases I would probably never need. When would I want to ask someone where to catch the train for Gdańsk?

As it turned out a lot sooner than I expected.

Moving from the Defence Intelligence Staff to MI6, the Secret Intelligence Service, had been quite a culture shock. The DIS had always been very conscious that it was a junior partner in the British Intelligence establishment, something MI6 was always happy to make clear. The Service, as I quickly learned to call what the DIS had simply referred to as Six, was only loosely attached to the Foreign Office. From being simply a Whitehall civil servant I found myself amongst a group of men, and at the junior level women, convinced that their superior intellect, innate sophistication and deep understanding of the 'real world' enabled them to be the ultimate guardians of the nation's future. It was an arrogance that, perhaps worryingly, I felt myself beginning to embrace. The Service was special and made its people feel special.

And it was secret. I told myself that I had joined the Service to do something for my country but the truth was I enjoyed being in a secret world, knowing what others didn't know, going where others couldn't go.

The MI6 head of station in Moscow at that time, Jeremy Grundig, was one of the breed now reaching the top of the Service who had been too young to serve in the Second World War. A generation that felt they had missed out on the action but could still feel superior to people, like me, who came of age long after conscription disappeared.

'Korea was my war,' he once told me.

He omitted to mention that the nearest he had been to Korea during his national service was a parade ground somewhere in Germany. He was a Cold War warrior confident he knew exactly where the world should be going but not knowing, or even caring, where it had come from.

It was Jeremy Grundig who suggested the trip to Yaroslavl.

'You should get to see more of the country,' he said. 'We don't have many opportunities to venture out. Take your wife, I'm sure she will enjoy it. Who knows, you may see something interesting.'

'Interesting' is perhaps not the most felicitous way to describe the man standing next to you being murdered.

Our immediate reaction to General Demirkan's murder was total shock. One minute an orderly group of diplomats and their minders were clustered around our guide, the next there was a spreading sense of confusion and then total pandemonium as it became clear what had happened. One of our KGB minders produced a gun which he waved around to no purpose. Another started shouting into his radio. The American Jacobs screamed at people to get off the street. Only Julia seemed to remain calm, her arms wrapped around the gently moaning wife of the murdered man.

A police car arrived and then two more. No sign of an ambulance. And no sign of the attacker.

A lorry load of soldiers appeared but the officer in charge clearly had no idea what to do. He tried to shepherd us back to our coach but Jacobs, who had clearly appointed himself our leader, was having none of that.

It was ten minutes before an ambulance arrived. Along with it came another police car from which emerged a civilian who promptly started to exercise his authority by pouncing on our tour guide, Oleg, and demanding to know why he had not been informed that a group of foreigners was visiting his city. Only after that did anything like a coordinated police operation stumble into action. Julia had given Oleg a description of the assassin but only two other members of our group had even noticed the man.

An official from the Australian Embassy had seen the man walking towards us but could only confirm the odd marks on the man's face.

A Japanese woman had seen the man hurrying away and described what he was wearing. She was surprisingly precise on everything from his boots to his headgear but her description could have fitted half the men in Yaroslavl, variety was not a characteristic of the clothing available in Soviet Russia.

Both the Australian and the Japanese confirmed that the man was tall, heavy and moved quickly, none of which helped very much.

Nevertheless the circle of soldiers and police were told to fan out through the town and track the criminal down. It was now almost fifteen minutes since the murder and the chance of tracking anyone down by this time, I thought, was non-existent.

A police photographer appeared. After taking pictures

of the body which the ambulance crew had left lying on the street he started taking photographs of every foreigner in sight. In Russia being overzealous in the presence of your superiors is always wise.

The civilian then announced that we must all accompany him for questioning. That struck me as not unreasonable in the circumstances but both Oleg and Jacobs objected strongly. The argument was only concluded when the civilian was called back to his police car where we could see him gesticulating into his radio. I don't know what the person at the other end said but the civilian suddenly slammed down the radio, shouted a command to his driver and screeched away. I never saw him again.

Oleg shepherded us towards the coach and this time Jacobs acquiesced. The body of the dead man was being loaded on to an ambulance with his wife still by his side. Julia ran over to her and the next minute they were both climbing into the ambulance. Oleg looked as if he was going to object but then thought better of it. The important thing for him was to get the rest of us off his patch. He gave an unsmiling wave goodbye and the coach set off back to Moscow.

The assassination in Yaroslavl filled all of our thoughts for the next few days. Ethan Jacobs and the US Embassy were treating the death as a major diplomatic incident. Their Ambassador seemed determined to outdo the Turkish Ambassador in the loudness of his protests about the Russian failure to provide proper protection. He insisted that every country that had been represented in our group should deliver protests pointing out that any one of us could have been the victim. That, I thought, was unlikely; General Demirkan had not been selected at random.

Julia had returned from Yaroslavl well after midnight to find a telex from London suggesting she travel to Ankara to attend General Demirkan's funeral. Packing her dress uniform she was off on the same flight as the general's widow and the poor man's body. He had been due to end his tour in Moscow the following month but this was not the return home he and his wife had been looking forward to. In accordance with Turkish tradition the funeral took place within a matter of hours and Julia was back two days later. To her surprise she had found one of the Defence Intelligence Staff bigwigs, the Deputy Director General Adam Joseff, at the funeral. Apparently he had met the dead man and afterwards he interrogated Julia at length about the circumstances of the murder.

By the time she returned every possible theory about the assassination had been explored, discounted, resurrected and reported back to ministries around the world.

The view of my service, expounded with vehemence rather than evidence by Jeremy Grundig, was that the KGB were entirely responsible. In a police state like Russia he insisted it was inconceivable that anyone else could have mounted such an operation. When asked why the KGB should have wanted to kill Demirkan he suggested that perhaps they had tried to recruit him and reacted violently when they were rebuffed. Even he must have realised how flimsy that sounded but his theory was endorsed with equal force by Ethan Jacobs.

The CIA man asserted that even if Grundig was wrong about their motive the KGB, which Jacobs always referred to as 'The Opposition' or 'The Other Side', had certainly killed the Turkish general. Perhaps Demirkan had discovered something embarrassing to the Russian regime, perhaps he had uncovered a mole in the Turkish Embassy or perhaps even in somebody else's Embassy.

Most people agreed that somehow someone within the sprawling Russian intelligence apparatus must have been involved, although nobody really had any proof.

Only two people seemed to discount Russian responsibility. The French military attaché in Moscow blamed everything on the Americans, not for the first time. Demirkan, he claimed, had once told him that the Americans were constantly interfering in Turkish affairs. And Adam Joseff back in London, perhaps relying on his conversation with Julia at the funeral, insisted that it just didn't smell like a Russian operation. Perhaps, Joseff suggested, it was the work of one of the exiled Kurdish groups the KGB had been known to support. He was immediately countered by Grundig who pointed out that such groups would have been quick to claim credit: a week after the murder nobody had tried to do so.

It was difficult to say what the Russians thought. They quickly rounded up all sorts of suspects: petty criminals, political dissidents and an Armenian student who happened to be in Yaroslavl at the time. Mugshots were sent to the Embassy but Julia reported that none of them even vaguely resembled the man she had seen.

Julia's description of the marks on the man's cheek had caused great confusion. Grundig insisted on calling him Scarface, like the American gangster Al Capone. Julia made clear that the marks were not scars. She made the mistake of mentioning they were more like Mongolian Spots; a friend of ours had given birth to a child with the

13

distinctive blue birthmark just before we left London. Jacobs had immediately pounced on this and began referring to the killer as The Mongolian even though Julia insisted that the man did not look at all Mongolian other than a slightly Asian cast to his eyes.

The day after her return from Ankara the Ambassador received a formal request from the Russian authorities for Julia to be interviewed. After much toing and froing a meeting was eventually agreed with a colonel of police. He arrived with two men introduced as his assistants, one of whom did most of the talking. Julia was accompanied by two of our Consular staff to make sure she said nothing that might be used against us. The interview provided the Russians with no information we had not given them at the time and provided us with no indication of where their investigation was heading, although as their questioning became more belligerent Julia felt that she would soon be seeing her own photograph amongst the suspect mugshots.

Some weeks after the murder we received an unexpected visit from one of the higher-ups in the Service. I was no longer the newcomer I had been when I first transferred from the DIS to MI6 but being stationed in Moscow meant that I still only knew a handful of my colleagues back in London. Justin Brasenose was one of the few I had come across before. About the time I first joined the DIS there had been a massive falling out within the Intelligence establishment during which Brasenose alleged, wrongly, that there was a Russian mole in the DIS.

I hadn't liked the man then but that was seven years ago. When he arrived in Moscow I immediately started to revise my judgement. Perhaps that was a sign that I was going native but I preferred to think that Brasenose had changed.

'Good to see you again,' he greeted me. 'Not as warm as our last meeting.' He might have been talking about the temperature outside, our previous meeting had been in the Caribbean, but I suspect he was remembering the heated nature of that encounter.

The old Brasenose had been a man in a hurry, willing to sacrifice anything and anyone on the altar of ambition. Seven years on he was where he always believed he belonged: at the Service's top table. He was recognised as part of the Intelligence establishment. Now he was content to look around not simply ahead. Considered reflection had replaced immediate reaction. The patronising had given way to the patrician.

He had come prepared for the Moscow weather and wore a woollen greatcoat in army green with wide wrap-over lapels which he somehow managed to make look stylish. The coat's soft-brushed jersey lining complemented the colours of his Liberty print scarf and the double row of leather buttons perfectly matched the gloves he held in one hand.

He announced that he was here to conduct a security review, although it soon became clear that physical security was not his area of expertise.

Julia and I were separately taken through the events in Yaroslavl in painstaking detail. Brasenose was far more conscientious in that respect than Jeremy Grundig had been. He wanted to know exactly why we were on the tour, who had set it up, who had suggested we were included, when did that happen, who said what on the coach, where were we all standing when the murder took place and on and on. He was particularly keen to know how the Russians had responded.

What did the tour guide Oleg say and do? What about our KGB minders? Were we sure only one of them was armed? When did the police arrive? How many? And the soldiers, what insignia did they bear? What rank was their officer?

Brasenose seemed permanently unimpressed with my answers. Had I really observed so little about the civilian who had taken charge and then suddenly vanished? Had I not heard anyone referring to him by name or title? Did the police car he arrived in have any special markings? Was his driver in uniform and if so what sort of uniform?

After that he spent a whole morning with Grundig and me going over yet again all the possible theories about the attacker, who by now was universally referred to in the Embassy as Scarface, much to Julia's annoyance. She insisted that Scarface was no better than Jacobs referring to the killer as The Mongolian.

'He's clearly a professional,' Grundig declared.

That much was obvious, but whose professional?

Brasenose went through the various groups that might have wanted to kill Demirkan as a representative of the Turkish state, Kurds for example or Armenians or Alevis. It was less than eighteen months since the Maraş Massacre when hundreds of Alevis, a minority Moslem sect, had been massacred in the town of Kahramanmaraş by the Grey Wolves, an ultra-nationalist militia trained by the Turkish Army.

'But surely they would have found it easier to carry out an assassination almost anywhere else,' I argued. 'Nobody would decide to mount an operation like this in the Soviet Union unless they had an established base here, but would they then risk upsetting their hosts?'

'And we know the Russians are upset,' Brasenose agreed. 'The KGB have been hauling in the various terrorist groups they support in the region and letting them know in no uncertain terms that political assassinations on Russian soil are totally unacceptable.'

And that implied something else. The KGB was itself not sure who was behind the murder, and that meant it was not them. The actions of their men on the ground suggested the same thing. They had no idea what was going to happen and had no idea how to react when it did happen. This led Brasenose to his own theory.

'The KGB are powerful but not all-powerful. We mustn't forget the military have their own foreign intelligence arm.'

He looked across at Grundig who nodded in agreement, as he usually did when someone further up the chain of command said something. 'You mean the GRU. That's a real possibility. They're not just a few soldiers playing games like our DIS,' he added in a gratuitous swipe at my old, and Julia's current, employer.

Brasenose continued. 'The GRU as you both know has tentacles all over the place. We're never really sure what they're up to and how much independent authority they have at any particular time. My guess is that they were planning some sort of operation and Demirkan stood in the way. No idea what but Turkey is right on the Russian border and it's sure to be high on their agenda. Ever since Kennedy put American missiles there and triggered the Cuban missile crisis the Soviet military have been obsessed with any threat from that direction.'

Satisfied he had solved the matter Brasenose headed off to the US Embassy to discuss other subjects with the

Company Station Chief Ethan Jacobs. The Americans were agitated by the discovery of counterfeit US dollars in the Far East which for some reason they were convinced presaged a KGB plot to flood Western Europe with fake currency. Brasenose, however, had different priorities. He later told me he had insisted on spending most of his visit discussing the situation in Poland and the likely Russian response to the increasing instability there.

Brasenose had arrived on 1st July, the very day that a wave of strikes started to spread across Poland in response to the government increasing the price of meat. Workers' Defence Committees were springing up and nobody seemed to know how to respond. And that was as true in the soundproofed rooms of the CIA and MI6 as it was in the corridors of power in Moscow and Warsaw. The hardliners in the Kremlin were known to have drawn up plans for military intervention.

There was no more discussion of the Turkish general's assassination until a few weeks after Brasenose had departed when a man from a small village outside Yaroslavl was convicted of the murder and found to be criminally insane.

Julia had been absolutely insistent throughout that she would be able to recognise the murderer again if he ever crossed her path. The dark vertical creases below both eyes were unique and unforgettable. From the mugshot published by the Russian authorities it was clear to us that the convicted man bore no resemblance to the man Julia had seen. They seemed to have latched on to Jacobs' reference to the killer as The Mongolian and picked on a peasant with a slightly Asiatic appearance. However, as he had admitted his guilt there had been no need for anyone in our tour group to give evidence and Julia was told that the Yaroslavl police had kindly given permission for her to leave the country whenever she wished. It was hinted to our Ambassador that her presence in the Soviet Union was no longer considered conducive to good relations between our two countries.

At the time relations between the United Kingdom and the Soviet Union were not at their best, I can't remember why, and the Foreign Office were keen that we did not appear to give way to Russian pressure. Although Julia and I were expecting to move on at the end of the year we were told that our posting would be extended for another twelve months.

'Bugger,' was Julia's unusually mild response when I told her the news. Three years ago we had been excited by the prospect of our first posting in Moscow, now we were equally excited at the thought of returning home. We had a long list of friends we wanted to see and things we wanted to do. Another year in Moscow meant another year without a decent curry.

We did return to London for a week in October, timed so that we could attend the retirement party of Adam Joseff as DIS Deputy Director General. Office gossip was that the Director General, General Fearmont, was determined to ease out the 'old guard' and had pushed Joseff into retiring early. However Fearmont had then been ambushed by the Cabinet Office who had vetoed the man he wanted to take Joseff's place. Instead he had been cajoled into promoting the existing Director Operations, considered in Whitehall to be a 'safe pair of hands'. I reflected that the one place where an office grapevine should not operate was in an intelligence agency devoted to secrecy but the opposite too often seemed to be the case.

Julia and I had both worked closely with Joseff and had come to appreciate his judgement enormously. His farewell was very well attended. General Fearmont made a competent if uninspiring speech. Amongst a stream of platitudes he commented that some old soldiers were tempted to hang around the barracks after retirement but he was sure that Adam would want nothing more to do with the messy world of Intelligence. I saw Fearmont's predecessor, Julia's uncle, raise an eyebrow at that.

Joseff certainly didn't seem to have lost interest in the work yet.

'Anything new on the Demirkan business?' he asked us.

There was nothing to report. 'I wonder what General Demirkan would have thought about the coup?' Julia asked.

Just a few weeks before, the Turkish military had staged another coup to put an end to the chronic political instability in the country. The coup was welcomed by most in the West and I was surprised when Joseff replied that Demirkan would 'quite rightly' have opposed it. The DIS were going to miss his contrarian thinking.

Our departure from Moscow was fixed for mid-November 1981. The tenants of our little house in Wimbledon had already told us they were going back to Australia in October so that fitted in reasonably well. When the time came we were packed and ready to go. Then Jeremy Grundig intervened.

'Something's come up. We may need you here for another week or two.'

As my replacement had already arrived that seemed odd and indeed there was virtually nothing for me to do. Julia and I spent most of the next ten days visiting the sights we had not got around to seeing during our time in Moscow. We rapidly realised that the reason we had not seen them was that there was not much to see, there was a limit to the amount of enthusiasm I could summon up for Stalinist architecture, heroic art and workers' museums. Most of Moscow's truly wonderful heritage lay inside the Kremlin and in those days was completely off limits.

The only matter of interest that came up at the Embassy was an encrypted message from Brasenose in London marked urgent which Grundig immediately decided was anything but. I had to agree with him, a Polish sailor jumping ship in Middlesbrough hardly seemed to be something of any significance to us. As it turned out we were, once again, completely wrong.

II

In the middle of the night a security guard inside Tees Dock on the north-east coast of England had been approached by a man who was clearly very hungry and apparently spoke very little English other than the word 'Police'. The police were duly summoned and when they realised that the man was Polish called in Special Branch. Somebody in Special Branch must have sensed that their visitor was not the usual drunken sailor mesmerised by the prospect of a life of luxury in the West, albeit the relative luxury of an area as economically depressed as Teesside, and contacted MI6. By the following evening we had concluded that we wanted to interview the sailor ourselves and he was being escorted down to London.

What made Kacper Nowak different was that he was not an ordinary sailor with little of interest to tell us but a serving officer in the Polish navy. As a Kapitan Marynarki, equivalent to a Royal Navy Lieutenant, he might not be privy to anything of great strategic interest but he had until recently been training with the Russian Navy in Kaliningrad, Russia's most important naval base. After twenty-four hours of gentle interrogation the Service had discovered that Nowak had nothing of particular importance to say on the subject of politics but concluded that he might have a lot to say on matters military and so had passed him over to the

Defence Intelligence Staff. The DIS had lodged him in the military prison in Colchester while they decided what to do next.

London wanted to know if we had come across any mention of Nowak. It took us five minutes to establish that we hadn't. Kaliningrad, a Russian enclave on the Baltic between Poland and the Soviet Republic of Lithuania, is a sealed area and we had never been able to obtain any useful intelligence about what went on there. A quick check with Julia established that the name meant nothing to the DIS Moscow team either.

'I'll go and check with Ethan Jacobs,' said Grundig. 'The Americans sometimes pick up intel on what's happening in Kaliningrad.'

But Jacobs hadn't heard of Kapitan Marynarki Nowak, and neither had the Swedes who were also at times surprisingly well informed. We reported our ignorance to Brasenose and would have forgotten all about it had not Jacobs called back two days later. Grundig sent me over to see him. The American had somehow got hold of a two-line summary of part of Nowak's military record. It simply recorded the date of his arrival in Kaliningrad from Gdynia and his departure ten days ago. His destination was shown as Wojewódzki Hospital, Gdańsk.

I forwarded the information to London. At the same time I decided to press Grundig further on why my return was being delayed.

In the event Grundig's assistant called me. I was needed urgently.

'You're in for a holiday,' Grundig greeted me. 'We need you to stop off in Warsaw on the way home. I can't tell you why, you'll be briefed there, but I can tell you this is the highest priority. And it's top secret and I mean top secret. You're to make no contact with our Embassy and keep well away from Professor Prince.'

'Who's he?'

'My opposite number in Warsaw.'

'And he's a professor?'

'Certainly not. That's just my name for him. David Prince is a pompous bore obsessed with Polish history. Should have been put out to grass years ago. As I say don't go anywhere near our Embassy. They're all unreliable. You'll be staying with Lars Sigurdsen, the Danish Ambassador, it's all arranged. You're staying there as his friend.'

I had met Sigurdsen a couple of times but we were hardly friends. He had been the Danish number two in Moscow and had just moved to Warsaw as his last post before retirement.

'I didn't know Sigurdsen had anything to do with our business,' I responded. 'Why is he briefing me?'

'Good God he's not briefing you. He's just doing us a favour. We needed an excuse for you and your wife to be in Warsaw.'

'My wife! Julia's coming with me?'

'Yes of course. Let me explain. The Americans have an operation running in Poland. What the Company calls Project Coronation. They need our help. Someone who knows some Polish to hold the hand of a local. They will tell you all about it. You just need to spend a couple of days with the Sigurdsens playing tourist and making sure nobody's on your tail. Then on Saturday you go to a foreign currency shop, I'll give you the address and the time, and you'll be slipped an envelope with instructions for what to do next.

You follow those instructions and on Tuesday you'll be flying home. That's all there is to it. And I repeat: no contact at all with our Warsaw Station.'

'You can't tell me any more than that?'

'I could but I won't. All will be revealed, as they say, when you get there. You're lucky. A few days' holiday in Poland will be a real tonic after this place.'

That seemed unlikely judging from the Foreign Office background report Grundig suggested I read.

For two decades the Polish economy produced what most Poles wanted: the reconstruction of their devastated country, jobs for all, education for the young and functioning health services. But by the end of the 1960s that was not enough. American TV shows like *Dr Kildare* introduced the delights of consumerism. To satisfy these new demands the government needed to modernise its industry and permit Western imports. Investments and imports had to be paid for but Western banks were more than happy to lend money. For a short period the Polish economy boomed. Then came the Arab-Israeli war. Oil prices and interest rates rocketed. Global trade collapsed and with it the Polish economy. The result was chaos. Millions of workers were now on strike.

Julia was unimpressed by Grundig's decision to arrange a 'holiday' in Poland with the Danish Ambassador.

'Who does he think he is? He's not my boss. I've a good mind to go straight home.'

Of course she didn't.

When we arrived in Warsaw we discovered that Lars Sigurdsen was at a Nordic security conference in Oslo but his wife made us welcome.

'Call me Freja,' she insisted.

A short, broad woman with homely features and, we discovered, a fierce intellect. She was more than happy to give us the benefit of her opinions in far from diplomatic language. In two days in her company we learned a lot about Danish politics – her particular hobby horse was what she called the absurd anti-Americanism of the radical left – and only a little less about life in Poland.

It was a pleasure to have visitors, Freja Sigurdsen assured us. 'Warsaw is becoming drabber by the day. Nobody comes here if they don't have to.'

So much for Grundig's promised holiday.

My first impression of the Polish capital was not promising. The enormous Palace of Culture that dominated the city was an almost exact copy of one of the so-called Seven Sisters in Moscow, the outlandish symbols of Stalinist architecture that similarly dominated the city skyline.

The Polish government had woken up to the economic benefits of tourism, and was busy building new hotels, but the number of Western tourists was still tiny and would soon start to decline again. As Freja explained, the economy, always fragile, was collapsing, rationing was getting worse and mounting popular discontent was running up against an unbending government.

In August the meat ration had been cut from 3.7kg per month to 3.0kg, prompting 'hunger demonstrations' across the country. The protests were peaceful but alarming. There were shortages of everything: food, coffee, cigarettes, soap. In Warsaw there were no spare tyres for the buses and the authorities announced the closure of non-essential routes. Even alcohol was rationed.

Nevertheless there was still plenty for a tourist to see. The

Royal Castle had been badly damaged at the beginning of the war and five years later what remained had been completely levelled by the Germans in a final act of barbaric vandalism. After years of debate the Castle's reconstruction had started in 1971. A decade later there was still much to do inside the building but Castle Square, which was actually more of a triangle, was returning to its pre-war glory. It was overlooked by a column reminiscent of Nelson's Column in Trafalgar Square, although much less than half as tall. This one was topped by King Sigismund III Vasa, under whose rule the Polish-Lithuanian Commonwealth had reached its widest extent and Warsaw had replaced Kraków as the capital.

'Isn't Vasa the name of that medieval warship they managed to raise in Sweden?' Julia asked. 'Why name a Swedish ship after a Polish king?'

'It's the other way round,' I replied, as usual happy to show off. I had read a Polish guidebook before leaving Moscow. 'The Vasa dynasty were hereditary kings of Sweden and the chap on the column here was King of Sweden for a time. In those days the Polish nobility elected their kings and they elected Sigismund. The Swedish nobility didn't like that so they kicked him off the Swedish throne and he spent most of his life trying to get it back. His sons became kings of Poland as well.'

I had forgotten the names of the sons of Sigismund III Vasa and never expected to be called upon to remember them. In that again I was wrong. Without Sigismund's younger son Jan Kazimierz, or John Casimir as the Americans called him, I would not have been in Warsaw and the CIA's Project Coronation would not have been born. I had no idea of that when I set off to receive my instructions.

27

The Pewex shops were a peculiar feature of Polish life. The chain of state-owned shops sold an eclectic collection of imported goods ranging from blue jeans to TV sets, canned drinks to toys. The shops also sold Polish goods like premium vodka normally destined for export. The drawback for the average Pole was that Pewex only accepted foreign currency which was not easy to obtain legally. For foreign diplomats, however, the stores were a magnet as prices were usually far lower than back home. It was an ideal place for a foreigner like me to be seen loitering.

I did not have to loiter for long. A man came in shortly after me and I immediately realised why there was no need to have any fancy passwords. We had met before, although I couldn't immediately remember his name. He was based in the US Embassy in Moscow. He gave no sign of recognition as he walked towards me and I hardly felt the envelope being pushed into my coat pocket. It all seemed very professional until, in a stage whisper, he mouthed 'See you on Monday.'

Flanagan, he was called, Robert Flanagan. I remembered as I emerged from the Pewex shop clutching two bottles of gin intended as a present for Mrs Sigurdsen. He had been in Moscow for about six months but I knew nothing about his place in the CIA set-up there.

I didn't open the envelope in my pocket until I was back at the Ambassador's residence, had handed over the gin and joined Julia in our room. I had expected to find something that might tell me what Project Coronation was all about but instead I simply found two return train tickets for the following Monday. It seemed that Julia and I were about to take a trip to Olsztyn.

After dinner Freja produced a large map and pointed out Olsztyn on the edge of the Masurian Lakes.

'A truly beautiful area,' she told us. 'There are said to be over two thousand lakes stretching from the lower Vistula right up to the restricted area on the Polish–Russian frontier. Very popular with Poles who have the money to get there. With fuel rationing as tight as it is now you need to stock up well before setting off. I've seen families leaving Warsaw with the children on the back seat surrounded by petrol cans. You're lucky to be travelling by train.'

Compared with London's major railway terminals Warsaw's new Central station was relatively uncrowded. We went downstairs to Platform 2 prepared for a long wait but the train to Olsztyn pulled away on time, trundling underground until it finally popped out and crossed over the Vistula.

The outskirts of Warsaw seemed to be block upon block of concrete apartment buildings interspersed with the detritus of light industry and trees looking forlorn without their leaves. I caught sight of a terrace of three brick-built houses and with a shock realised they were the first pre-war buildings I had seen. Seventy per cent of Warsaw had been destroyed during the war, much of it deliberately demolished by the German invaders.

After twenty minutes we were leaving Warsaw proper and rattling through the woods and small towns on its outskirts: Legionowo, Nowy Dwór Mazowiecki and, after crossing the winding Vistula again, Modlin. As the train rumbled to a stop it seemed to me just another insignificant town on the way north. I couldn't have imagined that the next time I arrived in Modlin it wouldn't be by choice and I would be in the back seat of a police car, its blue light flashing eerily on deserted streets.

As the journey continued we moved through countryside brown and lifeless and curiously hostile. In spring the smallholdings amongst the trees would no doubt come alive again and the trees themselves would burst into leaf. In the towns the allotments beside the railway track, so empty now, would be full of hunched figures determined to supplement diets made meagre by rationing. Cabbages, beans, radishes and tomatoes would spring up on land now abandoned to winter.

The landscape became more rural, flat unbroken fields stretching away to the horizon and carefully laid out orchards. The towns and villages had a few more pre-war buildings although the fighting here had been fierce. Further north the countryside became gently undulating. As we approached Iława the tree cover increased and wide empty spaces became less common. We had been on the main line to Gdańsk until Iława, there our route branched east towards Olsztyn. The first large lake, Lake Drwęca, appeared as the train approached Ostróda and stopped briefly at the gloriously elaborate station.

'Not long now,' said Julia.

I didn't answer. I was deep in a book about the region's history that Freja Sigurdsen had given me before we left Warsaw. Somewhere I realised we had crossed an invisible line that fewer than forty years before had divided Poland from Germany. We were travelling through a part of Europe where blood stained every acre of its soil. Even in recent times the history of what my grandfather's generation knew as Prussia was every bit as barbaric as it had been in the age of the Teutonic Knights. The First World War Battle of Tannenberg, at which the Germans totally destroyed the armies of the tsar, was fought around Olsztyn. Each station we passed had its own tragic story. Działdowo, ceded to Poland after the First World War by the Treaty of Versailles and where, after the Nazi invasion of 1939, German-speaking inhabitants tortured and then murdered hundreds of their Polish-speaking neighbours and for good measure set up the Soldau concentration camp nearby. Mława where the Germans built a forced labour camp and then massacred hundreds of inmates when the Red Army approached. And when the Russians arrived a new wave of rape and murder followed and eventually the wholesale expulsion of the surviving German speakers as German Eylau became Polish Iława, Osterode became Ostróda and Allenstein became Olsztyn.

Leaving the station at Olsztyn I saw Flanagan about 100 yards away. We walked towards him and he moved off, eventually stopping next to a small red car. It was parked in front of one of the near-identical four and five storey blocks that had been thrown up all over Poland and could as easily be office buildings as apartments. This one in fact turned out to be a school.

I introduced Julia and as I did so another man joined us. Flanagan introduced the newcomer simply as Jerry. Like Flanagan he was clearly American. Both were dressed in ordinary Polish working clothes and would have mingled easily with those walking past but for Flanagan's overpowering aftershave. Julia and I by comparison stood out like the proverbial sore thumb.

'Thank you for keeping your husband company Mrs

Dylan,' Flanagan said to Julia with a smile. 'We'll look after him now. I promise to have him back here well before your train back to Warsaw.'

Julia, unsurprisingly, looked bemused. 'I understood we were both on this operation. That's what I was told in Moscow.'

'Then there's been a misunderstanding. If you take a taxi from the station and ask for the Stare Miasto, the Old Town, you'll find plenty to do. The shopping may not be up to London but there's a wonderful castle and I'm told the cathedral is centuries old.'

'That's not the point. We're not here to see the sights.'

Flanagan was trying to be patient. 'Mrs Dylan this is where your husband's real work starts. I'm afraid this has to be secret. Intelligence is like this.'

I stepped in quickly before Julia could respond. 'There seems to have been a miscommunication somewhere. Julia is an Intelligence officer. In fact she's senior to me. We come as a team on this op.'

I thought he was going to argue but after a brief hesitation he smiled. 'OK, if that's what you want. It might be helpful to have a woman, we're meeting a guy who may respond best to a tender touch. Let's go.'

The four of us piled into the tiny, two-door car with Julia and I scrunched up in the back seat. It was one of the ubiquitous Fiat 126 models produced under licence in Poland and inside it was no bigger than the original British Mini.

Before starting to tell us anything about Project Coronation, Flanagan clearly thought he needed to explain the rules of the game.

'Just so there's no more misunderstanding let's be clear this is not a joint operation. The Agency's been working on this for months and you're only helping out on one tiny part of the operation right at the end. Today we're just here to buy something and pass it on to someone else. The party we're buying from is a bit simple and like I said he might appreciate the tender touch. He's a peasant and I mean a *real* peasant.'

'A soon-to-be rich peasant,' interrupted Jerry, the first time he had spoken since his introduction.

'A very, very rich peasant,' agreed Flanagan. 'Although knowing peasants he'll probably just hide the money under his bed. The point is he likes the English. Apparently his brother died in the war flying with the English Air Force and he thinks he can trust you guys more than us. So here's the plan. It's a bit complicated because not all the parties know each other and we don't want them to. That includes you. First we're going to meet a priest and you two stay with him for a while. Jerry and I will drive on and meet this peasant and our man Krypton.'

'Krypton's presumably not his real name.'

'No of course not. Anyway Krypton is bringing the money and the peasant is bringing the Crown.'

'The Crown?'

'The Great Crown of Jan Kazimierz. It's some holy relic that means a lot to the Catholics here. Seems a friend of our peasant, another peasant in the same village, died last year and on his deathbed told our peasant he had this ancient Crown hidden away. Sounds like a fairy tale but turns out it's true. We've seen the photos. Our experts in Langley checked it out. It truly is what the Poles call the Great Crown. The peasant tried to sell the Crown and that's where Krypton heard about it and told us. That's all there is. We meet the peasant and verify he has the Crown. Then Krypton pays the peasant and goes back to where he came from and we collect you and the priest. The peasant gives the Crown to the priest and we all shake hands and go home. Mission over. Oh, by the way, we haven't told the priest that Uncle Sam is buying the Crown, let him think our peasant is passing it over for the love of Poland and the Catholic Church.'

'Why is Uncle Sam buying the Crown?'

'That I don't know. Maybe somebody powerful in Washington has a Polish grandmother. Like I say our mission is finished when we hand the Crown over.'

I wasn't sure I believed him. 'The best plans are the simplest plans' was one of the Service mantras repeated on every training course. Project Coronation seemed much more complicated than it needed to be but Flanagan obviously wasn't going to tell us anything more. He had one more question for us.

'Are you carrying?'

'Carrying?'

'Are you armed? I know you English don't like guns but I wanted to check. This op is entirely peaceful. If we're stopped we're just innocent tourists who may have got a bit lost, at worst we'll be expelled. They find guns and we're off to the gulags.'

'No, we're not carrying.'

We soon left the industry of Olsztyn behind and drove on eastward through farmland and forests with the occasional sighting of an ice-covered lake off to one side or the other. Flanagan regularly cursed the feeble power of the Polski Fiat's two-cylinder 600cc engine, comparing it unfavourably to the gas guzzlers back home. Julia and I were more concerned with the contortions forced on our bodies by the lack of space in the back and with the noise from the engine right behind us. We stopped outside Mrągowo to admire the view and unbend. It also gave Flanagan an opportunity to watch the passing traffic for any sign that we were being followed. Satisfied that we were not we climbed back into the car as it started to rain.

Somewhere just to the north of us lay the town of Kętrzyn. Fewer than forty years earlier Kętrzyn had been Rastenburg and would have been a top priority for American and British Intelligence. Hidden in the nearby forests was the Wolf's Lair, Hitler's wartime headquarters.

We headed south-east before eventually turning off on to a series of forest tracks. By then the rain had stopped but the little Fiat still slipped around on the mud.

Jerry was consulting a hand-drawn map and, after making one wrong turn and precariously reversing back, we came across a green van half hidden in the bushes. We gratefully clambered out and looked around. The Syrena Bosto van was unoccupied and both the back seats and the compartment behind them were empty but for two large fuel cans tied to the floor.

III

Flanagan, cigarette in hand, prowled around while the rest of us stood silent beside the van. It was bitterly cold. Except for a few conifers the trees were completely bare. A few small patches of snow lay in the areas of deepest shadow.

After four or five minutes two men emerged from the woods. The shorter of the two advanced towards us with a wary smile on his face. He had a dark scarf hanging loosely around his neck with a dog collar beneath and introduced himself as Father Paszek.

The other Pole he simply introduced as 'My friend Walentowicz.'

Flanagan made the introductions on our side and I discovered that Jerry bore the surname Sokolowski. Julia was introduced as my wife and the two Poles were clearly not expecting her but said nothing.

Julia could sense their unease and to my surprise suggested that she would go for a walk to stretch her legs. She started to walk further along the track we had been taking but Flanagan stopped her.

'That's the way we'll be going. Why don't you try over there?' He pointed off at a right angle, where a narrow footpath disappeared into the trees.

Without comment Julia took his advice.

'Now Father,' Flanagan said, turning to the priest and

still talking in English. 'We're off to meet Mr Broniszewski. There's a hut by the water about a mile ahead, he should be there by now. We just need to make sure he hasn't brought any friends with him and that he really has the Crown. Then Jerry will return and give you the all-clear to come on down. Until then you just stay with our two English friends. Jerry should be back in half an hour or so. This is the moment we've all been waiting for: the return of the Great Crown to the true representatives of the people of Poland.'

Father Paszek made the sign of the cross but the two Americans clambered into the Fiat without seeming to notice. They started off gingerly along the track towards the lake that Flanagan had been so keen for Julia not to follow. Sokolowski had grabbed a bag from the boot and sat with it on his lap. I wondered what was in that.

For a minute or two neither of the Poles said anything and we stood in silence. At this time of year the sun set early, it was just past three but already the gloom had set in. The forest was eerily silent.

'These are dangerous times,' said Father Paszek eventually. 'Dangerous times for the world but dangerous times for Poland especially. We have one chance to restore our pride, our glory, to expel the Russians. If we don't seize the opportunity it will be lost for a generation or more.'

I wasn't sure what to say but it didn't matter, the priest clearly did not expect me to say anything.

'We Poles have always been surrounded by enemies. Swedes, Russians, Germans. Enemies outside and enemies within, Jews, socialists, atheists. We must awaken. The nation needs a symbol that will unite us all, that will resurrect the true Catholic spirit of Poland.'

I realised he was repeating words he had often uttered before. He wasn't trying to convince me of anything. He didn't care what I thought. He was explaining, not arguing, talking to me in the tone he would use to explain to a child that the first man was called Adam and the first woman Eve. I wondered why Flanagan regarded Paszek as the 'true representative' of the Polish people. The man certainly spoke with authority but it was the accumulated authority of the Church not of any personal charisma. He would be unremarkable without the character provided by his clerical collar; as my father might have quipped, colourless when collarless.

Silence descended again.

The rain came back and I clambered into the back seat of the van and looked at my watch. The two Americans had left twenty minutes ago. Suddenly Julia appeared, running towards us. Father Paszek got out to let her join me in the rear.

'Something's wrong,' Julia gasped. 'There are soldiers up there.'

I had assumed Walentowicz did not speak English but he shouted 'Quick, we go now.'

I started to object but just then there was the sound of a shot followed immediately by two more. The sound was unmistakable. Then three more shots a few seconds apart. They seemed to be coming from the direction of the lake but it was difficult to be certain.

Walentowicz grabbed at Julia, pulling her into the van with Father Paszek behind her. He started the engine and moved off as the priest was still pulling the door closed. Fortunately there were no seat belts to worry about. I thought

I heard a volley of shots further away but above the noise of the engine and the sound of rain on the van's metal roof I could not be sure.

I had no idea what might have happened to Flanagan and Sokolowski but right now they were not my priority. I had to trust that they could look after themselves. Walentowicz certainly wasn't going to wait for them. As the van squelched forward Julia explained that she had stumbled on two Polish Army lorries hidden in the trees. There was nobody with them but what was even more alarming was the sight of an unmarked 'bukhanka' with Russian plates. *Bukhanka*, Russian for loaf, is slang for the loaf-shaped 4x4 van, officially the UAZ 452, beloved by the Russian military.

I expected pursuit to appear behind us or the way to be blocked in front. If those troops had been waiting for us they would surely have cut off any escape route. Although we approached the metalled road without anything happening I wasn't about to relax. The truth is I was rattled. I hadn't been expecting any shooting. Neither obviously had Flanagan or Sokolowski. They had made a point of being unarmed.

Back in Moscow Grundig had said we were going on a holiday; he could not have been more wrong.

'You caught train to Olsztyn,' said Walentowicz. He meant it as a question.

'Yes we did.'

He turned east, away from Mrągowo and Olsztyn. 'Then we go to Ełk. You catch train there. It is more safe. We drive fast.'

He shoved his foot hard down on the accelerator but the tiny three-cylinder engine of the Syrena seemed to produce no more power than the two cylinders of Flanagan's Fiat.

When the possibility of being caught in a hail of bullets seemed to have gone Julia voiced what we were all thinking.

'What happened?'

Only the priest had any answer. 'Russians. They are everywhere. They are always everywhere. We must pray.'

I wasn't sure prayer would help, especially when we saw a flashing blue light coming towards us half an hour later. I felt Julia tensing beside me. However, the approaching police car merely signalled us to keep to the side of the road as three lorry loads of Polish soldiers thundered past, sending up waves of icy slush. We watched their lights disappear in the Syrena's rear-view mirror.

Julia's question hadn't been answered. What the hell had happened? Who had been shooting and had Flanagan and Sokolowski got away? What about the men they were going to meet? I had wanted adventure; I had found it and was now running away. How would I explain that? What should I have done?

There had been an air of unreality about the operation ever since Grundig had called me into his office in Moscow. I had never heard of the CIA needing a fairly junior member of MI6 to help with an operation in the field, let alone where that agent had no experience at all of the country concerned. And the operation itself, when I finally found out what it involved, was pure fantasy. Magic crowns and medieval legends in the twentieth century.

But there was nothing magical or medieval about what had happened at the lake. Father Paszek was no handsome prince coming to reclaim his crown. Those were real shots we had heard; they weren't magic dragons breathing fire. If that last volley had been fired by the soldiers Julia had seen, the chances were that whoever they were aiming at was now dead. There was no sign of knights in shining armour riding to the rescue.

The road ahead of us was largely empty. The scenery would be stunning in daylight. Poland's largest lake, Śniardwy, lay not far to the south of our route, but we could see nothing beyond the feeble yellow of the headlights. Snow began to fall. When we reached Elk the small town looked as if nothing had disturbed its slumbers for decades.

Walentowicz parked in a side street and disappeared, leaving the priest fingering the cross on his rosary and Julia and I wondering how much longer we were destined to spend bent over in the backs of cars and vans.

Walentowicz was away for nearly thirty minutes. When he returned he had three rail tickets to Warsaw. 'You take train to Białystok. Then take express to Warsaw. You have money for ticket?'

I handed over a bundle of zlotys and he looked satisfied. He turned to Father Paszek and launched into a stream of Polish that was so fast that all I could make out was that he wished us all a safe journey but warned the priest to sit well away from Julia and me.

Father Paszek took him at his word. Despite his short legs he took off towards the station at top speed and on both the train to Białystok and then on to Warsaw sat as far away from us as he could. We arrived back at Warsaw Central station without exchanging another word with him. Our last sight of the little priest was of him hurrying past the scaffolding that had become a feature of the five-year-old but already-crumbling station. He did not look back.

I still couldn't believe what was happening, partly

because I still didn't know what was happening. When we had returned to the privacy of our room at the Danish Ambassador's residence Julia and I looked at each other in mutual bemusement. Julia repeated the question we had asked ourselves in the car: 'What happened?'

One thing seemed obvious: we had walked into a trap. We were not being followed. Somebody was waiting for us. The only reason Julia and I had escaped was that they had been waiting for us at the hut.

'If they had stayed out of sight and allowed Jerry to come back and fetch the priest we would all have been caught,' I commented.

'So why didn't they?'

'Why didn't they what?'

'Why didn't they wait? Why charge in guns blazing?' Julia asked.

'They can't have known we were there. They can't have been expecting Father Paszek.'

Julia shook her head. 'I don't believe that. They knew there was going to be a meeting at the hut. They surely would have known who was going to be there.'

'Something unexpected might have happened,' I responded. 'Flanagan or this mysterious Krypton could have spotted the soldiers and tried to get away.'

'Perhaps,' she agreed. 'Or perhaps whoever was waiting there didn't want to catch Paszek. It could have been Paszek who told them about the meeting.'

Something else had been troubling me. 'Why open fire? The Americans weren't armed.'

'Yes I've been thinking about that. Perhaps Krypton was armed.'

Julia could be right. 'Or perhaps Broniszewski, the peasant who was supposed to have the Crown, brought a gun.'

That took us to the core of the whole business. Did we really believe the story of a medieval crown with the power to bring Poles together, uniting the nation to rise up against the Russian occupiers? It seemed more than improbable; it was utterly unbelievable.

'So what do we do now?' Julia asked.

'We get out of Poland as fast as possible. We were very lucky to get back to Warsaw without being arrested. It must surely mean they weren't expecting us to be there. Which is very odd. But to answer your question we have a flight booked for tomorrow morning, let's try to take it and see what happens. In the meantime, we need to tell someone what happened to Project Coronation. We can't wait until we get home; if we get home.'

'Grundig was absolutely insistent that we stay away from the Embassy,' Julia pointed out. 'You're not to contact the Station here under any circumstances.'

'No I'm not, although these circumstances do seem a bit extreme. But Grundig can't tell you what to do. You're not in the Service. It's a pity that the DIS doesn't have anyone at the Warsaw Embassy.'

'But they do,' said Julia. 'There's so much going on here, Fearmont posted someone to Warsaw two months ago. And I've met him. A passed-over major called Brampford. He stopped off in Moscow to see my boss when his posting was announced. Seemed a nice enough chap. Didn't speak a word of Polish or Russian. I could call the Embassy Duty Officer and try to reach him.'

'But if you phone the Embassy and somebody's listening in they'll discover where we are.'

'You're right. Nobody knows we're here and we should keep it that way. Let's see if our hostess has met Brampford on the diplomatic circuit and can somehow persuade him to drop by.'

Freja Sigurdsen was very happy to have anyone drop by but she hadn't yet met Major Brampford. However, she was sure the Danish military attaché who lived just next door would be happy to help. And so it proved.

Just after nine o'clock Freja's neighbour arrived with a portly and clearly perplexed British major expecting post-dinner drinks to celebrate a Danish battle he had never heard of. Mrs Brampford followed close behind her husband and was promptly whisked off by Freja.

Fortunately Major Brampford recognised Julia from their brief meeting in Moscow. We recounted everything that had occurred from the moment Grundig had told us we were both bound for Warsaw. Brampford simply listened and asked very few questions. Julia and I had discussed leaving out some of the names of those involved but decided that there was no point at this stage in paying any attention to Grundig's insistence that we not involve the Embassy. If we were arrested the next day, London would want the fullest possible report from Brampford.

'Thomas was told specifically not to contact the Station here but that can't apply to me,' Julia explained. 'London needs to know what's happened and we can't be sure we'll be allowed to leave tomorrow. In any case somebody surely needs to contact the Americans as soon as possible. Two of their agents are missing, they may be wounded or even dead.'

Brampford nodded. 'I've been told not to get too close to Six here. Don't know why. Their man Prince seems perfectly sound to me.'

Our Warsaw head of station, David Prince, had been around for a long time but I had yet to meet him. Back in Moscow Grundig had described him as a pompous bore but I discovered that just a few months earlier Prince had managed the exfiltration of a Polish dissident, Feliks Radlowski, from right under the noses of the Polish security services. It seemed odd that the DIS and MI6 in the same Embassy were keeping their distance. It wasn't until later that I found out why.

'I'll get something to London right away,' Brampford promised, 'and hope somebody reads it. Then I'll come out to the airport with you tomorrow.'

'That might not be a good idea. The authorities will know what you're doing at the Embassy and we don't want to draw attention to ourselves. I'll ask Freja to come with us. She'll let you know if anything happens.'

Brampford looked uncertain but eventually agreed. He and his wife left after that, but not before both of them had downed two more large brandies.

In Moscow I had been accustomed to constant surveillance and it seemed inconceivable that by now the Polish authorities would not have connected Julia and me to the events in the Masurian Lakes. But although Poland in those days was still a police state, the Polish secret police, the SB, were much less evident than the KGB had been in Russia. Poland's population had less reason to fear the police informer next door, the midnight knock on the door and sudden arbitrary arrest than the inhabitants of any other

Eastern Bloc country. But that did little to reassure me. The presence of an unmarked vehicle with Russian plates where the two CIA men had disappeared had been thoroughly alarming.

We slept very little that night and set off early with Freja Sigurdsen and a Danish Embassy driver. I half expected to see extra security at the airport but everything seemed to be normal. What I did see as soon as we entered the terminal was Major Brampford. That was not good news. As I had explained, the last thing I wanted was for us to be seen with him. Fortunately it was soon clear he had received the message. He was talking with another man but after the briefest of glances in our direction he marched up to the check-in desk. It seemed he was catching the same flight. We held back to keep our distance from Brampford. His companion stood waiting at the back of the hall and as Julia and I checked in I could see him watching us.

'He looks British,' Julia whispered to me in a tone that was supposed to be reassuring.

It looked as though Brampford had decided we needed to be watched all the way to London. In the departure lounge he was seated as far away from the gate as possible, looking oddly conspicuous. We joined everyone else near the gate and started to relax.

Suddenly the speaker announced a delay to our flight and Julia's hand tightened on mine but it seemed there had been a technical problem. We lifted off fifteen minutes late and touched down at Heathrow almost on time. There was a welcoming party.

IV

As we left the plane Julia and I were taken aside by a young, smartly dressed man who introduced himself simply as Sawyer. After collecting Brampford he led us down some steps to a waiting car. Then he collected our luggage receipts and disappeared.

We climbed into the car and without saying a word, the driver moved off but stopped again after three or four minutes. I was surprised to see Justin Brasenose standing outside an unmarked door.

'This way,' he said.

We followed him inside, along a short corridor and into a small conference room.

'You both know Richard,' Brasenose said as we entered, pointing at a powerfully built man who stood waiting for us. I had known Richard Mendale at the Defence Intelligence Staff. Then he had been Director Operations but had been made Deputy Director General when Adam Joseff retired. The Director General had apparently been keen to bring in some new blood but Mendale had lobbied hard and General Fearmont had reluctantly been persuaded that to ensure 'continuity' and preserve the 'organisational memory' Mendale should be allowed to step up.

Sawyer returned, poured us all coffee and then sat pen in

47

hand poised over a large black notebook. I don't recall him saying anything in the whole meeting.

Brasenose kicked off. 'What the hell's happening?'

He looked straight at me.

'I'm sure Major Brampford has already filled you in on most of it,' I started, but Brasenose immediately interrupted.

'Assume nothing. Just start right from the beginning. What were you told in Moscow and who by?'

It seemed to me that there was not much to tell but Brasenose and Mendale fired question after question at us and it rapidly became obvious that they had known very little about what I was doing in Warsaw. Even the Americans' name for their operation, Coronation, was new to them. When I mentioned the Great Crown of Jan Kazimierz I could sense Mendale's incredulity.

He looked towards Brampford: 'You mentioned a Crown in your telex, I thought it was an error in the encryption.'

Unsurprisingly we spent a lot of time going over the events in the Masurian Lakes. Julia, for example, was pressed hard for more details on the vehicles she had seen parked nearby. Was she certain the 'bukhanka' had Russian plates? Were there no other markings on it at all? Were the Polish lorries army or secret police, SB militia? What insignia did they carry? What did surprise me is that Brasenose and Mendale were not only interested in what had happened the previous afternoon but just as much in everything that happened before and after, starting with what exactly Grundig had told me in Moscow and ending with what we had told Freja Sigurdsen in Warsaw.

'Look, Thomas,' said Brasenose at one point. 'Something's gone badly wrong here. Now just think: did you say anything to anyone in Warsaw that might have put the other side on to what you were doing there? Could this Sigurdsen woman have mentioned something in a casual conversation with one of her lady friends? Did she have any visitors while you were there? Did either of you bump into anyone when you were playing tourist?'

After nearly two hours Brasenose decided we should take a break. He and Mendale left the room. When they returned the atmosphere changed, inquisition gave way to debate.

'Let's go over what we know,' Brasenose started. 'The Company's Station Chief in Moscow, Jacobs, approaches our man Grundig with a simple proposition. The Company have made contact with a potential asset in Poland but are having trouble reeling him in. The man's suspicious of American intentions. However, he seems to have a love of all things British. Could we send someone to their next meeting to reassure him? It's a pretty odd request but Grundig agrees. No mention of any medieval crown or Polish priests. There are some delays setting up the meeting but eventually everything's in place and Thomas is off to Warsaw. Grundig has the bright idea of Julia going along for extra cover.

'In Warsaw everything goes to plan. You're not under observation. You meet the Company team, Flanagan and Sokolowski, and you set off for Olsztyn and the Masurian Lakes. Then it all goes wrong. Bullets start to fly and, to coin a phrase, our American friends appear to disappear.'

'You mean we haven't heard what happened to them?' I interrupted.

'Not a word. We have complete silence not only from the two of them but from the Poles and from the Russians. Not even a hint that something is up. No imminent announcement of American spies being captured. I suppose that's not really surprising, it's hardly twenty-four hours since you and the priest very sensibly decided discretion was better than valour. One thing I can tell you is that the Company haven't heard anything either. We're meeting them later and all hell seems to be bubbling over on both sides of the Atlantic. I'm not sure Washington was fully apprised of Mr Jacobs' plans.

'But for now that's beside the point. What do we think happened? Let's start with this fairy tale about the Great Crown of Jan Kazimierz. What's that all about?'

Brasenose and Mendale looked at me but I wasn't going to be rushed. I had no more idea of what was happening than they did.

'There's only one thing I would say. The priest, Father Paszek, certainly believed that the Crown existed. It sounds odd but there was something almost messianic in the way he spoke about it.'

'Ah, Father Paszek. A controversial figure. If the Americans had told us he was involved we might have had second thoughts about becoming involved ourselves.'

'In what way is he controversial?' asked Julia.

'He's a fascist,' interjected Mendale.

'I wouldn't put it like that,' responded Brasenose smoothly. 'He's a Polish patriot who believes in a strong and independent Poland united by a common Catholic faith and what we now call family values. He's one of those men who come alive on a stage, or in his case a pulpit. Our man in Warsaw, David Prince, has met him and refers to him as the mouse that roars, you know like that Peter Sellers film. According to David he was just an obscure priest in Lublin until his sermons got picked up somehow and started being published all over the place. Someone has put some money behind him.'

'He's gaining quite a following,' commented Brampford, who until then had said nothing.

'The problem,' replied Brasenose, 'is that nobody knows where his followers are being led. He's not one of the modern generation of socially conscious priests throwing their weight behind this new Solidarity trade union; Paszek is very much old school.'

'Whatever he is,' said Mendale, 'the Americans are swimming in dangerous waters if they start playing politics in Poland. We should be steering well clear until we can see which way the tide is flowing.'

'Quite,' replied Brasenose. 'Let's get back to our Masurian mystery. Assume everything Flanagan said is true. He was planning to meet their agent, whom we only know as Krypton, and Krypton was going to lead them to an anonymous peasant who had in his possession this fabled Crown.'

'Not quite anonymous,' Julia interrupted. 'Thomas heard a name. Brzezinski or something.'

'Broniszewski,' I put in. 'Flanagan was talking to Father Paszek and told him he was off to meet Mr Broniszewski.'

'All right then,' continued Brasenose. 'Krypton leads them to Mr Broniszewski and, in order to protect Krypton's identity, from whom I wonder, he was then going to disappear and the peasant and the Crown would be brought to Father Paszek.'

'No.' It was my turn to interrupt, mildly irritated by the way Brasenose was treating us. I had been on the interrogation course and knew all about the little tricks like repeating back stories with minor changes to see if they were picked up. 'As I said, Paszek and I were to be fetched and brought to the peasant, who would remain at the meeting place.'

'Ah yes. And you were there because of this peasant's love for the English and distrust of America. Frankly the whole thing stinks. Why was Krypton bringing the money not Flanagan? If Krypton had the money and he was the only one who knew the peasant, why didn't he just buy the Crown and then pass it on to Flanagan for Flanagan to pass on to Father Paszek somewhere a lot more convenient than in the middle of a Polish forest in mid-winter?'

'I suppose the peasant insisting on a British presence made everything more complicated?'

'That I just don't buy,' said Brasenose. 'This man is about to become very, very rich. That's the phrase you said Flanagan used. And he holds back because of some sentimental nonsense about his brother having flown with the RAF over a quarter of a century ago. I think not. But the real puzzle is those shots you heard. Think about it. That Russian truck, what did you call it: bukhanka? The bukhanka and the Polish troops, how did they get there? Unless Flanagan and Sokolowski just by accident happened upon some sort of completely unrelated army exercise, which I don't believe for one minute, they were waiting for you. Someone had told them you were coming.'

'Perhaps the Americans were careless,' suggested Mendale. 'Poland is a police state after all, perhaps they tried to get around the petrol rationing and someone reported them. How did they get hold of a car in the first place? The Polish police may have been tracking them for days and had seen one of them scouting out the area. They wouldn't have needed to follow them from Olsztyn.'

'Possible, but I don't think so. They were waiting at the hut Thomas mentioned. How did they find that? And there's another question for us. Why start shooting before Thomas and Paszek arrived at the hut?'

I had asked myself the same question. 'Perhaps they just wanted to pounce before Krypton disappeared,' I said.

'Really? Instead of seizing you and Paszek? Why would they do that? They could surely have taken you all. They could have grabbed you at the same time they took the others or they could have let Krypton leave the meeting place and taken him later. And why shoot anyway? Believe me, two American agents in a show trial would be worth far more than two killed in a shootout. In any case, who was armed? You said the Americans weren't. I suppose the peasant might have had a hunting rifle. Or Krypton might have had a weapon. But would either of them try to take on two lorry loads of soldiers?

'And then, of course, why did they let you get away? They could have taken you there or on the way back to Warsaw or even at the airport this morning. Either they didn't want you, and if they didn't why not, or they didn't know you were there, which would mean they had been told all about the Americans buying the Crown but nothing about what the Americans had been going to do with it, nothing about you and the priest. That's possible; in fact, I can't see any other way of explaining why they pounced when they did, but it all seems very unlikely.'

Brasenose relapsed into silence for a moment and it was Julia who asked the obvious question: 'What happens now?'

For one moment I thought he was not going to answer. He might not have done if, to my surprise, Richard Mendale had not looked directly towards him. 'We really have to make some decisions about Warsaw, Justin. We can't let the position there just drag on. And,' Mendale added, turning to the man who had flown back with us, 'we need to bring you into the picture, Major Brampford.'

Brampford nodded. 'It's about time. I want to know why I've been warned off your Warsaw head of station David Prince. Why is he being kept out of all this?'

Brasenose hesitated but then thought better of it. 'Very fair questions, Major. So let me be straight with you. We may have a leak in the Warsaw Embassy. Perhaps within my Service.'

Brasenose sat forward in his chair. Mendale I noticed, in contrast, was rocking back and fro with an unreadable expression on his face as Brasenose continued.

'We've had a potential problem in Warsaw for a while. In fact for at least seven years. It started with an exfiltration operation Dick Mendale here was helping on. A potential Russian defector we were trying to get out suddenly disappeared. We later discovered he had been shipped back to Moscow and shot. We couldn't work out how the other side had got on to him.'

'So you decided I was the leak,' interrupted Mendale, a hint of bitterness still lingering behind the forced smile on his face.

'We had to explore every possibility. You were of course completely cleared. David Prince was head of station then and he conducted a very thorough review but found nothing. A couple of years later there were some important trade negotiations in Warsaw and we realised that the Poles seemed surprisingly well prepared for us. David conducted another review but again nothing turned up. But we weren't satisfied so we brought David home and in fact the whole Embassy staff has been rotated out since the first suspected leak. All seemed well until eighteen months ago.

'The Solidarity strikes had just started. The West needed to decide how to react. There was a meeting of the people on the ground, diplomatic and intelligence, in our Embassy. The Americans were there. They had a man close to the Solidarity leadership. A week after the meeting he disappeared. It may have been a coincidence, probably was, but we decided to tighten things up again. We sent David Prince back. He knows far more about Poland than anyone else and right now we need his experience. The situation there is explosive, the economy collapsing, strikes and protests everywhere. The Russians could invade at any moment and if they don't heaven knows how long the regime can survive.

'David's first task though was to review security again. I went out there with him. He did a first-class job but found nothing. I was convinced that it was all smoke and no fire. A string of coincidences. David himself had some cockeyed theory that one of the local support staff, he called her Esterka, had planted bugs inside the Embassy which we hadn't been able to find. Then the bombshell arrived. Six weeks ago the Americans claimed to have evidence that we did indeed have a mole in Warsaw. They couldn't give us a name but apparently the mole was one of us, someone inside the Service, and he was senior. The implication was our head of station or his deputy. David Prince or Euan Moss. We pressed them for evidence, pressed Jacobs because the story apparently came from Moscow, and eventually he came up with something more. The mole had been recruited seven or eight years ago, and critically, he had been recruited in Warsaw. At that time Moss was in South Africa. It had to be Prince. If, of course, and it's a very big if, the Americans are right.'

'What's their source?' I asked.

'They're certainly not going to tell us that. We wouldn't tell them. But they've assured us it's been totally reliable in the past. I suspect we'll have to bring David home again.'

'Are you sure Prince knew nothing about the Americans' Coronation project?' I asked. 'Could he have blown it?'

'Absolutely not. The Company have run the whole operation from Moscow. Even their own Warsaw Station was only brought in at the last minute to help with logistics. None of our Warsaw people have had any involvement.'

I thought about that for a moment. 'Why would they run it from Moscow? Is their source Russian? If he is, how did he come across a Polish peasant who happened to be sitting on a valuable medieval crown?'

'Good questions. Perhaps we'll get answers tonight.' Brasenose looked at Julia. 'I appreciate you have a home to move back into and you have leave booked but I'll need your husband tonight, we're meeting our American cousins.' He turned back to me. 'Century House, six o'clock.' The meeting was over and, it seemed, Brasenose and Sawyer were off.

I wondered how Julia, Brampford and I were going to find our way back to Immigration but Mendale quickly led us outside to another waiting car. No immigration formalities for us. Brampford was dropped off outside departures.

'Thanks for chaperoning these two home, John,' said Mendale. 'Keep your eyes and ears open when you get back.'

I hadn't realised we were being chaperoned, but then I hadn't realised Major Brampford had a first name either. I wondered what he would have done if we had been stopped at the airport. Realistically there was nothing he could have done. He had been told to fly back with us not to offer protection but simply to observe and report.

'I'll take you home,' announced Mendale once Brampford was gone. 'By the way, Justin Brasenose has agreed I might borrow you at some point, Thomas. I understand you now have a talent we might need. How's your Polish?'

'Passable but a long way from fluent.'

'I'll bear that in mind.' He paused and then seemed to change the subject. 'You'll find security's really been stepped up while you've been in Moscow. Bombs in Oxford Street do tend to concentrate minds. The IRA have got everyone looking over their shoulder.'

Our driver turned east on to the M4 into London.

'Good thing really,' Mendale continued. 'Somebody was on the ball at Colchester garrison last week, noticed a man "acting suspiciously" as they say. Interesting. When challenged the man ran off. A couple of off-duty soldiers chased after him and one managed to get close enough to make a grab at him. The man then turned around with a pistol in his hand and knocked the soldier out. One blow. Wallop. And the squaddy's suddenly lying there with his skull fractured. The other squaddy stops and puts his hands up thinking this is the end but the man just shouts at him and runs off again. Disappears who knows where. So of course we all think IRA. But maybe not. Couple of things were a bit odd. One the man doesn't shoot. He has a gun in his hand, two British soldiers right in front of him, perfect targets, and he just runs away.'

'Perhaps the gun was unloaded,' I suggested.

'Perhaps, but why loiter around a British Army base with an unloaded firearm? The second thing is even odder. The man shouts at the soldier in front of him, just yards away, but the soldier can't understand a word the man says. Obviously it's a warning, keep back, but it's not English. We don't know what language it was and believe me we have tried everything. Apparently it wasn't something you might learn in school, like French, and probably not southern European like Spanish or Italian. But it could have been pretty much anything else. Scandinavian, east European, Russian, Turkish, Arabic, Polish perhaps.'

'Why Polish?'

'Well that's where the guessing starts. Brasenose thinks I'm fantasising but I just have an instinct. We have a Polish problem at the moment and he's inside Colchester garrison. Kapitan Marynarki Kacper Nowak.'

'You mean that Polish sailor who jumped ship up north somewhere and wanted to defect?'

'Precisely. Although jump ship isn't quite right. He wasn't a crew member; he had stowed away in Gdańsk and clearly had no idea where the ship was going. He was as surprised as we were when he ended up in Middlesbrough. What's more it seems pretty obvious he had no plan to stowaway in the first place.

'He had no food. No change of clothing. No baggage of any description. And nothing to trade. He's a Polish naval officer, if he wanted to defect it would have been sensible to steal something we might want first, a code book perhaps, or bring some photographs. As a source of intelligence he's been useless even though he says he spent three months on patrol out of Kaliningrad. He's hiding something. I've interviewed him and even through an interpreter that's obvious. Your people in Six have had a go, we even found a Polish speaker in Five to try, but none of us are getting anywhere. Nowak is the most common surname in Poland, not that easy to get behind. He's given us lots of low-level background which adds up, I'm sure he really is a naval officer, he really has been in Kaliningrad recently and everything he tells us about his training, his school days, his home town seems to stack up. Well, nearly everything.

'The Company chap in Moscow told you Nowak had left Kaliningrad for the Wojewódzki Hospital in Gdańsk. Nowak denies that vehemently, which is not surprising, the Wojewódzki Hospital is for mental patients.'

'Well if he does have a screw loose,' I suggested, 'it's not likely anyone would be trying to help him escape. Unless the man with the gun had mental problems as well. Nobody in their right mind would try to spring someone from a prison in the middle of an army base armed just with a pistol.'

'Nowak's not really a prisoner, more a guest, but escape is only one possibility. There's another. Perhaps the objective wasn't to get Nowak out but to keep him there, permanently.'

'Kill him?'

'Who knows? It might all be pure coincidence. But there's something else that I'd rather keep to myself for the moment.' He smiled to himself and muttered enigmatically 'A coincidence too far.'

We got nothing more from him. Mendale was not a natural conversationalist, a former boss of mine had described him as laconic. The Deputy Director General relapsed into silence until we reached Hammersmith, where he stopped the car and disappeared towards the Tube. Twenty minutes later Julia and I drew up outside the terraced house that was about to become our home again. I fumbled with the locks and as the door swung open we both had the same sinking feeling. Something was very wrong.

We walked towards the back of the house and what used to be the kitchen. It looked as if a bomb had struck. A very wet bomb judging by the soggy state of the hall carpet and the water running down the back step into the garden outside. For reasons I was not interested in exploring there had clearly been a water leak in the loft above our bedroom. This had caused the ceiling to collapse and the water tank itself to fall through into the bedroom. This in turn had led to part of the bedroom falling through into the kitchen, a bedside table stood miraculously upright on the kitchen table.

'Welcome home,' said Julia.

The most sensible reaction came from the DIS driver who stood behind us holding Julia's suitcase. 'I'll put this back in the car,' he said.

I managed to find the main stopcock and turn off the water still spurting down from a pipe in the loft. To my surprise the telephone was still working and Julia did what she usually did in an emergency, phoned her uncle. Although he now based himself in Cornwall, Uncle Gordon kept a studio flat in Bayswater and ten minutes after we had arrived home we were off to collect the spare keys from his neighbour. Not the homecoming we had expected.

The day didn't get any better when I phoned our insurance company. The call seemed to be going well until I mentioned that the damage was so bad because the house had been left empty for longer than we expected.

'How long?' I was asked.

There was a sigh when I replied.

'I just need to check something, sir. I'll put you on hold for just a moment.'

I was left hanging on for five minutes and when the call was reconnected a different voice took over. After confirming when our tenants had moved out the new voice dropped his bombshell. Regretfully our policy excluded damage if the house had been unoccupied for more than six consecutive weeks. The claim could not be accepted. I could of course still submit a written claim and it would be reviewed by the claims manager but the policy wording was quite clear, six weeks.

'We'll see about that,' responded Julia when I reported the conversation to her. 'And let's be positive. At least we won't have to spend the weekend moving the stuff we left in storage back into the house. We can go down to Cornwall and visit the family. It will be nice to see everyone again.'

That seemed a pretty small positive to me but Julia was right, it would be good to see the family. In the event her phrase about 'seeing everyone' took on a totally unexpected meaning. The one person Julia was not expecting to see again, least of all in Cornwall, was the man she had seen kill General Demirkan in Russia.

V

Before we could go down to Cornwall I had an appointment
in Suffolk. I met Brasenose at Century House and we joined
the rush hour traffic out of London. Although officially
named 'RAF Mildenhall', the airbase was in reality part
of the US Air Force and Brasenose and I were escorted to
the meeting room by two uniformed American servicemen
wearing the distinctive blue berets of the Security Police.
Ethan Jacobs, the Company's Moscow man, was already
there. As we entered the room he quickly greeted Brasenose
before turning to me.

'What the hell happened to Flanagan and Sokolowski?
Where were you?'

He managed to make the questions sound like
accusations and I remembered his hectoring tone when the
Turkish general had been killed in Yaroslavl.

Brasenose was having none of it. This might be an
American base but Brasenose had the sense of effortless
superiority that comes as much from centuries of imperial
tradition as from five years at Eton College. 'Let's wait
until everyone's arrived shall we?' he responded quietly. 'No
point repeating ourselves. Perhaps you could rustle up some
refreshments, a cup of tea would be nice. Or coffee, that
might be easier for you.'

He smiled at Jacobs, who, without returning the smile,

opened the door and spoke to one of the blue-bereted servicemen standing guard outside the room.

'Interesting, your Security Police,' said Brasenose. 'You know they were set up originally in imitation of the RAF Regiment. Churchill had created the Regiment to protect RAF bases and after you chaps joined the war somebody thought it might be sensible to copy the idea. I believe they were called something like Air Force security battalions back then. And they were manned by what in those days were known as Negroes. Never very popular in this country, your segregation laws, still that's all changed now.'

Jacobs looked as if he was going to say something but thought better of it and went over to the window. A C-11 Gulfstream had just landed and we watched as five men, bundled up against the biting wind, came down the steps. Ten minutes later they joined us. Four were American, two VIPs and two bag carriers.

The two VIPs looked like actors playing good cop, bad cop. I knew enough about the way the Company was organised to realise we had two very different animals in front of us.

Blake Lorrimore represented the intellectual face of the CIA, the Analysts. Ivy League educated, expensively dressed, frighteningly intelligent and more at home in the country clubs around Washington than in the dirty world on the other side of the Iron Curtain. Chuck Hoeven, on the other hand, was from the other CIA tradition, the Operators. Ex-military, he had probably honed his skills at the sharp end in Vietnam or in the dirty wars the Company was always fighting in Latin America.

The last person to enter the room was our Washington Station Chief, Colin Asperton.

Asperton and Brasenose were two polished peas from the same public-school pod. Immaculately attired in expensively tailored suits and conservative shirts adorned with ties that were meant to be recognised and gold cufflinks discreetly bearing their initials or, more likely, their family crests. No doubt they had risen through the Service in similar ways: a spell in one of the more prestigious overseas Stations and an obligatory stint in Washington but most of their careers spent in Century House handling the Holy Grail of the British civil service: 'policy'. Brasenose was the elder and more confident of his status but Asperton now had the Washington role that Brasenose himself had used as a springboard to the top table. They were clearly more colleagues than friends. As I had seen when he visited Moscow, Brasenose was a detail man; Asperton, I suspected, was more impatient, more inclined to act first and tidy up later. He reminded me of the Justin Brasenose I had first met, back in my Defence Intelligence days.

When we were all seated and without any preamble Hoeven kicked off. We were in an American base talking about an American operation and to Hoeven that meant this was his meeting. He had questions he wanted answered. He looked straight at me. 'What happened?'

Before I could answer, Brasenose intervened. 'Let's not start in the middle,' he suggested gently. 'Perhaps you could give us a little more background on Operation Coronation first. What were you expecting to happen? How did all this begin? We're still a little in the dark over here, I haven't had a chance to chat to my colleague yet.' He nodded towards Asperton.

It was the other American, Lorrimore, who replied with the same half-smile as Brasenose.

'Of course. The beginning. I don't need to tell you the context. Poland is in a state of flux. Demonstrations. Strikes. General discontent. It could explode at any moment. What does that mean? It could mean the first Communist domino falling, the beginning of the end for Soviet rule in Eastern Europe. Or it could trigger a Soviet invasion, a Russian clampdown, tanks in the street. We know the Soviet military have plans for exactly that eventuality. And if they invaded today they would be unstoppable. The Polish government would probably welcome them in. The Opposition are still fragmented, too weak to organise any armed response. At the moment the Opposition are striking for bread not freedom, they're trade unionists who never look beyond the factory walls. You can't unite a nation by demanding higher wages for shipyard workers.'

'It needs a symbol,' interrupted Hoeven. 'Like the stars and stripes. And the Poles have one, the Great Crown of Jan Kazimierz, and we found it.'

'Let's really go back to the beginning,' resumed Lorrimore. 'In the Middle Ages the Polish-Lithuanian Commonwealth was the biggest and most powerful country in Europe. Far more important than France or England. But in the seventeenth century all that changed. The Poles call that period The Deluge. The Swedes invaded from one side and the Russians from the other. The Swedes captured Warsaw and the king, Jan Kazimierz, had to flee. He eventually ended up with a tiny band of men in Lwów, a Catholic king being crushed between the Protestant Swedes and Orthodox Russians. And there on April the first 1656, in the Cathedral, he swore the Oath of Lwów and in the presence of the pope's emissary dedicated his crown to the Blessed Virgin Mary.'

'And that's the crown you found?' Brasenose conveyed more than a hint of disbelief.

'That's right,' Hoeven took over again. 'That crown symbolised King Jan Kazimierz driving the invaders out of Poland. Until the Russians arrived in 1939 the people of Lwów kept it on display to demonstrate their love of God and country.'

'Well not quite.' The professor in Lorrimore disapproved of his colleague's cavalier attitude to history. 'The people of Lwów is an elastic concept. They haven't all been lovers of Poland. The city has changed hands time after time. Ukrainians, Austrians, Russians. There were a hundred thousand Jews in Lwów at one time. But the point is that the Crown was in the historical museum in Lwów before the war. Then, like Chuck says, the Russians arrived. While the Germans are invading from the west and looting everything they can find, the Russians invade from the east and take Lwów. The Russians aren't interested in looting, they're out to destroy Lwów as a Polish city. The contents of the Lwów Historical Museum are taken away to what they call the Black House and smashed beyond repair. But it gets worse. The Russians are kicked out and the Nazis arrive. Now we need to use some imagination.

'Suppose the Crown had managed to survive the Russians, what might have happened to it then? Was it looted by the Germans or vandalised by their Ukrainian fascist allies? Or did the museum staff manage to hide it? And if so what happened when the Russians came back at the end of the war?

'The Russians still had no love for the Poles of Lwów. The frontier was moved. Lwów was no longer in Poland, it was part of the Soviet Union. Ukrainian replaced Polish. Polish Lwów became what it is today, Ukrainian Lviv. Those Poles who had survived the war were shipped west to populate the land chopped out of Germany and given to Poland. Danzig's German population was expelled and the city rechristened Gdańsk and stuffed full of Poles from the Ukraine. In all the chaos the Great Crown of Jan Kazimierz simply vanished.'

'And now you've found it?'

Lorrimore looked across at Hoeven, who took up the story. 'We've found it. Seems a guy who worked at the museum, a curator named Dyrda, buried it in his back garden, right back when the war started. After the war he didn't know what to do with it. The Russians were back. The Ukrainians were taking over. And then all the Poles were told to pack their bags and take a train to their new home, in his case a place called Malbork near Gdańsk.'

Brasenose interrupted. 'So this museum curator shoved a priceless crown into his suitcase and when he reached Malbork buried it in his garden again and we're supposed to believe it stayed there until you came along.'

This time it was Blake Lorrimore's turn to respond. 'I suppose that's English sarcasm. It does sound like a fairy tale but I tell you, Justin, we've done a lot of research on this. Malbork was Marienburg before the war and Marienburg Castle was a shrine for the Nazis. The Hitler Youth had an annual pilgrimage to celebrate the Teutonic Knights who built the Castle. After the war the Poles claimed it as part of their history and turned it into a museum, a museum with a curator named Dyrda. Now can we prove this guy had come from Lwów? No. If any of the records in Lwów/Lviv did survive the war we can't access them, but we've spoken to his niece and she claims he worked in the museum in Lwów before the war.'

'The man himself is dead?'

'Yes, he died a year ago, in Bartoszyce. Seems his wife had already passed away and they had no children so when he retired in the late sixties he moved to Bartoszyce to be with his brother. The brother also died a few years ago.'

'So no confirmation of the story?' Brasenose persisted.

'Well we sent Jerry Sokolowski to look up the niece but he didn't get much. Seems she's a diehard Communist. Like I said, she confirms the family were originally from Lwów and her uncle worked in the museum there. Jerry tried to ask her about the Crown but she was already suspicious of an American turning up claiming to be looking for long-lost relatives. Jerry decided she didn't know anything and left.'

'Or perhaps she didn't know anything because there is no Crown.'

'Oh there is,' Colin Asperton butted in. 'I warned Blake that you would be sceptical but there's no doubt the Crown exists. Blake has found photos from the thirties showing the Crown in the museum in Lwów. Black and white of course. But he also has a picture of the Crown taken just a month ago, in full colour, and there's no doubt it's the same one.' He looked at Lorrimore for confirmation.

'Well we can't tell positively without examining it,' Lorrimore conceded, 'but the new photo is either genuine or an amazing forgery.' He opened his briefcase and took out two photos. 'You can have these. Comparing them, we think the Crown in the colour picture is the real thing.'

Brasenose changed tack. 'Well then let's get to the crux of the story. How did the Crown get from Mr Dyrda to you?'

Hoeven started to answer. 'We have an asset in Bartoszyce.'

Brasenose cut him off, his tone more incredulous than ever. 'You have an asset in a village in Poland that nobody's ever heard of?'

'You haven't heard of it because we don't tell the whole world where we have agents. Bartoszyce is right up by the Russian border, just thirty miles from Kaliningrad and yes, we have an asset there. OK it's just low-grade stuff but it's reliable. He knows the terrain; he can get over the frontier when we make it worthwhile.'

'I don't suppose he has a name?'

'Broniszewski.' Hoeven almost dared Brasenose to contradict him.

I knew that name. 'You mean the peasant we were supposed to meet at the lake? The man who was bringing the Crown?'

'That's him. Seems he had befriended Dyrda. Listened to the old man's stories about life in Lwów before the war. Listened to him going on about Poland's glorious history before the Russians destroyed everything. And eventually, just before he died, Dyrda showed him the Crown. Dyrda's mind was wandering a bit by then. Maybe he gave Broniszewski the Crown, maybe Broniszewski took it. Anyway, Broniszewski comes to us and says he wants to sell this thing. He's heard they have sales of old relics in London. Can we help him get it there? So we set up the meeting by the lake. I guess this is where you take over.' He looked at me. 'What happened?'

Again Brasenose stopped me answering. 'Haven't you missed something? There are a couple of characters you haven't mentioned yet. Father Paszek and the man who set up the meeting, I believe you call him Krypton. I don't suppose you'd like to give us his name?'

'No, we wouldn't.' It was Jacobs, the Moscow Station Chief, who answered, the first time he had said anything since the meeting started.

Brasenose turned towards him with a smile. 'So Krypton's one of your people is he? You're handling him from Moscow. Is he Russian perhaps?'

Jacobs said nothing and Lorrimore filled the resulting silence. 'Come along, Justin. Krypton's not relevant. Father Paszek is different. He could be central to this whole thing. You know of him, of course. He has some powerful friends back in the States. If the Communist regime falls in Poland and if the Russians don't intervene then we have to consider who may take over. The Agency's view is that the most likely scenario, if we do nothing, will be what back in the Prague Spring in 1968 they called socialism with a human face. You remember Dubček, the Czech leader? He thought he could reform the economy, introduce freedom of speech and still keep his country a loyal Russian ally. The Russians didn't agree, of course, and they marched in. But times are changing. After their problems in Afghanistan the Reds aren't so keen on invasions.'

'But socialism with a human face is no good to the United States,' Brasenose suggested.

'It's no good to any of us,' Lorrimore retorted gently. 'The Poles won't get genuine freedom; they won't get the free markets and the outside investment they need to grow their economy and we won't get an ally to help contain the Soviets.'

'It's simple,' said Hoeven. 'We need someone like Paszek,

someone who will stand up for their country, stand up to the Russians.'

'Unless, of course,' continued the more emollient Lorrimore, 'by standing up to the Russians we push Brezhnev into sending in his troops. That would be the worst possible outcome.'

'Brezhnev's senile,' Hoeven retorted. 'He's incapable of making any decisions. Now is the time to act. Who knows what will happen when Brezhnev finally goes?'

'You could be right, Chuck,' Lorrimore admitted. 'Paying a few thousand dollars to get Paszek this Crown doesn't seem like a bad investment.'

That brought us back to what had been called Project Coronation but now seemed to be a fully-fledged Operation Coronation. It was Colin Asperton who turned the spotlight on to me. 'The politics are all very interesting but we have an operation that seems to have gone wrong and two Agency personnel are missing, not to mention Krypton and Broniszewski. Let's hear from the man who was there. The question Chuck keeps asking: what happened?'

This time Brasenose made no attempt to stop me and for the second time that day I went through the events in the Masurian Lakes a little over twenty-four hours before. Nobody interrupted until I mentioned hearing the shots.

'What sort of shots?' Hoeven demanded.

'I'm not sure. Handgun perhaps. Not a shotgun and the first three not automatic.'

'And you're sure there were three and then three more.'

'I'm positive. After that I think there were more shots but my wife was scrambling into the car and Father Paszek's driver had started to move off.'

'You didn't think of going to investigate?' Jacobs wanted to know. 'You just left Flanagan and Sokolowski there.'

'Paszek was leaving. It wasn't sensible for Julia and me to stand around with no vehicle and people firing off guns. Your men had a car, I had to believe that if they could get away they would.'

'You mean you panicked. Your wife runs out of the woods screaming and you just want to get away.'

'I wouldn't put it like that.'

Brasenose intervened again. 'Are we to take it you've heard nothing from your team?'

'Nothing. Not a squawk. Not from Flanagan and not from Krypton.'

'You think they bumped into a Polish patrol?'

'Bumped into, no. It was a trap. Someone told the Reds we were coming.'

'Any idea who?'

Brasenose's question hung in the air. Eventually Hoeven answered. 'Well there's one obvious candidate, your man in Warsaw, David Prince.'

'But he didn't know anything about this operation. Wasn't that the whole point of bringing Thomas in from Moscow?'

'Are you sure?' Hoeven looked across at me suspiciously. 'You couldn't have just let something slip, at the Embassy? Perhaps your wife mentioned something to a girlfriend and it got back to Prince.'

'Neither of us spoke to anyone at the Embassy. I've never met David Prince.'

'Don't your Defence Intelligence people have a man in Warsaw? Brampford. Couldn't your wife have said something to him? Something quite innocent. Asking about the shops in Olsztyn, perhaps?'

'Impossible. We didn't meet Brampford until after we got back to Warsaw.'

'Well somebody blew it. Those troops didn't just turn up to admire the view. They knew our men were there.'

'Chuck's right, Justin,' put in Asperton. 'We have to do something. We all like David but the evidence is piling up.'

'What evidence?'

'Our source is reliable,' insisted Hoeven. 'And there's only one person who fits the description he gave us: Prince.'

'Really? And who is this source?'

This time it was Lorrimore who answered. 'You know we can't tell you that. What would happen if it got back to Prince?'

Brasenose bowed to the inevitable. 'All right. As it happens this afternoon I had Prince recalled again. We'll keep him out of Warsaw until this is all over.'

'And keep him away from anything connected to Operation Coronation.'

'Of course.'

There was no more to be said.

On the trip back from Mildenhall Brasenose and Asperton sat in the back of the car discussing the meeting that had just ended as if I was not present, and yet at the same time they were both careful not to say anything that junior ears should not hear. What was obvious is that the two men were not seeing eye to eye.

Brasenose remained sceptical about every part of Operation Coronation. He didn't really believe any of the Great Crown of Jan Kazimierz saga and was in any case dubious about the wisdom of, as he put it, 'upsetting the apple cart' in Poland. Asperton, on the other hand, was much more bullish. The former Polish leader Edward Gierek, who had been in power for a decade, had been ousted the previous year and his replacement, Stanisław Kania, hadn't lasted long. A matter of weeks earlier he had been replaced as Party Secretary by a military man.

'The new regime can't last. Either the Russian tanks will roll in or something revolutionary will happen,' Asperton insisted. 'And we can help shape that revolution.'

'And if the revolution fails?' Brasenose asked.

'Then the Russian tanks roll in. Either way that's the likely outcome but it's possible the revolution will work. With strong leadership it could unite the people, win the support of the military and frighten Brezhnev into staying away. It's a risk worth taking.'

'A risk for whom? It won't be our blood on the streets if it all goes wrong.'

Asperton changed the subject. 'What are you going to do about Prince? Lorrimore and Hoeven are right, we have to do something.'

'Let's talk about that in the office, Colin,' replied Brasenose, perhaps conscious of my presence. The remainder of the journey was devoted to the performance of the English cricket team, currently escaping the British winter by touring India, and the chances of France winning the rugby Grand Slam again.

When I got home I discovered that the Mildenhall meeting was to be repeated the next day, with Julia playing my part. Richard Mendale had phoned to say that the Director General, General Fearmont, wanted her in his Whitehall conference room at nine o'clock sharp next morning. The Defence Intelligence Staff and the CIA, Fearmont had announced, were going to conduct a review of what he called their 'joint operation' in Poland.

'Like suggesting that an elephant stepping on a mouse is a "joint operation" because the mouse contributes its squeak,' was Mendale's comment.

I spent the next morning in the flat phoning builders and becoming increasingly depressed at both the cost and the likely duration of the repairs our house would need. Julia phoned at lunch to tell me that the conference with what Fearmont insisted on calling 'The Agency', a term hardly anybody else ever used, had been a complete waste of time.

The Americans were obsessed, Julia reported, with the idea that she must have somehow given our plans away. Fearmont, rather than standing up for her, had just made matters worse. No doubt, he suggested, she had tried very hard not to say anything untoward but was there really no conversation with anyone in which she had perhaps mentioned going to Olsztyn or me meeting Flanagan at the Pewex shop? It had been a mistake of Six, he insisted, to have encouraged her to take part in the operation. She had not been trained in this sort of thing. He was not blaming her for anything but they had to determine where the leak had come from and in particular if there was any way in which David Prince could have discovered anything at all about Operation Coronation.

I could imagine that Julia would have become increasingly angry. Eventually the point came when she had had enough but it was the American Lorrimore rather than her own Director General who had finally called an end to the discussion.

At that point Fearmont had raised the totally unrelated matter of Kacper Nowak. Julia could only imagine that Fearmont had wanted to show that the DIS also had its secret operations and that in terms of the British Intelligence establishment there were some matters better handled by the DIS than by MI6. Six had given up on Nowak, he implied, and passed it on to the experts in his department. Of course if the DIS discovered anything useful about Soviet naval capabilities he would pass it on to the Agency. In the meantime if there was anything the Agency could do to help to provide more background on the Polish defector they would be very grateful. Jacobs merely repeated the information that he had already passed over in Moscow. Nowak appeared to have been dismissed from the Polish navy and sent to a mental institution in Gdańsk. Fearmont didn't ask how the Agency had acquired this information and when Julia herself asked, Fearmont had rebuked her, pointing out that in the world of Intelligence sources always had to be protected.

Julia was not happy. Not only had Fearmont patronised her during the meeting but he was now sending her off on a thoroughly pointless jaunt to Essex.

'He wants me to spend the afternoon at the MCTC,' she told me.

'The what?'

'The Military Corrective Training Centre in Colchester, the place we're keeping that Polish sailor Nowak. Apparently it's Mendale's idea. He wants me to check something. I'll see you back at the flat this evening. See if you can find some of my uncle's decent whisky and have it waiting for me.'

In fact, Julia had forgotten all about the whisky when she finally arrived at the Bayswater flat. I opened the door to her and without even taking off her coat the words came rushing out.

'The world's gone mad. Do you want the good news or the totally incomprehensible, absolutely insane, simply impossible news?'

I knew Julia wanted to start with the totally incomprehensible, absolutely insane, simply impossible news so I said: 'Let's start with the good news.'

'You can be so boring,' she replied. 'But it is very good news. I spoke to my uncle about the insurance company turning down our claim.'

'Don't tell me he's got them to change their minds. He knows somebody in the company.'

Julia looked nonplussed. 'How did you know? The company's chairman is a crossbencher like Uncle Gordon and they know each other well. Uncle phoned him and explained we had been away on highly secret, government business and this chap promised to sort it out. And he did. There will be a claims assessor at the house first thing in the morning and they'll settle everything. We might even end up with a better kitchen than the one we lost. I told Mendale I'm taking the day off tomorrow to sort it all out.'

I didn't know what to say. It was marvellous news and I was very grateful to Julia's Uncle Gordon. But I still felt a little hypocritical. I suppose I had married into the British establishment and this is how the old boys' network worked, but I knew that my father would be horrified if I told him.

'It's all right for some,' I could hear him say, 'but what about all the poor sods who don't know anyone in the House of Lords? It's their premiums that will have to go up to pay for people like you.'

In theory he was right, but I certainly wasn't going to reject the offer.

'So if that's the good news what's the simply impossible news?'

If Julia was disappointed by my reaction to the good news she didn't say anything, her other news was pushing everything else into the background.

'I've found a killer. Fearmont sent me down to Colchester as I told you. Apparently Mendale wanted me to go through the surveillance videos from outside the base and see if I noticed anything suspicious. There's a camera there that records everything on cassettes which they keep for a week and then record over again. It seemed like a complete wild goose chase to me. There were a whole pile of these cassettes and I had no idea where to begin. I should have been suspicious when the sergeant waiting for me said that he had been told I should start with one cassette in particular. It turned out to be one of the ones recorded on the day the man with the gun appeared. An hour into the tape I saw him.'

'You mean they actually have a tape of this chap waving a pistol around?'

'No. He was just walking past, rather slowly but not in a particularly suspicious way.'

'Then how did you know it was him?'

'That's the point. That's why Mendale wanted me down there. Mendale must have known.'

'Known what?'

'He must have known what I would find. That I would recognise the man because I had seen him before. There's absolutely no doubt. It was the man who shot General Demirkan in Yaroslavl.'

VI

I was stunned. There could be no possible connection between the assassination of a senior Turkish general in Russia and the apparent defection of an insignificant Polish naval lieutenant. There had to be a mistake, and yet I knew Julia well enough to be sure that if she said it was the same man then it was the same man.

Julia explained that she had rushed back to Whitehall and immediately confronted Richard Mendale. He was not at all embarrassed when she demanded to know why he had sent her off to look for something he already knew was there.

'I needed confirmation.'

The two soldiers who had tried to seize the gunman the week before had provided very detailed descriptions. In particular they had both commented on the peculiar vertical marks on the man's face. That rang a bell with Mendale, impossible as it seemed at first. He had looked out Julia's report on the Yaroslavl assassination and the descriptions matched exactly. Not just the clefts on the cheeks but height, hair colour, complexion, weight. It couldn't be a coincidence; the man in Yaroslavl and the man in Colchester were the same.

Fearmont had dismissed the idea immediately but had agreed to Julia being sent down to Essex to check out the video. Now that Mendale's guess had proved to be correct, Fearmont shamelessly took ownership of the discovery.

'He immediately phoned the Americans,' Julia told me.

'Why on earth did he do that?'

'I think he just wanted to show them that our department was ahead of Six. It was a piece of one-upmanship. Six had interrogated Nowak and found nothing whereas we had been able to discover a link with the Demirkan killing. We now had evidence that the man lurking outside the Colchester garrison was a KGB killer.'

I was sure Julia was right, that is exactly how Fearmont would have thought. He should of course have contacted my Service and MI5 right away but I suppose he wanted his moment in the spotlight. Fearmont always took centre stage in his own productions. I wondered whether egos grow in the Army, and elsewhere, as a consequence of repeated promotions or is an oversized ego a prerequisite for repeated promotion?

We had another meeting scheduled with Lorrimore and Hoeven the next morning and no doubt there would be plenty to say about the new development. However, when I arrived at work Brasenose had other things on his mind. He called me in right away.

'Something's come up, the meeting with the Americans is off. They've flown to Sweden. It seems their agent Krypton has turned up alive and well in a place called Ystad. If we behave ourselves they may let us know what he has to report, or they may not. These days liaison with the Company tends to be a one-way street.'

Brasenose's cynicism proved to be unfounded. Later that day we received a message from Blake Lorrimore that he would be flying back from Sweden to Washington that evening via London. Perhaps we could have a quick chat during his stopover at Heathrow.

Before that we had to deal with the issue of a KGB assassin prowling the streets of Colchester.

Based on the sightings by the two soldiers who had tried to grab him, and Julia's recollections, a photofit picture had been produced and given to every policeman and soldier in Colchester. That still left a high degree of nervousness about Nowak's security but we discovered that General Fearmont had already solved that problem. Nowak would be moved, he announced without consulting anyone, to a safe house as far away from Essex as possible. His deputy, Richard Mendale, had already found somewhere suitable in the West Country.

When both MI5 and MI6 suggested that moving Nowak around the country might be more of a risk than keeping him where he was, Fearmont was adamant. The military facilities in Colchester had been compromised. He had spent thirty years in the Army and knew that military standards were not what they had been when he had first been commissioned. Just look at how the killer had been able to evade the two squaddies who had approached him before.

More importantly, the killer clearly knew where Nowak was being held, far better to hold him where nobody could find him. The Mongolian, as the Americans insisted on calling the man we equally ridiculously now called Scarface, was clearly a professional assassin with the full resources of the KGB behind him; bribing his way into a prison would be well within his capabilities.

'He's probably made arrangements with local Communists already,' Fearmont insisted.

Finally he produced his clinching argument. He had

spoken to Chuck Hoeven to tell him that he would be personally taking charge of Nowak's interrogation the next morning and the American had congratulated him on the steps he was taking.

Whatever the wisdom of Fearmont's plan, the underlying question remained. Why would the KGB want to kill, or alternatively rescue, a Polish naval lieutenant who seemed to have no knowledge of any value? On that question we were no nearer finding an answer.

Brasenose disappeared for lunch with Richard Mendale at a quiet restaurant near Waterloo where the tables were set discretely well apart. When he returned all that he would say is that everything still smelled. There was no news from the Americans now in Sweden and Nowak was still clamming up. Both men were convinced that Nowak was hiding something but what and why they had no idea.

It seemed to me that the two men had spent most of their meal gossiping. Mendale had reported dismissively that his boss, General Fearmont, and Chuck Hoeven were now the best of friends. They had agreed, reported Fearmont, that from now on there would be a full pooling of knowledge between their two organisations, the DIS and CIA. But, added Mendale with a smile, nobody in the DIS had been told that Hoeven's colleague, Blake Lorrimore, would be stopping off in London this evening. Whatever Fearmont might imagine, Her Majesty's Defence Intelligence Staff were not in the same league as the US Central Intelligence Agency.

One thing Brasenose and Mendale agreed on was that Scarface, the man with the gun spotted in Colchester, was even more of an enigma now than he had been before.

'I just don't buy this KGB assassin line,' Mendale had said. 'It's just too neat. I was never totally convinced that Demirkan's murder was down to them. What was the motive? We knew Samet Demirkan, he was a gentleman, he wasn't involved in any funny business in Russia. He stood up to the fanatics on both left and right. It's much more likely that some Kurdish group shot him.'

The police believed they had traced Scarface to a hotel in Chelmsford. He only stayed one night, paid cash and used the name Byron. The hotel didn't ask for any ID and there was no other trace of anyone called Byron.

'They may have some fingerprints from his hotel room,' Mendale had reported, 'but they don't match any in the records and in any case we won't know for sure if they belong to him until we find him. Apparently this Byron spoke some English but not a lot, not enough for him to bluff his way into a prison or convince anyone he was a local. If the KGB wanted to send an assassin over here they must have had hundreds of better candidates.'

The other subject of lunchtime conversation had apparently been David Prince. Brasenose was not going to tell me what had been said but clearly my name had come up.

'You and I need to have a word about your future,' announced Brasenose. 'You did well in Moscow and normally your next role would be back here in Century House. The rather irregular way you joined the Service meant you never had a proper induction. You need to spend time on a country desk here and get to really understand how the Service operates, lose some of those rough edges that didn't matter when you were in Defence Intelligence. But right now our priority is Warsaw. That's where we really need people on the ground. Pulling David Prince back is going to leave a massive hole. I'm not suggesting you're ready to take his place, but perhaps a temporary posting would be helpful, supporting his replacement until the situation there calms down.'

By starting to learn Polish I had known I was opening the door to a future assignment in Warsaw, that was one of the attractions of adding another language to my repertoire. But at the present moment Julia and I rather wanted some time back in London. We were looking forward to spending time with family and friends and enjoying a normal domestic life for a while. Travel was in our blood and we both loved the idea of living abroad again but right now we had other things on our mind, like starting a family. Nevertheless we both understood the Service well enough to realise that if I was being offered promotion saying no was not a sensible option.

In any case, Brasenose wasn't asking for my thoughts. His mind had already moved on.

'I've known David Prince for a long time and I don't believe he's a Soviet mole. But of course we've made mistakes before.'

Brasenose paused and for the first time I sensed an indecisiveness in him. 'It's eighteen years since Kim Philby took the one-way ride to Moscow. It's to our eternal shame that we never really doubted him. Others did but inside the Service we were blind for a long time. The Americans were right about Philby and we can't ignore them now. But I won't have David Prince persecuted on the basis of a source we're not allowed to know anything about.'

He paused again. 'I've consulted colleagues and we've

decided that in this case a degree of honesty is called for. I'm going to tell David that the Americans have concerns about him and we need to conduct an investigation. We need to go through everything he's done in Poland. You'll be part of that investigation and we might need to temporarily post you to Warsaw. But the first thing you need to get up to speed on is Feliks Radlowski.'

The Radlowski affair had been a major triumph for the Service. Feliks Radlowski was one of the first of the Polish intellectuals to link up with the working-class trade unionists who formed the Solidarity trade union. Despite constant harassment by the SB secret police he became a leading figure in the various underground protest movements. The SB had a reputation for being more subtle than most of their Soviet bloc colleagues but when they decided it was necessary they could be just as brutal. After spells in prison failed to dissuade Radlowski, the SB had decided that a fatal accident was needed. They arranged a gas explosion at his apartment.

Somehow David Prince had learned about the plan and when the explosion occurred in the middle of the night Radlowski wasn't there. He was in a friend's flat having his hair altered to look like the photo in a British diplomatic passport belonging to a junior member of the Embassy's commercial team to whom he happened to bear a vague resemblance. Twenty-four hours later Radlowski was in London. Shortly after that he moved to Chicago, where he was now coordinating the support American trade unions were providing to Solidarity.

Thinking about Prince's role in the Radlowski affair, I could understand Brasenose's hesitation.

'If Prince is a Soviet agent, why would he help Radlowski escape?' I asked.

'I suspect that's what Blake Lorrimore wants to talk about tonight. Radlowski is effectively working for the Company now, in fact working for Blake. He's helping them channel money to Solidarity through the AFL-CIO, the equivalent of our Trade Union Congress. If Prince really is a Russian agent what does that imply about Radlowski? Blake has put his reputation behind Solidarity. He already has Chuck Hoeven saying that the Company should be supporting nationalists like Father Paszek instead. Now he must fear that if Radlowski is unreliable the Company's money may not even be reaching Solidarity. And that gives us a way to make this more palatable to David.'

'How?'

'Obviously we can't tell David that the Americans have a source that implicates him in the leaks we seem to have in Warsaw. Instead we'll tell him the Americans have had suspicions about Radlowski. They thought he might be siphoning off money for his own account but now they've started to think he may even be a Communist plant. That's why they have concerns about David. Was he part of an SB or KGB operation to plant Feliks Radlowski in the US? Was the whole story of David helping Radlowski escape assassination part of an elaborate deception by the Reds?'

'It sounds a bit far-fetched,' I said.

'Yes, but it does have one advantage. It's true. The Americans are starting to think that if David is a mole then it follows Radlowski is a plant. We're just reversing that logic.'

When, that evening, Brasenose and I met Lorrimore in

a VIP room at Heathrow he did indeed want to talk about Radlowski but Brasenose was far more interested in what had happened to Julia and me in Poland. What had the mysterious Krypton said about that and the disappearance of the two Company agents Flanagan and Sokolowski?

Although Lorrimore was impeccably dressed, his suit somehow uncreased, he seemed less assured than he had been at our previous meeting. The American fiddled unconsciously with his elaborate cufflinks. When he started to speak he was surprisingly forthcoming, more so, I suspected, than his colleague Chuck Hoeven would have been. But at the same time his voice managed to convey the impression that he did not entirely believe what he was about to say.

He sat back in his chair and spoke without looking directly at either of us. 'Let me tell you Krypton's story.'

VII

Krypton is a cautious man. He has to be to survive. He was nervous about making the exchange at a place chosen by someone else but in the circumstances he had no choice.

Broniszewski, the peasant who was bringing the Crown to the exchange, knew the area in a way that Krypton did not. Two thousand lakes stretch across hundreds of miles from the Russian border to the Vistula, linked by streams, canals and small rivers. Broniszewski assured his handler that he knew them intimately, Krypton should trust him, there would be no problems. Broniszewski had chosen a hut on the southern shore of one of the middling sized lakes as the location for the exchange to take place. It was a popular picnic spot in spring and summer but at this time of the year there would be nobody around. A path led away from the hut along the eastern side of the lake but soon petered out. In autumn the marshes on the northern shore attracted the occasional hunter looking for duck or geese but the boggy ground was now hard and the water iced over, although the ice was still treacherously thin in places.

Three days before the meeting Krypton reconnoitred the area carefully. He drove his four-wheel drive Lada Niva along the road from Elk towards Mrągowo. He passed half a dozen trails and paths leading into the forest that Broniszewski had pointed out to him on the map. The peasant had suggested using one particular track but when the time came Krypton wouldn't be using any of them.

There was no sign of life and he hoped it would be the same when he came again. He drove on for three miles before returning along the same road and driving off into the trees along one of the paths he had seen earlier. As soon as he was confident the Lada could not be seen from the road he stopped and hiked the rest of the way to the lake. He didn't want anyone visiting the hut in the next few days to find his tyre tracks.

The hut itself was set a short distance back from the water, partly hidden by a clump of tall alder trees. A rickety wooden jetty looked as if it hadn't been used for years even though Krypton could imagine holidaymakers laboriously bringing their canoes to the lake when the winter months were well behind them. In the surrounding forest the trees were by now largely leafless but still dark and forbidding. Here and there a few patches of the snow that had fallen briefly the night before covered the ground. The silence was disturbed only when fragments of ice splattered down from the canopy above.

Experience had taught Krypton to plan in excruciating detail but even then expect something to go wrong. It was clear that if on the day of the exchange he approached the lake on foot, or even worse tried to approach by car, he could easily be trapped at the hut when the unexpected happened. He had no intention of letting himself be caught like that.

He had acquired a five-metre dinghy with a small outboard motor which he hid on a smaller, connecting lake to the west. In three days' time he would use the dinghy to travel from there along a small river to the peat bog on the northern shore opposite the hut. He could wait there and make sure there was nobody in sight before crossing over to meet Broniszewski and the Americans.

He had arranged to meet Broniszewski inside the hut. If the Americans were on time they would arrive shortly after.

It was a risky plan; the lakes were already icing up.

On the day of the exchange there was a bitter wind and clouds scudded across the sky. The radio had forecast light rain turning to snow later. Krypton found his dinghy where he had left it. He transferred the money for the Crown from the Lada to the dinghy which settled alarmingly, he had overlooked the weight of the sacks. Then he set off for the rendezvous. When he reached the peat bog he carefully studied the southern shore of the lake through his military-issue BPOC binoculars. There was no sign of movement although even with the field glasses it was harder than he expected to peer into the gloom around the hut.

To avoid making any noise Krypton didn't use the outboard motor. Instead he pushed off and rowed slowly along the eastern side of the lake. He arrived at the landing stage below the hut and tied up. He was early and cursed his impatience. There was no sign of Broniszewski. Leaving the money in the dinghy he walked through the trees to the hut. It was empty and as quiet as the grave. Even the birds were silent. Krypton stood unmoving for a moment. The silence was unnatural. Quickly he turned and hurried back towards the dinghy. He was almost there when he felt rather than saw a movement beside him. He turned and found himself looking into the stumpy barrel of a Makarov semi-automatic pistol pointed at him by a masked figure in a camouflage jacket and dark jeans.

A second man approached, also masked and also gun in hand. Neither said a word. Instead they motioned him towards the dinghy and frisked him. His own pistol was discovered and thrown far out into the lake. He knew the Americans had insisted on being unarmed but he had not been so stupid. One of the men ordered him to turn around. He expected a bullet in the back of the head but instead the two men tied him up and threw him into the dinghy. They made no attempt to gag him but warned him that if he made the slightest sound he would be killed. They then disappeared with the cash into the trees.

They couldn't have gone far because after five minutes they returned empty-handed. They checked that he was where they had left him but made no attempt to inspect the ropes binding him. One of them laughed and told him to be a good boy and then they were off again, this time in the opposite direction, towards the hut.

The two men were amateurs, Krypton concluded. In their position he would have made sure there were no witnesses left alive. He tried to untie himself but although his attackers were not professionals he was thoroughly trussed. Eventually he managed to wriggle around in the bottom of the boat and reach his box of fishing tackle. Pushing the box over with his feet he manoeuvred to feel inside. He found the gut hook with its 10cm blade. Expecting the men to return at any moment, Krypton managed to grasp the hook in one hand and saw away at the rope on the opposite wrist. It was painstakingly slow but after around twenty-five minutes he was able to free himself. As he finally did so and looked cautiously over the side of the dinghy he heard shots.

He didn't wait. He needed to get out of there, and

quickly. At first he used his oars to avoid alerting anyone but a man came bursting out of the trees. Krypton lowered the outboard motor into the water and jerked on the cord to pull-start the engine. Fortunately the motor clattered into life. He briefly looked back and saw one of the men who had jumped him, now with his face uncovered. He was running along the path beside the lake carrying a red and black bag of some kind. There were more shots, automatic weapons, but it wasn't clear who was shooting at whom. The shots didn't come anywhere near the dinghy.

Hunched down in the boat Krypton had only one thought: escape. He didn't look back again. When he reached the Lada he abandoned the dinghy and immediately drove off, expecting pursuit at any moment. It didn't come. He had escaped. The two Americans, Flanagan and Sokolowski, were not so lucky.

VIII

'Do you believe him?' Brasenose asked when Lorrimore had finished Krypton's story. 'Two mystery men jump out of nowhere, carry off the cash and then get jumped themselves. Did Krypton describe the men?'

'Yes, but nothing particularly distinctive. Tall and fit. It was cold and wet that day and both wore some sort of woolly ski hat hiding parts of their face, maybe what you call balaclavas. Military style clothing but definitely no insignia. One spoke Russian with a Polish accent.'

Brasenose smiled. 'So they spoke to your man Krypton in Russian?'

Lorrimore smiled back, realising his mistake. 'Yes they did, our man is Russian, but then you'd guessed that. We wouldn't be running the operation out of Moscow otherwise.'

'But you're still not going to give us his name. Even though your man is now in Sweden. Is he out permanently or will he go back to Russia?'

'Don't push me, Justin. I'm telling you more than some of my colleagues would like. Krypton's reliable, he's served us for a long time, that's all you need to know. Krypton didn't see Flanagan or Sokolowski and has no idea what happened to them. And he didn't see the man he was supposed to be meeting, Broniszewski, so he doesn't know if he brought the Crown.'

'And how did he get from Poland to Sweden?' Brasenose asked.

'You don't need to know that. We had something set up in case he had to come over in a hurry.'

Lorrimore suddenly looked across at me. 'Did Flanagan and Sokolowski tell you anything about the money? Did they tell you how much we were planning to pay for the Crown?'

'Not exactly. Just that the peasant who was selling it would be "very, very rich".'

'Those were their exact words?'

'Yes. Why?'

'It's just odd. Flanagan was authorised to offer up to $10 000. That wouldn't take much carrying but Krypton said the money was in two large cases and the men had trouble getting it out of the boat. Even in Poland right now $10 000 wouldn't be enough to make someone really rich.'

'So what are you implying?' Brasenose asked.

'I'm not implying anything. Like I say it's just odd. Chuck's not worried but to me it's an inconsistency and I don't like inconsistencies.'

We weren't going to learn any more but the story Lorrimore had just recounted didn't ring true. I couldn't decide whether he was holding something back or Krypton had been less than honest with the Americans.

Lorrimore changed the subject. He was clearly disappointed that we had uncovered nothing more on the leaks from our Warsaw Embassy. As far as he was concerned David Prince was the mole and it was up to us to do something about it.

'You've really got to grill the guy,' he said. 'We've lost

two men in Poland, remember, and we've still no real idea where things went wrong. There's a mole somewhere and Prince has to be it. There's nobody else who fits the bill. I tell you, Justin, we are very confident about this one, although I have to admit we can't figure out how Prince could have got on to Operation Coronation if your man here, or his wife, didn't alert somebody. There's a lot going on in Poland and we really want to work with you Brits on it, but we can't do that as long as Prince is in place.'

Brasenose nodded. 'Prince arrived back in London today and we will interrogate him tomorrow. You're welcome to stop over and join us. Obviously there are lots of questions to ask about Radlowski and you might be better placed to ask them than we would. I understand Radlowski is working for you now.'

Lorrimore ignored the last remark. We all knew that Radlowski was nominally employed by the AFL-CIO trade union group. Lorrimore seemed surprised by the offer to attend the interrogation but turned it down.

'I have to be back in Washington tomorrow, like I say there's a lot happening. The White House is really getting alarmed about the situation in Poland, they think the wheels could come off at any time. You need to remember that the Polish-American lobby is pretty strong back home and there is a lot of pressure on us to make sure that if the wheels do come off they roll in the direction we want.'

'I understand perfectly,' said Brasenose. 'We still have fifty thousand British Army troops in West Germany and we don't want the Soviets practising real live war games in Poland. Tell me, is it just a coincidence that everything we do at the moment seems to revolve around Poland? We have your Operation Coronation, this sailor Kacper Nowak turning up apparently with a KGB assassin on his tail and then doubts about Prince. All surfacing at the same time.'

Lorrimore laughed. 'I don't think the fact that the Polish government could fall at any moment has anything to do with your man Prince or with this sailor Nowak. And with the greatest respect, I don't buy the story of Thomas' wife identifying a man in the street in England as the scarfaced Mongolian she saw just for a few seconds when that Turkish general was killed in Russia. In this business we see conspiracy where anyone else would see coincidence and nine times out of ten we're wrong.'

'But there's always that one time in ten when we're not.'

'We'll see. I think they're calling my plane. Let's you and I keep in touch.'

As we walked back to our car Brasenose asked me if I had heard Lorrimore's plane being called. I hadn't.

'Neither had I,' said Brasenose. 'He didn't want us trying to connect Coronation, Prince and Nowak and he may be right. But the Company are still keeping things from us.'

'Like Krypton's identity,' I suggested.

'Yes, like that, although I have hopes we will soon find that out. And when we do perhaps we'll find an answer to the question that's been troubling me since you first reported back on your adventure by the lake. How did a long-standing Company asset, who we now know to be a Russian being run out of the Company station in Moscow, just happen upon a peasant with a magical crown a thousand miles away in Poland? That's not coincidence, that's conspiracy.'

IX

Brasenose wanted to keep his interview with David Prince under wraps and had decided that it would be conducted not at Century House but at the Ministry of Defence training rooms we used in Borough High Street, opposite Southwark police station. I was not invited to attend. Instead, after wading through the latest briefings on the situation in Poland, I took the afternoon off.

Julia had taken over planning our house repairs, thank goodness. She had spent much of the morning with the unusually obliging claims assessor, happily devising ways of remodelling the house and lining up someone to project manage what now seemed to have become a major refurbishment.

When I returned to Bayswater I discovered that the only thing left to do was collect her car. I had sold my own car when we moved to Moscow but nothing would make Julia give up her flame red MG. A photo of Julia powering her MG up the Wiscombe Park hill climb had sat amongst our wedding photos in the Moscow apartment. The car was now in a shed behind her uncle's house in Cornwall. If I was coming with her I had half an hour to get to Paddington station.

'Richard Mendale offered me a lift down,' she said, 'but I knew you would want to come. A weekend away from work and a chance to see your family.'

'Why was Mendale going down?' I asked idly.

'To escort Nowak of course,' she replied, obviously amazed that I could have forgotten General Fearmont's decision to move the Polish sailor well away from London. Cornwall was certainly remote and it was difficult to imagine the KGB looking for him there.

Julia and I arrived at Penelowek, the Grimspounds' house on the north Cornish coast, in time for dinner.

There are numerous charming villages in this part of Cornwall, most with one or two larger, grey-walled Victorian houses built to house the local landowners and their numerous servants. The first Lord Grimspound clearly liked the design of these houses but not their village locations. Instead he had built his own summer residence in splendid isolation roughly halfway between Delabole and Port Isaac. He could look out in every direction at views uncluttered by any other sign of human habitation. The nearest village, Pendoggett, was hidden from sight by a fold in the land. The outlook in most directions was of flat, characterless fields. The one exception was the spectacular panorama looking north out to sea. Perhaps to hide the drab uniformity in the other directions Grimspound had planted rows of trees which were now permanently stooped by the winds sweeping in from the sea.

Julia's uncle had inherited the grey stone house after the war and it had a comforting sense of solidity and permanence. I always enjoyed staying there. In the early days of my relationship with Julia it had been difficult to think of her uncle as anything other than my boss, only at Penelowek did it start to seem natural to follow his instruction and call him Gordon. My own family lived thirty miles away and since my father's stroke it suited everyone for us to stay at Penelowek.

We had approached the house along narrow Cornish lanes from Delabole. As always the first sight of the sea made my spirits rise.

Gordon and Anne, Lord and Lady Grimspound as the locals insisted on calling them, had greeted us warmly. I was surprised to find our old colleague Adam Joseff relaxing in the drawing room. I knew that when Gordon Grimspound and Adam Joseff had been Director General and Deputy Director General of the Defence Intelligence Staff they had become firm friends, but I had no idea that when Joseff had retired he had moved to a house only twenty minutes away from Penelowek.

'Adam's joining us for dinner,' Anne announced. 'I gather his house is becoming rather crowded with this Polish chap moving in.'

I looked at Joseff in astonishment. It certainly hadn't occurred to me that Mendale might borrow Joseff's house to lodge his Polish guest.

'Richard needed somewhere in a hurry,' Joseff explained, 'and as he'd been down here a couple of weeks ago he knew that I had a large house sitting full of nothing but my books.'

'And your stamp collection,' put in Lord Grimspound.

'Yes of course that,' Joseff acknowledged, with no hint of embarrassment. 'One needs something to do in retirement. Anyway, it seems the new DG wanted Lieutenant Nowak well away from Colchester and Richard thought that a stay at the seaside was just what was needed.'

It was nearly four years since General Fearmont had taken over from Julia's uncle as Director General, so he could hardly be described as the 'new DG', but that did perhaps say something about Joseff's own view of the world.

'Obviously,' he continued, 'I'm not involved in interviewing the gentleman but as a guest in my house we have exchanged a few pleasantries. He strikes me as a nice enough young man but of course it's difficult to tell, my Polish is rather limited. Perhaps that's where you will be able to help, Thomas, I gather you've been learning Polish. I think Richard would like to have a word with you tomorrow, pick your brains as it were, see if you can find a way to persuade our visitor that he has nothing to fear from us.'

'You think that's what's holding him back?' Julia asked. 'He's frightened.'

'As I say, it's difficult to know what's going on in his head. But one thing I can tell you with the benefit of my grey hairs: he's no spy. His nerves are shot to pieces. He's anxious to please. He's giving us all sorts of details about the ship he served on, about what it was doing in Kaliningrad, the Russians he worked with there, about his naval duties. It could all be bluff, he's not giving us anything much that we didn't know already, but the way it's come out has been too natural to have been rehearsed. But then he'll suddenly clam up. He stops talking, not because he's been trained to resist interrogation but because he's scared of what he might say.

'It's when he gets on to more personal matters that he starts to become evasive. For example, he says he hardly ever sees his parents and they know nothing about his life in Kaliningrad or Gdynia. That's just not believable. I'm willing to bet that he goes home to his family every opportunity he has. He's that sort of young man. He may be a lieutenant but he's not a leader, he needs people around him he can rely

100

on, he needs his family. So why does he tell us that he has nothing to do with them?'

Joseff left the question hanging in the air. It struck me that he had certainly done more than exchange a few pleasantries with his guest. I wondered what sort of game he and Mendale were playing and whether Julia's uncle also had a role to play. Joseff had already hinted that they had something in mind for me. This was not going to be the relaxed weekend away that I had been expecting.

All became clear when Richard Mendale appeared the next day on his way back from the station. Julia had gone into Wadebridge with her aunt and I had been hoping to stroll along the coastal path that ran near the house, but Mendale's arrival put paid to that. Instead Gordon Grimspound led our visitor into the drawing room.

Moving Kacper Nowak to Cornwall had been entirely General Fearmont's idea, Mendale explained, but when the DG himself arrived at the safe house near Rock he soon had second thoughts. The rail journey down to Cornwall had been much longer than he had expected due to overnight storm damage around Dawlish and when he finally arrived at Bodmin Road station someone had tried to take his taxi. But what really upset the DG was to discover Richard Mendale's predecessor as Deputy Director General, Adam Joseff, welcoming him at the door. His mood was not improved when one of the men Mendale had installed to guard Nowak happened to mention that Fearmont's own predecessor as DG, Lord Grimspound, lived only a few miles away.

'This simply won't do,' Fearmont had pronounced. 'We really must put things on a more professional footing. I will talk to the powers that be to acquire the requisite funding to buy a more suitable safe house for such eventualities as this.'

His mind was not put at rest by Mendale pointing out that this was the first time in living memory that the DIS had actually needed a safe house and that if ever one were needed again he was sure that MI5 would be able to oblige.

Fearmont spent nearly three hours with Nowak and the interpreter that MI5 had provided. He got absolutely nowhere. 'To nobody's surprise but his own,' Mendale commented sarcastically.

'That interpreter is missing something,' the DG had concluded. 'There's no point in carrying on here. I shall return to London right now. I suggest that we tell Mr Nowak that he's going straight back to the military prison in Colchester unless he bucks his ideas up and starts telling us why the Russians want to kill him.'

Mendale had personally driven Fearmont back to the station, largely, I suspected, to ensure that he didn't change his mind and return to the house.

Mendale settled back into an easy chair. It reminded me of the way I had seen him so often back in my DIS days, pushing his chair back on to two legs and waiting for someone else to speak first. But this time he was holding court. 'Kacper Nowak,' he announced without further preamble. 'What's he hiding? There's something he's not telling us, something about why he is here. Or rather why he left Poland, because one thing is certain, he had no idea where he was going. I think he just jumped on the first ship he saw. He's running away from someone or something. But he's not going to tell us who or what. I suspect we are what he is running away from. We represent authority, the state, the police perhaps. If we want him to open up we have to approach him very differently. We've told him about the man outside the barracks, even showed him the photofit of the man Julia identified. He didn't recognise the description but it still shook him and yet still he doesn't trust us.'

'You need to be able to play good cop, bad cop,' Gordon Grimspound suggested.

'Not exactly. We need someone who will not remind him of cops at all. Perhaps somebody like you, Thomas. Somebody his own age. Somebody who can speak his language, literally in your case.'

'But I'm just as much a representative of authority as you are. To him we are all cops.'

'Not necessarily. Sitting opposite him in Adam's house with a notebook in your hand, of course you'll seem like a cop. But strolling along the beach with no security in sight like old friends he might just open up. He needs to unburden himself. He must feel that. We just have to provide the right circumstances.'

'And how do we do that? I can't just turn up saying "I want to be your friend, let's go for a walk".'

'Of course you can't. No, you can't be anything to do with us. But suppose the local Lord of the Manor asked us to tea. And suppose his son-in-law wanted to practise his Polish. Then the two of you might decide to go for a walk? And what's more natural than for son-in-law to ask his new friend why Kacper is here, why has he left his native country? Although of course not as directly as that.'

I looked across at my former boss for advice but Gordon's only comment was to remind Mendale that although he treated Julia as a daughter, she was actually his niece and therefore I was not his son-in-law. It was his way of giving me time to think.

'Why would the Lord of the Manor invite a lowly Polish refugee to tea?'

'That's the easy part,' insisted Mendale. 'A retired admiral with a nephew-in-law who wants an opportunity to speak Polish hears there's a Polish naval officer in the vicinity. Of course he extends an invitation to a traditional Cornish cream tea.'

I could sense that this was no sudden idea that had struck Mendale as he sat sipping his Assam tea. I looked towards Grimspound again. This time he nodded.

'What have we got to lose?'

Clearly Julia's uncle had been forewarned of Mendale's plan: what have *we* got to lose he had asked. No doubt Adam Joseff had discussed it with him the previous evening. And no doubt Mendale had cleared the plan with my boss Justin Brasenose as well. That's what he meant by saying Brasenose had said he could borrow me. But it still smacked of desperation. If Nowak would not talk to professional interrogators why would he talk to me?

Despite my misgivings it was agreed that Kacper Nowak would be invited for tea later that afternoon. Mendale had invented an elaborate story to explain to Nowak why the invitation was forthcoming. This involved vastly exaggerating the prominence of members of the aristocracy in modern Britain and suggesting that it was perfectly normal for someone in Admiral Lord Grimspound's position to extend hospitality to a visiting naval officer. It seemed pretty lame to me.

After Mendale had left I asked Gordon what he really thought about the plan. He took a moment to answer.

'Adam and Dick Mendale have been at this game much longer than you or I. If they think this is the way to make that young man cooperate then I trust that judgement. But it's all very irregular. I don't know what's happened in the DIS. In my day nobody would have ever considered going outside the chain of command in this way. I don't like it. General Fearmont may be a fool but he is an honourable fool. If Dick thinks General Fearmont is obstructing the department's work he should go over his head, not behind his back. Go to the Minister if necessary. And Adam should retire gracefully, we all should.'

Then he smiled. 'Am I just sounding like a boring old fart?'

I assured him he was not and that the DIS was certainly not what it had been in his day. That was true. Fearmont had changed the tone of the organisation. I noticed that Mendale, who used to be known as Dick, was now Richard even to the recently retired Adam Joseff. I wondered how long Julia would last in the DIS if stuck back behind a desk in Whitehall.

The tea with Lieutenant Nowak was a stilted affair. Anne's skills as a hostess were legendary but even she found making conversation in the circumstances difficult. I was surprised to discover that Nowak really did have very little English. As the MI5 interpreter had not come with him conversational duties fell entirely to me. It rapidly became obvious that my own Polish still left a lot to be desired.

Nowak was not entirely what I expected. Adam Joseff the previous day had described a man consumed by fear but Nowak did not seem the naturally nervous type, although at times he showed a flicker of anxiety if the conversation took an unexpected turn. At one point Anne asked if he had any friends in England. He replied that no, all his friends were in Poland, with an unexpected stutter in his voice.

'You must miss them,' said Anne.

Nowak nodded. He was quiet for a moment before confiding that his best friend, Tadeusz, had just died.

'He had an accident,' he told us, 'on a ship.'

'Oh, he was a sailor too. I am so sorry,' Anne responded.

Nowak gave an odd little smile. 'No, not a sailor. When we left college I joined the navy. Tadeusz chose a different path, the Służba Bezpieczeństwa.'

I was shocked. Nowak's best friend was a member of the SB, the secret police. I must have shown my surprise. Nowak continued softly, 'Who would think the navy is a safer career?'

I wasn't sure what to say and didn't translate that last remark. Gordon had missed the reference to the SB but he picked up on the word *marynarka* meaning navy and tried moving the subject away from the death of Nowak's friend to naval matters. I worried that Nowak would think we were trying to pump him for secrets but the subject stirred his enthusiasm. He started to speak more quickly and kept losing me in a welter of naval terminology. Gordon and Nowak at times seemed to be understanding each other better than I did. It was not just technical expressions that lost me. Grimspound asked Nowak if he knew the story of the 'Piorun'. I had no idea what a piorun was. I discovered later it means thunderbolt, but Grimspound was referring not to the weather but to the sinking of the *Bismarck* when the Polish destroyer *Piorun* had single-handedly charged the German battleship.

Nowak smiled, of course he knew the story: Captain

Plawski had steamed in at full speed after signalling to the German admiral 'I am a Pole.'

Somehow the conversation moved on from Polish prowess at sea to Polish prowess on the football field. Gordon's devotion to the sport still struck me as odd; every other navy or army officer I met seemed to be obsessed with rugby. Julia had been amazed the previous year to receive a furious letter from the famously uncomplaining Anne because her husband had insisted on changing their long-established Sunday routine when the BBC had moved *Match of the Day* from Saturday evening to Sunday afternoon, an experiment that unsurprisingly failed. My own father had been finally convinced that he might after all have something in common with my prospective wife's family when he discovered that Gordon, like him, was an avid follower of Plymouth Argyle.

The qualifying games for the 1982 World Cup in Spain had just been completed. In the previous World Cup in Argentina, England, unlike Poland, had failed to qualify. This time, Gordon enthused both Poland and England were through.

'But,' Nowak insisted, 'England only just. You were lucky against Hungary. The Hungarians didn't need to play well because Hungary had already qualified, like Poland.'

That comment prompted a vigorous debate between Grimspound and Nowak during which Julia said nothing, I did nothing but translate and Anne cleared the tea things away. Now was the moment when I was supposed to invite Kacper Nowak for a friendly stroll on the beach and get him to divulge all. Although he was now relaxed I still didn't think there was much chance of Mendale's scheme working. It was Anne who inadvertently changed everything.

'Perhaps we should have a real drink,' she suggested. 'Would Kacper like to try some English vodka?'

Nowak's English may have been sketchy but he certainly caught the word vodka, although linking it to the word English was clearly too much for him.

Anne produced a bottle of Vladivostok Vodka. 'Made in Warrington,' she announced, pronouncing it Varrington like the recent TV adverts. Nowak examined the bottle suspiciously but when Anne invited him to try it he poured himself a very generous measure and waved away the suggestion of a mixer. It was not long before he happily accepted a second even larger glass while I hoped he was not noticing that my vodka and tonic was far more tonic than vodka.

I needed to find a way to separate Nowak from the others. The light was now fading and a walk on the beach in the dark seemed an odd thing to propose. Far more attractive might be a visit to the pub in the nearby village of Pendoggett. At this time of year there would only be a few locals propping up the bar. I had the feeling that more alcohol might be just what Nowak needed. He agreed immediately to my suggestion.

Julia's uncle suggested that Nowak might find Port Gaverne more interesting than Pendoggett. The tiny hamlet had once been a bustling port handling phenomenal quantities of pilchards in the eight-week late summer season and for the rest of the year shipping out slate from the nearby Delabole quarries. When the railways reached north Cornwall in the 1890s all that ended. Now it was well off the beaten track, especially in December, with just a few houses leading down to the barely used quay. The walk along the clifftops to Port Gaverne was one of Julia's favourites but today the darkness made that impractical. That reminded me of one potential problem.

Nowak had arrived with one of Mendale's men, an army sergeant called Bennett who seemed to have been given the dual responsibilities of prison guard and bodyguard. Bennett insisted on sitting in the car outside the house despite the bitter cold, presumably on Mendale's instructions and despite Anne Grimspound's pleas to him to join us all for tea.

'I need to speak to your driver,' I said and Nowak's face immediately fell.

'I'll speak to him,' Julia said and quickly marched out of the house. She was away for some time but was smiling broadly when she returned.

'Tell Kacper it's all arranged. Bennett will drive us all there and will then nurse an orange juice in a corner of the pub. I'll keep him company so you two boys can talk about football again.'

I translated what she had said and Nowak accepted it without question. I suspect he was quite at ease with the prospect of my wife being banished from any serious drinking. He had no way of knowing that Julia had a better head for alcohol than I had, having never endured the disapproving frowns of my teetotal mother.

Port Gaverne sits in the bottom of a steep-sided valley where a small stream empties into the sea. Whitewashed houses huddled under slate roofs cling to the hillside. Bennett dropped us outside the pub, just a few yards from the quay, and then he and Julia drove back up the steep slope we had just descended to park at the since-demolished Headlands

Hotel. As it was high tide the option of parking on the tiny beach was not available.

When we entered the almost empty pub the Polish sailor seemed at home for the first time. Perhaps it was the smell of the sea or perhaps it was the double vodka I ordered for him. We found a corner seat away from the door where we would not be overheard. Five minutes later Julia and Bennett arrived but made no attempt to join us. I was sure that Julia had taken the opportunity to phone Mendale and wondered how he had responded to our change of plan.

Nowak looked around the pub with interest but seemed in no hurry to continue our conversation. I described some of the peculiarities of English life, including the licensing hours that required the landlord to stop serving drinks at 10.30. I knew from past visits that in this case what that meant was the landlord locking the front door and then carrying on dispensing drinks to the locals until the last one left.

'Won't the police catch him?' Nowak asked.

'The local policeman is no doubt a regular here,' I explained. 'He'll drop in for a pint later.'

Nowak nodded; that, after all, was how everything worked in Poland.

I bought him another double vodka.

I needed a way of moving the conversation in the direction Mendale was expecting. I found it by accident.

'What happened to your friend? Tadeusz did you say he was called?'

Nowak fell silent and I thought he was not going to answer. Eventually he responded.

'Tadeusz Modjeski. We were at school together. We played together always. My mother called Tadeusz her second son, I only have sisters. The Russian killed him. He shot him. He would have killed me too but I ran away. I ran away and left Tadeusz.'

Nowak looked at me as if imploring me to forgive him for abandoning his friend. I didn't know what to say.

'What happened?'

I thought he wasn't going to answer. His sat looking into his glass, wherever his thoughts had gone they weren't focussed on anything happening in a pub in Cornwall.

'The Russian shot Tadeusz. Why? We had done everything we were told to do.'

He grabbed me by the arm. They say that vodka has no odour but the smell of alcohol on Nowak's breath was unmistakable.

'I promise we did everything right. Everything according to plan. We crossed the border from Russia. All our papers were in order. Then we drove to Gdańsk and again all the papers were correct. We took the Chinese cases out of the van.'

'Chinese cases?'

Nowak looked surprised at being interrupted. It was as though he was talking to himself. I needed to remain silent and just let him speak.

'There was a label on one of the cases in Chinese. The Russian took it off. In the docks we took the cases to the warehouse and the Russian joined us there. We found the big box just as we were told. There were two cases inside and we put them on a trolley and replaced them with the cases we brought. Then Tadeusz and I pushed the trolley a long way, to the other side of the docks. There was nothing else to do, everything was finished.'

Nowak paused and this time I said nothing, trying to make sense of what Nowak had said. He and his friend and a Russian had smuggled two 'Chinese' cases out of Russia into the docks at Gdańsk and hidden them inside a container, removing whatever was already there. What would anyone want to smuggle out of Kaliningrad?

'We started to leave,' Nowak suddenly continued. 'Me in front, Tadeusz behind. And then pop. The Russian shoots Tadeusz in the back of the head. Tadeusz falls on me and I swing round. The Russian is aiming the gun at me. I had the torch in my hand and I just threw it at him. He moved but the torch hit him on the hand, or the arm, and he dropped the gun. He jumped at me but I ran. I ran and ran. I could hear him after me but he couldn't find me. The torch had fallen in the water. I climbed up on to a crane and didn't move until he had gone. I left Tadeusz. I didn't go back.'

I thought Nowak was going to start crying but he just shook his head.

'What happened next?' I asked, although I could guess the answer. It would have been more sensible to ask him about the Russian but in the event it didn't matter.

'Look out,' Julia screamed.

I swung round. A man was standing in the door levelling a gun at me, or rather at Nowak. I lunged at Nowak as the man fired. Somebody screamed. Blood spurted on to me. I saw Julia launching herself at the man in the doorway. Behind her I was aware of Bennett pulling a gun from under his jacket. The man fired again and Julia fell.

X

I seemed to be running across the room in slow motion, each step gluing itself to the floor. All I could see was Julia splayed back against a bench, blood everywhere. By the time I reached her she was starting to stand up. I reached to put my arms around her but she pushed me away, blood still pouring from her nose. 'Get after him!'

I didn't want to let go of her but she shoved me again, 'Go on, we'll lose him!'

I ran outside but he, whoever he was, had gone. I heard a motorbike and saw the red rear light ascending the opposite side of the valley. The road there curled around the hillside and away towards Port Isaac. There was no way of following him.

Unsurprisingly, only Julia had followed me outside the pub, nobody else wanted to take the risk.

'It was the man I saw in Yaroslavl,' Julia said groggily. I hardly registered what she was saying.

'Are you all right?'

'He hit me with the gun barrel,' she replied, turning to look at me. 'He was aiming at you.'

'No. He was aiming at Nowak. I thought he'd shot you.'

'No, not me.' Suddenly Julia pulled her arm away. 'My God, Bennett.'

We rushed back inside. There was pandemonium. The

landlord shouted at everyone to keep calm while he tried to speak to the emergency services on the phone. Miraculously there had been an off-duty nurse in the pub and she was now holding what looked like a bed sheet against Bennett's chest. I looked around and saw Nowak still seated where I had left him, rocking back and forth. Someone had given him a scarf which was now wrapped tightly around his arm. His eyes were fixed on the empty glass in front of him, a glass, I realised, which bore the imprint of his blood-soaked palm.

What a mess!

I tried to talk to Nowak but without success. He sat mumbling to himself but I had no idea what he was trying to say. It seemed to be something about his mother. After checking that Bennett was alive Julia disappeared outside again. She had recovered sufficiently to find a phone box and call her uncle. By the time the police and ambulance appeared Gordon had managed to summon Richard Mendale who, brandishing a warrant card I didn't know he possessed, had quickly taken charge. Bennett was laid out on an empty table, the nurse still at his side, Nowak was entrusted to Julia's care and Bennett's gun had mysteriously vanished. When the first policeman arrived he was informed that the Chief Constable had just called and wanted him to phone the police headquarters in Exeter immediately. By that time Julia had found Bennett's car keys and spirited Nowak back to Penelowek.

'Disappear,' Mendale whispered to me as the police siren approached.

It was a long walk back to Penelowek and there was plenty of time to think about what had happened. There had been an instant when I really thought Julia had been killed. I realised that nothing else that had happened really mattered. Obviously General Demirkan's killer had managed to follow Nowak from London and then tried to shoot him. Why I had no idea and right at that moment I wasn't sure I cared, even though Julia had not actually been shot. In fact, judging by the speed with which she had reacted to the situation, she had hardly been injured.

As I walked, the comfortable familiarity of the surroundings made the events back in Port Gaverne seem almost surreal. The sound of the sea breaking against the cliffs behind me took on a hypnotic rhythm, broken only by the hoot of a barn owl somewhere ahead. I needed to stop thinking about what might have been and concentrate on what had actually happened.

For now I could forget trying to discover why the same man would assassinate a Turkish general in Russia and try to murder of a Polish naval lieutenant in Cornwall. The urgent question was how had he turned up in a pub in Port Gaverne? The more I thought about it the more improbable the whole thing seemed. It was simply impossible for one man to have kept track of Nowak all the way from London. Mendale would have made sure Nowak had no tracker device on him. So therefore Nowak had either been followed by a team, MI5 would probably have put at least eight watchers on to an assignment like that, or somebody told the gunman where the Polish sailor would be found. I couldn't believe that Mendale wouldn't have spotted a team of eight people, however professional, in an area like north Cornwall. So somebody on the inside must have revealed Nowak's movements.

By the time I reached Penelowek I had decided that

it must have been Nowak himself who had contacted the gunman, although not of course realising what was going to happen.

I found Julia, the Grimspounds and Nowak sitting in silence in front of a roaring log fire. Julia had found time to wash the blood off her face and reapply her makeup but was still clearly upset. Nowak was pale and unmoving. Anne Grimspound had produced a makeshift sling but he wasn't using it.

When it became obvious I had nothing new to report Anne announced she would make up a bed for Kacper Nowak.

Her husband shook his head. 'I don't think that will be necessary, my love.'

He was right. Mendale arrived in a police car and announced he was taking Nowak to the Royal Marine base at Lympstone near Exeter. When Nowak left he still hadn't said a word since being shot at.

I had already called my boss, Brasenose, and no sooner had I put down the phone than General Fearmont rang asking for Julia. He was clearly shaken. His main priority seemed to be ensuring that Julia spoke to nobody about what had happened until she had reported back to London.

'That includes the civilian police,' he insisted. 'Refer them to me if necessary.'

It was not necessary, as the only police we saw departed with Mendale.

Sleep did not come easily. Julia had already gone through all the possibilities I had considered on the walk back from Port Gaverne but we still rehearsed them all again. Eventually we lay in silence, Julia's hand resting on my arm. I had seen violent death before and it seemed likely that we had been lucky to escape with our lives when the shooting had started in Poland. But the shooting I had just witnessed had a startling immediacy. I could still feel the bullet intended for Nowak whistling past and I couldn't throw off the paralysing sense of shock that had hit me when I thought Julia had been shot.

We woke late and after an unusually subdued Sunday lunch set off for London. I could tell that Julia's mind was not on her driving by the way she stuck to the speed limits until well past Exeter. Only then did she start to put the MG through its paces even though the weather was getting worse by the minute, with warnings of snow on the radio. I assumed she was thinking about the previous evening but, perhaps to distract herself from the events in Port Gaverne, Julia's thoughts had gone back to Operation Coronation.

'You know those photos of Jan Kazimierz's Crown that the Americans gave us? I showed them to Anne.'

'You did what!'

'Come on, Thomas, it's not a major security breach. My aunt is totally trustworthy and a photograph with nothing written on it is hardly an official secret. There was something about the Crown that struck me as odd and Anne said exactly the same thing. It's certainly not a crown worn by a medieval king. It's a hoop crown, like the one used for the Queen's coronation. It has a base, the circlet, worn on the temple and fitting around the head, and then arches rising from the circlet up over the head. The arches go up to what's called the monde, a round orb that joins the arches together, and there is a cross on top of the monde. The problem with the crown in the photo is that the circlet is far too crude. It has no ornamentation at all. No self-respecting king would have worn a crown with no jewels on the circlet. Crowns are supposed to demonstrate wealth and power.'

'So you think it's a fake?'

'Well, that's what's odd. Attached to the circlet are six half arches each bearing enormous pearls. And both the monde and the cross on top of it seem to be delicately engraved, although it's quite difficult to tell from the photos. It's almost as if chunks of a genuine and elaborate hoop crown have been cut off and stuck on a really ordinary gold circlet.'

'I agree it's odd but I can't see that it has any particular significance. If Hoeven and Lorrimore are right then the Crown they're talking about was in Lviv before the war and at that time people thought it was real. It doesn't really matter if King Jan Kazimierz actually wore it.'

Julia smiled. 'You could be right,' by which she meant 'You're probably wrong.'

As soon as I presented my pass at Century House on Monday morning I was told that Brasenose wanted to see me urgently. I went straight to his office but his secretary reported that he had been called to an urgent meeting at the Cabinet Office; she did not know when he would be back. He had left instructions that I was to make sure I was right there when he did return. Clearly the proverbial was already hitting the fan.

As I sat waiting for Brasenose to return it struck me that Julia had been right, the shooting in Port Gaverne was in danger of pushing Operation Coronation from my mind. The disappearance of the American agents Flanagan and Sokolowski was undoubtedly more important than the unexplained appearance of a Polish sailor, but for the moment Nowak was taking priority.

I had avoided questioning by the Devon & Cornwall Police but Brasenose had quizzed me ruthlessly on the phone, both immediately after the attack and again before leaving Cornwall the previous day. I was sure the inquisition would continue as soon as he was back from the Cabinet Office meeting. I was right.

'From the top,' Brasenose instructed the moment he returned. 'Let's have it all again. What exactly did Nowak say to you about the death of his friend?'

'He mentioned during the tea that he had a friend called Tadeusz Modjeski who had recently died. He said Tadeusz had an accident on a ship. Then he mentioned that his friend had worked for the SB, the security police.'

'But he gave no indication of Modjeski's role in the SB? No mention of his rank, for example?'

'No nothing like that. It was just a casual comment. Then later in the pub, when he'd had quite a lot of vodka, I asked him again about how his friend died. Completely out of the blue he said the Russian killed him.'

'You're sure about that: the Russian, singular, not the Russians, plural?'

'No he was talking about a specific Russian, I'm sure of that. He said that he and his friend had done everything the Russian asked them to do but the Russian had then pulled out a gun and shot Modjeski in the back of the head. Nowak had managed to escape. He didn't say much more before the door of the pub opened and all hell broke loose.'

'Ah yes, enter the mysterious gunman. The gunman your wife insists was the same man that she had seen in Yaroslavl and had picked out on the video from Colchester?'

'That's right.'

'But you can't yourself be sure of that. You didn't actually see the man who shot General Demirkan.'

'That's true, but I trust Julia.'

'What about the gun? Could you identify that?'

I tried to picture the gunman coming into the pub and firing. 'It happened so quickly. I can't remember hearing the shot. Just seeing the man by the door. It was a big gun, long barrel. No, I couldn't tell you what it was.'

'Well one of the soldiers who saw Scarface in Colchester looked right down that barrel and gave us a very good description.' Brasenose opened the drawer in his desk and produced a pistol. 'He thinks it was one of these.'

He balanced the gun in his hand, thirteen or fourteen inches of lethal metal.

'What is it?' I asked.

After being stationed in Moscow for so long I thought I knew as much as anyone about Soviet weaponry. This didn't look Russian but then I realised it wasn't. It was American and I had seen one before. I answered my own question.

'It's a .22 calibre suppressed High Standard pistol.'

'Quite,' said Brasenose. 'Not very common, a rather specialised weapon. The silencer is integral. It will take a ten round magazine but it also has a slide lock; lock the action closed with that and you have an almost silent single-shot pistol, just the thing to shoot someone at close range without being seen.'

'On a street in Yaroslavl, for example.'

'Exactly. During the war the Americans wanted a gun like this for their covert operations. The High Standard Corporation of Connecticut produced this thing and quite a few ended up in Eastern Europe. And it's still used by the Company today.'

'But you can't think Scarface has been working for the Americans.'

'No,' Brasenose replied, 'I don't. The point is that back in 1939 High Standard started exporting their silenced pistols.'

'Who to?'

'That's exactly the problem. Their very first customer was us. We still have some, you may have seen somebody using one in training.'

I was silent for a moment. Brasenose couldn't be suggesting Demirkan's killer was using a Service issue weapon. 'But all our pistols are tightly controlled. We'd know if one of these had been signed out.'

'Nowadays that's perfectly true but it wasn't always like that. Anybody who's been around for a few years could have kept their personal weapon.'

Brasenose sat back in his chair and let that sink in. When I said nothing he sighed and moved on.

'You did well. Getting Nowak drunk was clever. So now we know that he's running away from a Russian. Unfortunately that doesn't narrow things down very much, and we don't know why. What was in the cases he says they switched? It looks as though someone is trying to smuggle something out of the Soviet Union into Poland and then on to the West.'

'You mean that if you're trying to get contraband from Kaliningrad to somewhere like the US it would be much easier to move it across the border into Poland first rather than try to ship it directly to the US?'

'That's right. There are no ships going from Kaliningrad to North America and in any case there would be less chance of American Customs crawling all over any consignment if its origin were marked as Poland rather than Russia. Of course those cases needn't have been destined for the US. Poland is opening up; there will be shipments leaving Gdańsk for all sorts of places. Whatever was smuggled in from Kaliningrad could be absolutely anywhere now.'

Brasenose might be right, although I wasn't wholly convinced. It seemed to me that if you want to get something out of the Soviet Union then get it completely out, don't send it somewhere else where it might be intercepted. Adding in that transfer inside the docks in Gdańsk must have added enormously to the risk.

'What do you think was in the cases?' I asked. 'Drugs? That might explain the Chinese connection.'

'I've no idea what was in them. But the idea of smuggling drugs from the Far East through Kaliningrad, the most heavily patrolled port in Europe, is insane. And I don't believe those cases came from China, that's a complete red herring. Nothing comes into Kaliningrad from China. The Russians and Chinese have been at each other's throats for years. Since the Soviet invasion of Afghanistan they're almost at war. I never thought I would see the day when Islamic Mujahidin in Afghanistan, armed by the Americans to fight the Russians, were being trained across the border inside China, but that's what's happening.'

'Perhaps Afghanistan is the answer. The Russians must have control over a lot of poppy fields there. Could they be producing heroin themselves and are now shipping it to the West?'

'As you say, perhaps. It's the sort of game the other side might play. But if that's what's happening it wouldn't be some petty gangster doing it, it would be official. And the fact that Nowak said they passed through the border so easily suggests the same thing. Having said that, if this is some sort of KGB op it's a very unusual one. Why would they bother routing contraband through Poland and above all why kill the men helping them?'

Brasenose moved on. 'Tell me, when the pub door opened and the gunman came into the pub do you think Nowak recognised him?'

It was a question Julia and I had asked ourselves. I tried to think back but the truth is that when Julia shouted her warning my attention switched completely away from Nowak.

'I don't know. Julia told me that the DIS had shown Nowak the Colchester video and he didn't recognise anyone. Why don't you just ask Nowak now?'

'That's a bit complicated, for a couple of reasons. First we've lost him.'

'Lost him? How can that be? He was at Lord Grimspound's house and then Mendale took him away.'

'That's right. I don't mean we can't find him; I just mean he's no longer ours. Procedurally your little pub crawl was a disaster. Our masters on the Joint Intelligence Committee are not happy. You can see why they're sensitive. So far we've managed to keep the story out of the papers. A mentally deranged man letting off a gun in a Cornish pub is not headline news. There was a shooting party staying nearby so if there are any more questions Fearmont has suggested we try linking the story to them. Personally I think suggesting someone mistook our man for a pheasant might be somewhat implausible. Thank goodness nobody was seriously hurt.'

'So Bennett's OK?'

'He will be. We're lucky there weren't many people in that pub. If any of them talk to the local press and there's a hint of what really happened we may have problems. We haven't issued a D-Notice and we don't want to; the press don't like being told what they can and cannot print. But we can't have people shooting off guns in country pubs. And we can't have the DIS running around pretending to be James Bond. There are protocols to follow and Fearmont and Mendale have ignored them all. I've just received a lecture on the wisdom of my letting you get involved with them. The upshot is that General Fearmont's wings are not just going to be trimmed but practically torn off. From now on the DIS don't get involved in any operations in this country and certainly don't start setting up safe houses, all that is handled by our friends across the river.' He meant MI5. 'Nowak belongs to them now. I don't know where exactly he is and we're not going to find out. Somebody leaked the fact that he was in Cornwall and nobody wants to risk that happening again. If our friends learn anything more we will be told in due course. But it looks as though they won't find anything soon. Nowak has had some sort of nervous breakdown. He's in the hands of the shrinks.'

Brasenose looked at me. 'You realise that this could mean his whole story is fiction. If the Americans are right, the last record of this man in Poland is of him entering a psychiatric hospital. Now he's in another one. Are we really sure that in between he was loading and unloading cases on the docks in Gdańsk and seeing his best friend getting shot?'

'Well somebody certainly shot at him in Cornwall. He's not making that up.'

'But it could be someone like him. Suppose this Tadeusz

124

Modjeski is not a secret policeman but someone Nowak met in an asylum. And suppose they escaped to England together, got off the boat in Middlesbrough but we only picked up one of them.'

'And the other one managed to find a gun and follow Nowak all over the country?' I couldn't keep the disbelief out of my voice.

Brasenose sighed. 'Yes it's totally far-fetched, although it's what General Fearmont seems to favour. He wants that photofit emblazoned across the newspapers; he doesn't seem to realise that publicity is the last thing we want right now. And you're right, there is no way this man could have followed Nowak for days on end from Middlesbrough all the way down to us here, then across to Colchester and then to Port Gaverne. It simply could not be done, not by one man. MI5 are correct, somebody told him where Nowak was. Somebody in the DIS or someone in our own Service.'

'Well at least we can be sure it couldn't have been David Prince,' I commented. 'He wouldn't have known Mendale was taking him down to Cornwall.'

'Ah but Prince did know Nowak was in Cornwall,' Brasenose replied. And without a hint of embarrassment he added, 'I told him.'

I said nothing and waited for him to explain.

'While you were having your weekend away in Cornwall some of us were working. As I told Lorrimore, we had set up a series of formal sessions with Prince. It's a pity Lorrimore couldn't be there, we had one of those American polygraph machines the FBI sent over. If you believe a machine can detect lies, which I don't, then Prince is the most honest man in the building. We'd already been over Prince's life a hundred times and he's been under surveillance off and on for months, he can't spend a penny without us knowing where the money's come from and where it's going. And we've never found anything. So four of us spent nearly seven hours with him on Friday. Johnny Munday was there.' At that time Johnny Munday was MI5's most renowned spy-catcher. 'By the end of the day even he had to admit that if it wasn't for this source the Americans claim to have there would be no reason at all to suspect Prince of anything.'

'So what are you going to do?' I asked bluntly. 'You can't just leave it there.'

Brasenose did not reply immediately. He was clearly surprised by my tone. I was at least twenty years younger than him and in those days that mattered. In the Service hierarchy was all-important.

'Mr Dylan,' he eventually replied with an unexpected formality. 'In our world we like to rely on evidence but sometimes one just has to rely on judgement. I don't like the word instinct but the reality is that's what it all comes down to. Who do our instincts tell us to trust? Can I trust David Prince whom I've known for nearly twenty years? Can I trust you, a newcomer? Can you trust me?'

I said nothing. There was no point in saying that of course he could trust me. And I realised I did not know him well enough to know if I could really trust him. He still hadn't told me why he had told Prince that Nowak was in Cornwall.

'After we had finished interviewing Prince on Friday I needed to reach a decision. What next? There is a lot going on in the world at the moment, crises all over the place, but one place where right now we urgently need someone who really understands what's happening on the ground is Poland. We need someone with sources he trusts and who trust him. And that man I believe is Prince. His number two, who's now a new man, Rembury, is perfectly sound but we put him there for a specific purpose, to handle Prince's key source. Rembury is a field man not an analyst, the advantage of Prince is that he's both. If I'm wrong about Prince then heaven knows what will happen, but at some point we have to rely on instinct and my instinct is that Prince is trustworthy. Warsaw is my desk and my decision is that Prince remains in post.

'That of course will not please the Americans so I phoned Blake Lorrimore. You remember he told us he had something important to attend to that meant he had to return to Washington. Well I finally tracked him down on the golf course but it seems he had spent the morning in a meeting with his own team.'

'With Chuck Hoeven?'

'No, not Hoeven. Lorrimore's own people, analysts. They had produced another report on that dissident, Radlowski, the man Prince got out of Warsaw. They're now as certain as anyone in this game can be that Radlowski is legitimate. Everything he's done in America has been checked out.'

'Then if Prince is working for the other side why would he have helped Radlowski escape?'

'That's exactly what I asked. Lorrimore thinks the Poles just wanted Radlowski out of the country. He was stirring things up and developing too high a profile to be silenced in the usual way. So they arranged for Prince to spirit him out of Warsaw. That way they got rid of a troublesome dissident and built up Prince's credibility at the same time.'

'Do you believe that?'

'The strange thing is I'm not sure Lorrimore believes it. There's something odd going on over there. There's clearly not much love lost between Lorrimore and Hoeven. There have been a lot of changes since Reagan arrived in the White House and made Bill Casey Director of Central Intelligence. The rules President Carter put in place to stop the Agency mounting covert operations here, there and everywhere, his Executive Order 12036, were watered down. Just a fortnight ago Reagan passed his own Executive Order, number 12333, which still banned assassinations but gave the Agency much wider authority. As Blake Lorrimore put it, the cowboys are back on the range and Chuck Hoeven is a cowboy king.

'I still don't understand why Hoeven won't tell us who their source is. We may joke about the Company being reticent when it comes to sharing anything with us but when the chips are down they usually come through. He must realise that if we knew more about their source we could try to work backwards from that. Instead of groping around in the dark we could start looking for Prince's supposed handlers where we might actually find them. Where did their source pick up the info that seems to incriminate Prince? Is the source diplomatic or Intelligence? If it's Intelligence is it KGB or GRU or some smaller specialist outfit? We know the source is Russian but has he always been Moscow based? Could he have access to SB files in Warsaw? If we just knew whether Prince is supposed to be working for Russian Intelligence or Polish it might help.'

'You put all that to Lorrimore?'

'Of course, but he knows it all himself. Lorrimore's not a field man but he's been around a long time. All he could say was that Chuck Hoeven won't agree to any details being shared. There must be something very special about this source.'

'Well there's one thing that's different about him or her,' I suggested.

'Lorrimore referred to he,' interrupted Brasenose, 'the source is a man.'

'OK he. But there is one thing about this man that strikes me as incredibly unusual. He has no name.'

Brasenose raised an eyebrow. 'Isn't that what we've been talking about?'

'What I mean is no name at all, no code name. He is just referred to as the source but there must be a code name, there always is, a unique name that can be used to hide the real name. If they are so obsessed with keeping his identity secret there must be some sort of cover, a pseudonym of some kind. I can't believe that every time anyone in the Company needs to refer to him they call him The Source.'

Brasenose nodded. 'You're right, it's odd, but does it get us anywhere?'

'Well it makes me think that the Company want to keep not only the source's real name secret but also the code name.'

'But why would they do that?'

'Because it's a code name we already know. A name we've already tried to get behind.'

Brasenose saw what I was getting at immediately. 'Krypton.'

'Yes, Krypton. Surely it's possible. Isn't it too much of a coincidence that the Company won't tell us anything about a Russian asset who claims to have discovered a mystical crown in Poland and won't tell us anything about a Russian asset who claims to have discovered a mole in our station in Poland?'

'Perhaps, when you put it like that. But it really would be one hell of a coincidence.' Brasenose mulled the idea over. 'It's possible but unlikely. The Company has been very successful at recruiting agents in the Soviet Union over the last few years. We shouldn't jump to any conclusions. We may know more when we identify Krypton.'

I was puzzled. 'You think we can do that?'

Brasenose smiled again. 'I hope so. We have photos of him.'

XI

'We have photos of Krypton? Where did they come from?'

'Our man in Stockholm.'

Brasenose sounded thoughtful. 'It's not like the Company to block us out completely. They asked for our help on Project Coronation, you and your wife could have been killed, and now they won't share anything more about it. I don't like that. We're supposed to be allies, partners. So when I heard they were flying to Sweden I arranged for our man to be waiting for them. They flew into Sturup in an American Air Force plane so it wasn't very difficult to spot them. They were met by more Company men and they all drove off to the most expensive hotel in Ystad where they spent less than an hour before driving back to Sturup, but now with one extra in their party. I believe they met Krypton in Ystad.'

'And our man managed to photograph him?'

'Amazingly yes. If the man who accompanied Hoeven from Ystad to Sturup was Krypton we have a reasonably clear shot of him.'

I found that astonishing. Krypton was one of the key men in the Company's Operation Coronation, which had just been blown wide open with two of their own men missing, quite possibly dead. And yet when they pick him up in Ystad nobody is alert enough to notice our man taking photographs. When I said this to Brasenose he just shrugged.

'My theory is that Hoeven was astonished when Krypton turned up. The Company had assumed that he had met the same fate as Flanagan and Sokolowski. This wasn't a carefully planned extraction, Hoeven rushed off to Ystad and summoned whatever support he could find. His only thought was getting Krypton out of there as fast as possible. It seems Krypton made his own way across the Baltic. I'd love to know how the hell he managed that.'

'You think he had help?'

'Well if he did and it wasn't the Americans it can only have been the other side. Either that or he was unbelievably well prepared and even then you would need superb contacts to get out of Poland so quickly. As I keep saying, this whole thing stinks. Our American cousins can be surprisingly subtle at times and unbelievably arrogant at others. Chuck Hoeven is a man on a mission who thinks he's invincible. He had obviously set up some sort of cover for Krypton in Sweden which he thinks is foolproof, at least temporarily. So when Krypton contacted him and said "I've arrived" he just dropped everything and flew over there. He collected Krypton, took him back to Sturup and then his local people went back to wherever they came from, Lorrimore flew to Stockholm and on to see us and the others got back into their Gulfstream and off they went.'

'So Hoeven took Krypton back to the US?'

'Yes, which must imply they consider that he's been burned, that there's no way they will ever be able to put him back into Moscow. And there's more. Our man has now come up with a name. Karacek. Someone arrived at the hotel the previous night, checked in using that name and appears to have left with Hoeven. We'll need to follow that up.'

Brasenose pushed back his chair. He had finished with Krypton and now wanted to move on to something else.

'That's all very interesting but the issue right now is David Prince. Lorrimore is more relaxed about my decision than I expected. But in order to keep the peace with Hoeven he wants us to keep Prince in London until the Company find out what went wrong with Operation Coronation. I've agreed for the moment. So you go to Warsaw. Spend a couple of days with Prince first. I had dinner with him on Friday evening and filled him in on developments, including Coronation and Nowak.'

'So that's when you told him Nowak was in Cornwall.'

'Yes, perhaps I shouldn't have done that. But I trust him and Cornwall's a big place. He couldn't have traced Nowak to a pub in Port Gaverne.' He sounded defensive. After a moment he continued in a more subdued tone. 'Your old friends on the Defence Intelligence Staff have made a total balls-up of this. After their adventures in Cornwall I'm afraid General Fearmont and Richard Mendale will probably be moving on; if I'm wrong about David Prince so will I.'

On that note I left to find the Warsaw head of station.

David Prince was older than I expected. I remembered that back in Moscow my Station Chief had referred to him dismissively as Professor Prince and he did look more like an avuncular professor than most of his sharp-suited, smooth-tongued colleagues. Like the rest of the civil service MI6 valued the generalist over the specialist. Anyone being fast-tracked to the top could expect to be moved from Jakarta one day to Prague the next and perhaps Paris the day after. Prince, however, had found his niche and stayed there. Poland had become 'his' territory even on his spells back in London. He was our Polish expert and was very conscious of the fact. In his own mind his local knowledge was there to be admired and used but not to be questioned.

The first thing he told me was that he had been around long enough not to take offence when someone thought he might be a Soviet mole. What he really meant was that he had been around long enough not to show that he was offended when accused of being a Soviet mole. He was clearly unhappy to be kept in London when the situation in Warsaw could explode at any time. Brasenose had promised him it would not be for long.

Prince began by telling me I needed to understand Polish history but he started with geography. 'We talk about Eastern Europe but the first thing to remember is that if you look at a map Poland is right in the centre of Europe. Everything kicks off there. Now my boy: which side was Poland on in the First World War?'

It was a trick question and I was not about to be patronised by anyone. 'It wasn't on any side. Poland had been wiped off the map at the end of the eighteenth century. It was carved up between Prussia, the Austro-Hungarian Empire and Russia. It didn't exist in 1914.'

'Well done, you've got it exactly right and precisely wrong. The Poles were on both sides in the First World War, some fought for Germany, some for the Austro-Hungarians and some for the tsar. You're wrong to say Poland was wiped off the map because Poland never existed. Poland is a made-up country just like most of the countries of Europe. What people don't understand is that before industrialisation society consisted of a few aristocrats supporting one king or another and below them lots of serfs living side-by-side but speaking different languages. The idea of Poland as a nation didn't exist.'

I had read enough about Poland's medieval history not to be convinced by that. 'But it had existed. The Polish-Lithuanian Commonwealth was the largest country in medieval Europe, bigger than France, much bigger than England.'

'There you go again. The Polish kings were for a time the most powerful in Europe, you're right, but theirs wasn't a country, it wasn't a nation. Most of the nobles were Poles, they spoke Polish, but their subjects spoke hundreds of different languages. You can't say the serfs were Polish just because their masters were. A peasant speaking Ukrainian wasn't Polish one day and Russian the next because the King of Poland had lost territory to the Tsar of Russia.'

I was not going to give up. 'Surely the Ukraine's an exception. Poland and Russia have fought over that for centuries.'

Prince shook his head in exasperation. 'You just don't understand. Poland, Russia. You're talking about nations when nations didn't exist.'

'Of course they existed. Just look at us. Look at France.'

'Yes look at us, look at France. When you say Poland was wiped off the map there were still thousands of Scots who refused to consider themselves British, thousands of Englishmen who had suddenly become "Americans" and let's not talk about the Irish. When Napoleon led 600 000 troops into Russia he did it for the glory of France. It was a French Army but if you had been sat at their campfires I doubt if you would have heard much French, the soldiers would probably have been speaking Polish or German or one of a hundred other languages. It was the same old story. Those at the top give history their names, those at the bottom just give their blood.'

He paused, expecting me to argue, but I wanted to find out where the conversation was going.

'Industrialisation and the railways brought peasants off the land,' he continued. 'And they allowed dangerous new ideas to spread. Socialism in the cities and land reform in the countryside. Troublemakers started to preach that if the workers or the peasants acted together things could change. Revolution was in the air. Now if you're a landlord or factory owner how do you stop that? How do you persuade the peasants that their interests are the same as the landowners? The answer is you find a common enemy. And that enemy was anyone who was different, who spoke a different language or went to a different church or, best of all, spoke a different language and went to no church at all.'

'Jews.'

'Especially Jews. Then along came Bismarck with a really novel idea. He would turn Prussia into the heart of an empire that would be united by just one thing: the German language. All his subjects had to speak German. Some, like those who had previously spoken Danish or French, might be Germanised. The Masurians who lived in the lakes where you had your little adventure spoke a language close to Polish but as they were Protestants they were considered suitable for Germanising. But as most Polish speakers were Catholics, they couldn't be Germanised and had to be exterminated. As he famously put it: God created wolves but we still have to shoot them.

'And in the East the tsar was having a similar idea:

Russification. After centuries as a multilingual empire the tsar decided that the way to end unrest on the borders of his empire was to make everyone Russian, the Polish language had to be eliminated.

'So suddenly we had a new phenomenon: linguistic nationalism. Nations are to be defined by a common language. So what happens to those who still speak Polish? They invent a new country. The First World War ends in defeat for Germany and Austria, two of the powers that, as you put it, wiped Poland off the map, and Russia has collapsed into civil war. There are millions of Polish speakers who no longer owe allegiance to the Kaiser, the Austrian emperor or the tsar. On top of that the American President needs the support of Polish-American voters and so he makes the creation of a Polish homeland an overriding priority. Poland is born, or if you wish, reborn although with borders no historian would recognise.

'The problem is that more than a third of the new nation do not speak Polish at home and many do not speak it at all. They speak Ukrainian, Ruthenian, German, Belorussian and a host of languages nobody has ever heard of: they would have to learn Polish or leave. And of course the real outsiders, nearly one in ten of the population, spoke Yiddish. In some areas, like Warsaw and the poverty-stricken borderlands near Russia, the Jewish percentage was much higher. For centuries Jews and non-Jews had lived side-by-side. When all the wealth lay with the nobility, poverty had drawn the poor together. Now the new nationalists tore that apart. They invented a global conspiracy: Jewish capitalists in the West and Jewish Communists in the East were conspiring to dominate the whole world.'

I understood what he was saying but couldn't see how it was relevant now.

'The ghastly fact is,' I interrupted, 'that that's not the position now, not after the gas chambers, after the Holocaust. The Jewish population was destroyed.'

Prince shook his head. 'I'm not talking about anti-Semitism. I'm talking about nationalism. People like Father Paszek are slap bang in the middle of that tradition. They need an enemy. Anyone who is not a true Pole, not a devout Catholic. Jews still, but especially nowadays Russians and Ukrainians, the people who have stolen the Polish lands to the east. Poles talk about "The Kresy", the borderlands, territory that should be Polish. The present inhabitants may not be Jews but they're not Catholics either, to Paszek they're all heretics. Do you know the most important date in Poland since the end of the Second World War?'

I was mystified by his change of subject but without waiting for me to say anything Prince answered his own question.

'Sixteenth October 1978.'

The date meant nothing to me. 'Something to do with Solidarity,' I suggested.

'No. Sixteenth October 1978 was the date the Archbishop of Kraków, Karol Józef Wojtyła, became Pope John Paul II. You can't imagine the impact that had in Poland. The nation united in celebration, even the Communists. That was the moment the government stopped sloganising about "the people" and started talking about "the nation". That's when we first heard about Father Paszek. Don't be misled by the radical priests lined up with Solidarity. They're not the authentic voice of the Church in Poland. Remember it's only a couple of years since the Bishop of Lublin gave his famous sermon about the dangers of free speech.'

I looked mystified again and Prince explained with the mixture of authority and quiet superiority that my professor at Durham used to employ when I struggled with the arcane vocabulary of Dante's Tuscan dialect.

'The august bishop, Zygmunt Kamiński, used the example of England to demonstrate the absurdity of free speech. You won't believe it, he told his congregation, but in London anyone can stand up at Hyde Park Corner and make idiotic attacks on the government and even insult the Queen. That's not freedom. Real freedom doesn't mean the freedom to say anything you like, it means the freedom to tell the truth, the truth as people like Paszek define it. That's why this Crown of Jan Kazimierz is so important to him. It represents his truth, it's a symbol of Polish nationhood and the authority of the Church, it helps reinvent a Polish history that never existed.'

'You think it's real then? There actually is a Crown out there?'

'It was real. It was there before the war. Whether the Crown has survived and somehow made its way to the Masurian Lakes is another question. I have my doubts. The point is that the Crown links to the Oath of Lwów and that is potentially very powerful. The Oath wasn't the great historic symbol the Company seem to think it was, a cross between the Declaration of Independence and the Magna Carta, but a good propagandist could make it into one. Brandishing Jan Kazimierz's Crown would remind Poles that Lwów was once the heart of the nation and it's now occupied by their enemies. Paszek doesn't just want to overthrow the

Communist government, he wants to recover the lands he claims Poland has lost in the Ukraine, in Lithuania; he wants to rip up the map and start again.'

Now it was my turn to shake my head. 'But that just won't happen.'

'Perhaps, but there are others who share his dream. You've heard of Mark Jaszczak?'

I shook my head.

'An American millionaire, some sort of commodity speculator. Polish parents. He's been funding Father Paszek. Complete nut and dangerous.'

Prince sat back and looked directly at me. 'These are very dangerous times. The Company are pouring tens of millions of dollars into Afghanistan, arming complete madmen on the principle that Russia's enemy has to be my friend. People like Mark Jaszczak want to do the same in Poland. If there's an Afghan type bloodbath right in the centre of Europe we won't be able to avoid getting sucked in. The Second World War started in Poland, I don't want to see that repeated.'

Prince spoke with emotion and sounded totally convincing but I couldn't help thinking that if he were a Soviet mole this was exactly how his reports would be coloured.

I wanted to bring the conversation back to more immediate concerns.

'So you don't like Operation Coronation. But what do you think happened in the lakes? What happened to the two American agents?'

'I don't know but my guess is that they are dead. If the Soviets had them they would be putting them on display, two American spies so close to Kaliningrad, it's a propaganda gift. What I don't understand is why anyone would start shooting. My theory, and it's only a theory, is that the Polish soldiers didn't fire first, Krypton did. I think the Americans stumbled into a trap, Krypton came along, realised what was happening and opened fire. Of course he wouldn't admit that to the Americans. He probably found soldiers blocking his way and decided to shoot his way out. In the crossfire the Americans were hit. If they were simply wounded they may yet reappear next time there is a prisoner exchange, but I wouldn't bet on it.'

'And the men Krypton says stole the money he was bringing?'

'Who knows? There's something missing in all of this. What happened to the Crown? Did it ever exist? The peasant you were supposed to be meeting could have invented the whole story, pretending to Krypton that he had a medieval crown to sell. He might have been working with the two men in balaclavas. Perhaps the authorities heard rumours that they were trying to sell a fake Crown and followed them to the lake. When the police pounced the men pulled out their guns and the firefight started. The two Company agents being there was just bad luck.'

Like he said, it was possible, but I thought improbable. For one thing, why would Polish police investigating a suspected fraud be accompanied by the Russian bukhanka Julia had spotted?

I moved the conversation on to the practicalities of my temporary move to Warsaw. Prince appeared to be perfectly open about his work in Poland. There were two matters which he made clear were particularly sensitive. The first concerned the leaks from the Embassy.

'They've been going on for years which rules out just about everyone there. We've swept the building time and time again and found nothing. But I have an idea I've been working on with my deputy, Paul Rembury. You don't need to know what it is; Paul will tell you when the time comes. We've called that operation Esterka. The other is Firefox. I have a source in the SB, the security police. Not high up but well positioned and totally reliable. I got a dissident out a while ago just before he was about to be arrested and probably killed. Firefox tipped me off. The Opposition must realise that I have a very well-placed source and I don't want to jeopardise him. We've put Rembury in the Embassy primarily to handle Firefox. So far I don't think the other side realise Rembury is part of my team and we must keep it that way. So stay away from Firefox and let Rembury manage him. Again you don't need to know any details.'

That seemed like a sensible precaution. 'I contacted Rembury after speaking to Brasenose on Friday night,' Prince continued. 'I told him to give Firefox the names of Kacper Nowak and his alleged friend Tadeusz Modjeski and see if he can turn anything up. And we've asked him to listen out for anything about a special operation a week ago in the Masurian Lakes. But don't expect too much. It's not like phoning directory enquiries. Even if he finds anything Firefox may not be able to arrange a secure handover quickly.'

We spent most of the day talking and I warmed to him. I could see why Brasenose instinctively trusted him. He seemed open and helpful, with a bright intelligence and old-fashioned courtesy once you got over his innate pomposity. He encouraged trust, just like a good spy should. But who was he spying for?

When I got home I found Julia sipping a whisky which was unusual, she had been cutting down on alcohol recently. Her day had not gone well. We had both planned to take leave on our return from Moscow but she had agreed with Mendale that she would come into work until the Nowak business was sorted. That way she would take her leave when the repairs to the house were complete. But when she had arrived at the DIS offices in Whitehall this morning Mendale was nowhere to be found. He had gone off to the Cabinet Office with the DG but only Fearmont returned.

Fearmont was not in a good mood, something that was only made worse by finding that Julia was in the office.

'The JIC obviously had a go at him,' Julia told me, referring to the Joint Intelligence Committee meeting he and Mendale had been summoned to attend along with Brasenose.

'He told me there are going to be changes in the DIS and from the look on his face I suspect he won't be around for long. Neither will I, he made that plain. I'm off back to the RAF. In the meantime I had to listen to a stream of complaints about Mendale taking Nowak to Cornwall as if the idea of moving Nowak away from Colchester had been nothing to do with our dear Director General. Fearmont seems convinced that everything that happened in Cornwall was some kind of conspiracy by the DIS old guard, including my uncle, to discredit him. The upshot is that I'm being moved to police liaison for the rest of the week and then I'm to take the leave I'm owed in preparation for my next posting.'

Julia's mood was not improved by my announcing I was off to Warsaw. My suggestion that she come over with me for a couple of weeks was met with derision.

'Have you any idea how much there is to do fixing the house? If I get any spare time I shall go down to Cornwall again, I've had quite enough of Poland.'

After a very nice meal in a Greek restaurant in Inverness Mews I tried to interest Julia in Warsaw again by repeating Prince's history lesson. Julia was not convinced, although for a brief moment her intellectual curiosity was raised.

'Is he right? All this stuff about linguistic nationalism. You're the linguist. Is language so important?'

'It's not about language. It's about diversity. Not so long ago there were literally hundreds of languages in Europe and each represented a more or less unique culture. As Prince says languages nobody today has ever heard of. One of my linguistics professors wrote a paper on the Podhale archaisms of the Goral language. I've completely forgotten what the Podhale archaisms are but I remember that Goral was a language spoken in the mountains of southern Poland right up until the Nazis arrived. The Gorals were a people who have now just disappeared like the Masurians.'

I found the subject fascinating. Julia did not. I would be going to Warsaw on my own.

XII

It was arranged that I would leave for Warsaw on Thursday morning. In the meantime, and in addition to ploughing through yet more briefings on Poland, Brasenose had the bright idea of searching through the shipping movements into and out of Gdańsk at the time that Nowak alleged that his friend Tadeusz Modjeski had been shot. I wasn't sure what I was looking for but by the end of Tuesday afternoon had produced what I hoped was a comprehensive list which would be circulated to our stations around the world. I was just about to call it a day when Brasenose appeared at my desk, an unusual event in itself.

'Our bird has flown,' he announced.

'Which bird?' I asked.

'Our scarfaced killer. We've had a confirmed sighting of him at Heathrow but it's too late to do anything about it. The airport authorities put his photofit up yesterday and two people recognised it right away. They were sure they had seen him in the airport on Sunday night. We have now confidently identified him as a passenger who boarded a flight to Copenhagen. He was travelling on a Finnish passport in the name of Mikkonen. I'm sure that will turn out to be fake.'

He had only just stopped speaking when I had a phone call from Julia, she had news on exactly the same subject. The

Devon & Cornwall Police had managed to establish that Scarface had arrived at Bodmin Road station on a train from London on Saturday morning.

'What's really embarrassing,' Julia reported, 'was that he seems to have arrived in Cornwall on the same train as General Fearmont.'

When I reported that to Brasenose his face creased into a smile. 'That's rather a coincidence. Perhaps we are on to the way that Scarface found Nowak. If he followed Fearmont down from London that might explain how he was able to establish not only that Nowak was in Cornwall but exactly where in Cornwall the DIS had found their safe house.'

I recalled that General Fearmont had been involved in some sort of altercation with a tourist at the taxi rank outside the station when he arrived. Could it be that the tourist had not been trying to steal his taxi but rather trying to find out where he was going? If Scarface had been told that Fearmont was on his way to the West Country to interrogate Nowak it would not have been difficult for him to wait at Paddington station hoping to identify the DG. No doubt the KGB's London station could produce a photograph of the general. If, of course, Scarface was actually working for the Russians.

Brasenose agreed. 'But the real question,' he said, 'is how did Scarface find out that Fearmont was going down to Cornwall and would lead him to Nowak? Somebody must have told him. Somebody in the DIS.'

'Or David Prince,' I said. 'You told him on Friday night.'

'Perhaps, although I don't recall telling him that Fearmont personally was going down.'

I said nothing. I was beginning to like David Prince but, unlike Brasenose, was not about to let instinct alone guide me. I liked Prince even more the next day when he took me to lunch at his club. We returned after sampling an excellent claret to find that Brasenose had been waiting for me in his office. Prince came with me.

When Brasenose's secretary showed us in we found our man in Washington, Colin Asperton, standing with his back to the room, silently studying the photos of pre-war ocean liners that covered one wall. I couldn't read the expression on Brasenose's face. He simply looked at us and started speaking before we had even sat down.

'Gentlemen. Something a little unexpected has occurred. The Great Crown of Jan Kazimierz has turned up in Finland.'

'How did it get there?' Prince asked.

Neither Brasenose nor Asperton answered him, each looking at the other as if to say you first. It was Asperton who gave way, turning directly to Prince as he spoke.

'David, you know the awkward situation we are in with regards to you and the Americans. Justin had a very useful conversation with you last Friday and as a result we are of course quite certain of your loyalty. Unfortunately our American cousins have yet to come round to that point of view. I am afraid the unlamented Mr Philby cast a very long shadow. This operation is crucially important to the Company. The new director, Bill Casey, takes a keen interest in developments in Poland. You may be aware that he himself has contacts at the highest level in the Vatican where, unsurprisingly with a Polish pope, the prospects of what one might call the re-energising of the Catholic Church in Poland are a particular priority. We all need to be cognisant of that dimension. As you know, our relationship with our American colleagues is fundamentally important for the

Service. I think on this occasion, therefore, we need to defer to their wishes. I know Justin has already briefed you on the history of Operation Coronation but going forward it would be best if you do not participate in any detailed planning for the next stage. In as much as the operation concerns future political developments in Poland we will of course be greatly dependent on your expertise but I think it would be better if we continue this conversation with Mr Dylan alone.'

Prince and I looked at Brasenose and I hoped he would say something to puncture Asperton's pomposity. Prince, after all, reported to Brasenose. Asperton's authority came only from his closeness to the Americans. But Brasenose merely nodded. 'We know Hoeven is making a mistake,' he said, 'but for now we have to go along with him. You and I should speak later.'

'I understand,' said Prince and left the room with more dignity than I would have shown in similar circumstances.

Brasenose had the grace to look embarrassed. He gestured to Asperton. 'Colin, perhaps you would be kind enough to outline the state of play to Thomas.'

Brasenose and Asperton spoke to each other with the measured politeness that an Englishman might use to explain the rules of cricket to a dim but important foreigner.

'Certainly, Justin.' Asperton turned to me. 'While you and Prince were at lunch I received a transatlantic call from Chuck Hoeven. When he arrived in his office this morning he was given some news that he considered should be immediately communicated to us. As Justin has just said, it would appear that the Great Crown of Jan Kazimierz was not lost during the unfortunate events in the Masurian Lakes. Chuck has received information that the Crown is in Helsinki and is available to purchase. He intends to do exactly that, after which Operation Coronation will continue as planned. He will again require our cooperation.'

'If Thomas is going to be thrown right into the middle of this,' said Brasenose, 'he really needs to know exactly what's going on.'

'Of course,' replied Asperton, turning back to me. 'Have you heard of a man named Mark Jaszczak?'

'Yes,' I replied. 'A Polish-American millionaire with a strong interest in Polish politics.'

'And a strong interest in US politics as well,' interjected Brasenose.

'Indeed,' continued Asperton. 'I believe Mr Jaszczak is a major donor to the Republican Party, although I'm not sure that is entirely relevant at the moment. Mr Jaszczak has a particular interest in this Great Crown and is willing to provide the funds needed to purchase it. He will then pass the Crown on as intended to Father Paszek. Indeed that is what he intends to do in Finland this evening.'

'Father Paszek is now in Finland?' I asked in surprise.

Brasenose made no attempt to hide his smile as Asperton explained that that was not what he meant. 'Father Paszek, of course, must remain in Poland. Mr Jaszczak is flying to Helsinki at this very moment to purchase the Crown. He will then come here to meet you. The transfer of the Crown to Father Paszek will take place in Warsaw.'

'Why does Jaszczak want to meet me?'

'Because you are required at the transfer. It is hoped that can be effected over the weekend. Mr Jaszczak has a private jet and you will fly to Warsaw with him on Friday.'

'No he won't,' Brasenose interrupted. 'Thomas will be in

Poland as a British diplomat. He goes tomorrow evening. The less overt connection he has with this business the better. If anything goes wrong we must try our best to ensure that the Americans, and Jaszczak in particular, take any flak that may be coming. I don't like this whole thing Colin, as you know, but if the orders from our political masters are that we cooperate then cooperate we must, but we are cooperating with an allied intelligence agency not taking part in a millionaire's private fantasy.'

'Understood, Justin, understood. Now to turn to Prince's question, how did the Crown get to Finland? We don't know. Nor do we know how the Party selling the Crown got in touch with Jaszczak.'

'So the approach was made directly to Jaszczak not through the Company?' I interrupted.

'It would appear so. And similarly Jaszczak is in contact directly with Father Paszek. This time the fewer people who know what's going on the better.'

'I still don't understand why I'm wanted when the Crown is handed over.'

'That I can tell you,' said Asperton. 'It seems that Father Paszek would rather not be directly involved at this stage. Things are tightening up in Poland and there are spies everywhere. He will send along a representative, someone you know but Jaszczak does not. Your job is to vouch for the authenticity of this intermediary. That's all. Once you've done that you leave the scene.'

'And who is this intermediary?'

'A man called Walentowicz. I gather you met him last time.'

I remembered Father Paszek's driver, who just nine days

ago had hurried us away from the lake when the shooting started.

'Yes I met him, briefly.'

'Well it seems you're going to meet him again. Let's hope this time things go smoothly.'

So one way or another I was off to Poland, quite possibly for years. When I returned to Bayswater that evening I realised Julia and I had a lot to discuss. Almost by accident we had reached a turning point in our lives. We had both chosen careers, Julia in the RAF and me in the DIS and now MI6, in which either of us could be given what was called an 'unattached posting', meaning long periods of separation. We had spent nearly every day together for the last five years and living apart would be a shock. It was something we had talked about when we decided to get married but had then put out of our minds. Julia, having been brought up in a naval family, was perhaps comfortable with the idea; to my surprise I found that I was not. But it was Julia who had decided to do something about it.

I discovered that Julia had bought fillet steak, usually a sign that we were celebrating something. She greeted me enthusiastically and immediately produced a large gin and tonic. It was obvious that she intended to make my last evening in London very special, although oddly she hadn't poured a drink for herself. Perhaps, I thought, she might even change her mind and spend her leave with me in Warsaw. In fact she had something quite different on her mind.

'I'm resigning my commission,' she said.

'That's a big step. Are you sure? You would be letting Fearmont win.'

Julia looked perplexed, almost disappointed. 'I'm

resigning my commission,' she repeated and when I still didn't respond properly, added, 'I'm pregnant.'

We looked at each other for a millisecond before I crushed her in my arms. There must have been hundreds of things I should have said and I said none of them. I was speechless. Two years of fruitless trying in Moscow had led to a tacit agreement not to even discuss the possibility of Julia becoming pregnant. When I did speak it was to utter the stupidest words possible.

'Are you sure?'

'Of course I'm sure. I got the results this afternoon.'

'That's wonderful,' I finally managed, and was conscious of how inadequate that sounded. I was going to be a father, there would be three of us. Perhaps I should have been thinking about the new addition but all I could actually think about was Julia. 'Are you all right? Shouldn't you be resting?'

'Thomas, I'm pregnant. I'm not ill. It's what we wanted.'

I realised I was more flustered than she was. Julia was right, a child is exactly what we had been desperately hoping for but now that it was happening I was full of doubts. Of course I wanted a family, but was I ready to be a father? Could I really look after a child? Could I look after Julia? There was so much to learn. I looked at Julia and suddenly realised she had no doubts. We would not just manage, we would triumph.

The rest of the evening was a jumble of the momentous and the mundane. When should we tell Julia's aunt and uncle and my family? Not yet, it's too early. What name shall we choose for the baby? It's far too early for that as well. What coat should I take to Warsaw? The warmest obviously.

Eventually we returned to the subject of Julia resigning her commission. In those days it was virtually automatic for a female officer who became pregnant to leave the RAF, indeed most resigned when they married.

'The point is,' said Julia, 'I'm not cut out for the RAF. They will never let women become pilots. And I can't stay in the DIS, there's going to be a wholesale clear-out after what happened in Cornwall. They announced this afternoon that General Fearmont is retiring at the end of the year, three weeks from now, and Richard Mendale has already gone. He's been made assistant to the military attaché at the Embassy in Washington. It's a non-job. The DIS will become pen-pusher land and that's just not me.'

I was shocked to hear about Fearmont and Mendale but Julia was right. The world was changing, and my world was about to change even more. I was about to become a father, unless something that Colin Asperton would probably describe as 'unfortunate' was waiting for me in Warsaw.

XIII

Mark Jaszczak flew into RAF Northolt the next morning. After stopping off at the nearby Polish War Memorial he arrived at Century House just before midday. Colin Asperton had decided to delay his return to Washington to be here. Jaszczak arrived with Chuck Hoeven but not the fabled Great Crown of Jan Kazimierz.

'That's locked in a safe on my plane,' he informed us. 'My man Dragan will make sure it stays there.'

I had expected Jaszczak to be a powerfully built bull of a man but physically he was quite the opposite. Short, wizened and bespectacled, he nevertheless strode into the meeting room as if he owned it. After perfunctorily shaking hands with Brasenose, Asperton and myself he seated himself at the head of the table.

'We are about to make history,' Jaszczak announced and then launched into a speech he had obviously delivered many times before. Poland had suffered for nearly three centuries but now freedom was coming. The people were awakening and the embrace of the Russian bear would be thrown off. But the people couldn't do that on their own, they needed help and they needed leadership. They needed patriots like Father Paszek to give them courage and hope, to rekindle the spirit of Jan Kazimierz, King John II Casimir Vasa. Jan Kazimierz's Oath of Lwów had united all Poles in defence of his Crown, the very Crown that he had just acquired on behalf of the people of Poland.

He sat back as if expecting a round of applause. Only Chuck Hoeven responded enthusiastically.

'The way the Agency sees it the situation in Poland can't last. Revolution is in the air; the government is losing all authority. The Polish Army won't turn on its own people so the only thing that can stop the coming revolution is the Russians. We know Moscow can't decide what to do. One faction thinks the army should have been sent in months ago. Another believes the Party just has to wait the troubles out: buy off the trade union demands by increasing wages, pay for the extra wages by increasing prices and just watch Solidarity collapse. That's happened before, the unions give a little, the government gives a little. But this time it could be different. We just have to make sure the Opposition are properly prepared, that when the time comes the whole nation rises up. We have to make it impossible for Russia to intervene. Brezhnev must understand that the cost to him would be too high. He can't afford another Afghanistan.'

'Afghanistan is not the same,' said Brasenose. 'The natives there have always been armed to the hilt and nobody has ever managed to conquer them. Let me tell you we British have tried often enough and always failed. The Russians could have learned a lot from our experience. Poland is very different. It has been occupied by one power or another for centuries.'

Jaszczak interrupted him impatiently. 'And we have fought off those powers. Look at the Germans. I've just landed at an airbase called Northolt. Do you know which squadron was based at Northolt during the last war? The

303 squadron, a Polish squadron, with the highest number of kills of any squadron in the Battle of Britain, higher than any English squadron let me tell you.'

'That was different, they were flying the best fighter planes in the world. You're talking about unarmed civilians taking on the Red Army, the most powerful army in Europe.'

'Who says?' demanded Hoeven. 'The mighty Red Army is creaking at the seams. It's overstretched in Afghanistan.'

'What's more,' insisted Jaszczak, 'there are officers in the Polish General Staff who understand the situation. They don't want the Russians marching in again and they will act if the people rise up. The Polish Army is a conscript army, they won't turn against their own people. We have humint on that. When the chips are down Poles will unite to fight the invader. It's happened before, it will happen again.'

I wondered idly where Jaszczak had picked up a word like humint. HUMINT is a term sometimes used to distinguish intelligence gained from human assets rather than say SIGINT derived from intercepting signals, but I had never heard anyone use it the way Jaszczak used it in normal conversation.

Asperton smoothly changed the subject. 'Nobody doubts the fighting spirit of the Polish people, Mr Jaszczak, and Her Majesty's Government is committed to bringing democracy to the whole of Eastern Europe. What my Service needs to be assured of before we commit more resources to this project is that we fully understand some of the finer details. Put bluntly, Mr Jaszczak, where did this Crown come from, how do we know it is genuine and above all, how will you ensure it reaches Father Paszek?'

'The Great Crown is genuine all right, you think I would

pay another half a million dollars if it wasn't. We checked that out weeks ago.'

'But you only bought the Crown yesterday,' pointed out Brasenose. 'How can you be sure the Crown you bought in Helsinki is the one that Flanagan and Sokolowski were hoping to buy in Poland?'

'Don't worry, the seller was verified,' said Hoeven.

'You mean Broniszewski, the man you were supposedly meeting last time? You're telling me a Polish peasant managed to travel from one end of the Baltic to the other with the Crown in his suitcase across some of the most heavily policed parts of the Soviet Union?'

'Not Broniszewski, no. The men who stole the Crown from him,' Hoeven replied.

'And stole my money,' interrupted Jaszczak.

'Perhaps,' Asperton put in, 'it might facilitate matters if we started at the beginning. Chuck, it might be useful if you just bring us all up to speed on developments since our Mildenhall meeting.'

I realised that this was not the conversation the two Americans had expected. They were here simply to tell us what to do next. As Flanagan had told me in Olsztyn, this was their operation and we simply had a walk-on role. I thought Hoeven was going to plead the old Intelligence world standby 'need to know' but he evidently thought better of it.

'There's not much to tell. Father Paszek was contacted by someone offering to sell the Crown. He contacted Mark Jaszczak here who arranged to fly to Helsinki with our agent Krypton. A man turned up as arranged and Krypton identified him as the man he had seen at the lake. Krypton handed over the money, retrieved the Crown and brought it back to Mark. That's it.'

'So what actually happened at the lake? What happened to your officers?'

'We still don't know for sure. Krypton didn't have a chance to interrogate this man.'

'I told him to just check the Crown against the photo,' interrupted Jaszczak. 'It's the Crown that's important.'

It struck me that Hoeven ought to be more interested in what happened to his two men but he said nothing.

Jaszczak was continuing. 'Half a million dollars is a lot of money, takes up a lot of space. We had hired a car and loaded the money in the trunk and Krypton just handed the keys over and walked away.'

'And where is Krypton now?' Brasenose asked.

'On his way back to the States,' Hoeven replied. 'We can't risk taking him to Poland. From now on this is Mark's show, I'm heading back this evening as well.'

'How was Father Paszek contacted and why did he then contact you?' Brasenose asked. 'How do we know the Soviets haven't set this whole thing up? They could have grabbed the Crown at the lake and are now trying to lure you into some sort of trap.'

'That's my risk,' snapped Jaszczak.

'Not entirely. Our man will be with you.'

Hoeven snorted. 'Operation Coronation has been approved; we're going ahead. We're here to make sure it succeeds.'

Before Brasenose could ask anything more Asperton moved on. 'Thank you, Chuck. That brings us on to what happens now and Mr Dylan's role.'

Brasenose interrupted. 'Thomas is flying to Warsaw this evening. He is there as a British diplomat. I don't want questions being asked about why he arrives in an American private jet.'

Jaszczak nodded, 'Good point. We will meet tomorrow night in my hotel, Hotel Bristol. My business manager in Poland is meeting one of Father Paszek's colleagues tomorrow to arrange how we hand over the Great Crown. I'm not doing that until I am sure security is watertight.'

'You have a business manager based in Poland?'

'Of course,' replied Jaszczak dismissively. 'I've invested a lot of money in that country. We're trying to turn round some of their manufacturing facilities. You won't believe how far behind the Communists are, everything's still done by hand. The market opportunities are enormous once we knock things into shape.'

Brasenose, I suspected, didn't want to sit through another lecture on Jaszczak's vision for Poland's future and rather abruptly drew the meeting to a close. We all stood up.

'I'll show you to your car, Mr Jaszczak,' said Asperton.

As they left Hoeven turned to Brasenose. 'Operation Coronation has been approved at the highest levels. You would do well to remember that.'

'Oh I am well aware of that,' replied Brasenose. 'I'm just hoping that your Mr Karacek will prove to be more reliable on this matter than I believe he has been on another matter.'

'How the hell,' snarled Hoeven, before stopping himself and following Asperton from the room.

Jaszczak was charging ahead, turning right at the end of the corridor.

'Not that way,' I heard Asperton murmur. 'That's not the way out.'

When Asperton returned he made no attempt to hide his annoyance. He turned on Brasenose right away, ignoring my presence completely.

'What the hell did you say to Hoeven? Who's Karacek? Why haven't I heard about him?'

'Karacek is the cover name the Company set up for Krypton in Sweden. We've just discovered a bank account in Ystad in that name which the Company have been shovelling money into for years.'

'And how do you know that?'

'Swedish Security have him on their radar.'

Brasenose clearly saw no need to tell his colleague that he had put a tail on Hoeven.

'And Prince?'

'What about Prince?'

'Hoeven says you asked about Karacek and Prince.'

'I didn't mention the name Prince. I was fishing by suggesting that Karacek might have been unreliable on something else. Interesting that Hoeven jumped to the conclusion I was referring to Prince. Perhaps Thomas is right.'

'Thomas? Right about what?' Asperton looked at me but Brasenose answered.

'Thomas has a theory that Krypton is the source of the information that supposedly incriminates David Prince.'

Asperton took a moment to think about that. 'Hoeven has given me no reason to suppose that to be the case.'

'Hoeven is a bloody fool,' said Brasenose forcefully. 'He learned his craft in Vietnam where he couldn't avoid sticking out like the proverbial sore thumb. He's never learned how to be discreet. It's amazing. Two cars with diplomatic plates leave the American Embassy in Copenhagen, one being driven by the CIA's Copenhagen Station Chief. They take the ferry across to Malmö in Sweden and then drive to the airport at Sturup. There they are met by the CIA's Stockholm Station Chief who has just flown down. Half an hour later a US Air Force plane arrives bearing two very senior CIA directors and their Moscow Station Chief. Then they all drive off in convoy to an insignificant little port across the sea from Poland. And Hoeven expects nobody to notice. The Swedes are not stupid. Their Security Department were on the alert the moment the diplomatic cars arrived unannounced from Denmark and the Americans filed a flight plan for landing a military aircraft at Sturup. The hotel in Ystad was probably being watched by plain-clothes Swedish police within moments of the Americans arriving there. It's a pretty poor reflection on our own man that he didn't notice the surveillance himself.'

Asperton jumped in at that. 'So we had someone there, how did we manage that?'

Brasenose ignored that question. 'Anyway the next day when our man is back in Stockholm he had a visitor. A very correct representative of Swedish Security who asked him very politely to explain what the hell is going on in Ystad and why a representative of British Intelligence seemed to have been following a team from American Intelligence around southern Sweden. And why, he wanted to know, when the Americans had flown away, did our man go back to Ystad and start asking questions about the man the Americans had taken with them?'

161

Glancing across at me Brasenose explained|: 'Of course we try to cooperate with the Swedes although it's not always easy, they're a very independent lot. But we rely on them to keep an eye on the Soviet Navy in the Baltic and it wouldn't have helped our relationship to try to stonewall.'

He continued: 'Our man might not be very good at recognising surveillance but he is a quick thinker. He tells our Swedish friend most of the truth. We don't know what the Americans were doing. They came to London for a routine meeting with our people. Then suddenly in the middle of the meeting they announced they had been called home and had to go. But we discovered they had filed a flight plan to Malmö. London thought that was discourteous at best and out of curiosity asked our man to pop down to Malmö to see what was happening. I'm not sure the Swede believed what he was hearing but he opened up about their concerns. And the thing that had really got them worried was that we weren't the only ones trying to find out what the Americans were up to. You can't keep secrets in a place like Sweden, US Air Force planes arriving at a civilian airfield cause people to ask questions. Next morning two other men flew down from Stockholm to Malmö, drove to Ystad and started poking around.'

'Did the Swedes say who?' Asperton asked.

'Two supposed diplomats from the Russian Embassy. The Swedes have identified them as GRU, Russian Military Intelligence.'

Asperton at first said nothing. He was as surprised as I was.

'I wonder if they discovered anything.'

'Well they certainly discovered the name Karacek,'

Brasenose replied. 'They talked to staff at the hotel where he was staying. The Swedes don't think they found out about Karacek's bank account. But the name's enough. Perhaps,' he said to Asperton, 'you should tell your friend Hoeven.'

I was trying to think through the implications of what Brasenose was saying. The Russians were asking questions about Krypton. The Company obviously regarded Krypton as one of their prized assets. He presumably had some sort of responsible position, perhaps in the military or even with the GRU or KGB. Krypton was now in the West and the Russians must surely have realised he had disappeared. They would be looking for him and throwing every resource they had at the task. Even if the GRU hadn't followed him to Ystad it wouldn't take them long to realise that the man Hoeven had met was the man they were looking for.

'So,' I said, 'the Americans know Krypton's identity, by now the Russians must know it, we're the only ones in the dark.'

'Yes,' said Asperton, who had clearly been rethinking his position. 'That is rather illogical. I need to talk to Chuck Hoeven. Once he knows the Russians are on to Krypton there is no need at all to keep his identity a secret. I will do that now, before Chuck leaves the country.' He looked at Brasenose. 'Of course I won't tell him that you had him followed while he was in Sweden.'

'I didn't say that.'

'No, but we both know that's what you did.'

Brasenose merely smiled. I followed him back to his room.

'Did you notice,' I asked, 'that Jaszczak referred to having lost a lot of money when Krypton was jumped at the lake?

That fits with what Flanagan and Sokolowski said, they talked about a peasant becoming very, very rich. So why did Lorrimore tell us they were just paying a few thousand dollars?'

'I can tell you that,' Brasenose replied. 'Hoeven has been keeping things from Lorrimore. In particular Lorrimore didn't realise Jaszczak was so deeply involved in Operation Coronation. He has only just found that out and he's not happy about it. He can't believe Hoeven has told a maverick like Jaszczak about an asset as sensitive as Krypton. Lorrimore thought Flanagan was buying this Crown out of Company funds. Now he's discovered that Jaszczak has been putting his own money Hoeven's way and it's not entirely clear where it's all been going. Jaszczak is the wildcard in all this. Since the Polish economy started opening up he's invested a lot of money over there. Mainly in the south, in Katowice and Kraków but also in Torun and Warsaw. He's providing employment and seems to think that will make him a big man in Poland but that's not how things work over there. He may see himself as a Polish patriot but the Communists just see him as one more American capitalist, they want his money not his politics.'

When we reached his office Brasenose glanced at his watch and waved me away. 'I need to call Blake Lorrimore in Washington. He should be at work by now.'

An hour later, just as I was about to set off for Heathrow, Brasenose called me back to his office.

He was on the phone to Asperton, clearly Hoeven had finally given us Krypton's real identity. 'Konstantin Kirilov' I heard Brasenose saying. 'A colonel in the KGB. I'll make a note of that and have enquiries made. What does this Kirilov do?' Asperton didn't have that information. 'That's a pity,' Brasenose commented, 'but we'll find out.'

When he had put the phone down Brasenose turned to me.

'You heard that. Krypton is Colonel Konstantin Kirilov. He's the senior KGB man in Kaliningrad, quite a coup for the Company.'

'I thought Asperton was saying he didn't know what Kirilov did.'

'That's right. He doesn't know, but I do. Lorrimore told me when he gave me Kirilov's name half an hour ago. I didn't tell Colin Asperton that. We have to be cautious. Operation Coronation is Chuck Hoeven's and I don't want him finding out that Blake Lorrimore is talking to me about it. The CIA is a very large organisation and inevitably there will be people pulling in different directions. Hoeven's a powerful man. He's been around a lot, Far East, Near East and now he's in charge of operations in Eastern Europe. Colin quite rightly is sticking close to him and I don't want him accidentally dumping Lorrimore in the mire.'

I smiled to myself. The point of having a Station Chief like Asperton in Washington was for him to act as the gatekeeper between the two agencies. But not only were Lorrimore and Brasenose exchanging information without telling Hoeven, quite clearly they also weren't telling Asperton.

Brasenose removed a photograph from a file on his desk and pushed it across to me. It was the picture our man had taken outside the hotel in Ystad. Hoeven had his hand on the shoulder of a man I assumed to be Kirilov. Two other men, clearly Americans, stood beside them while Lorrimore and Jacobs stood behind. I studied the Russian with interest.

Receding hair and an alert, sharp face, he carried himself with the same swagger as Hoeven. This was a man used to having his orders obeyed, quite a catch for the Americans. I wondered idly how he had been recruited. I would be willing to bet he had approached the Company, not the other way round.

'We had him down as a classic KGB career man,' commented Brasenose, 'no idea that the Company had recruited him. It would appear he joined the KGB in Leningrad, then transferred out to Vladivostok where he seems to have risen very quickly. I suppose Kaliningrad has many of the same sort of issues because he moved directly from number two out there to number one in Kaliningrad. We don't really know anything else about him. He doesn't seem to have had anything to do with intelligence or counter-intelligence. The only time his name has cropped up was in a report a couple of months ago about a KGB team visiting North Korea. Assuming it was the same Colonel Kirilov, that seems to be the only time he has been outside the Soviet Union.'

Brasenose stood up and walked over to the window. The view towards Pearman Street was uninspiring on the best of days and this was not the best of days. Dark grey clouds hung low over the city. Brasenose was still mulling over his telephone call with Lorrimore. When he spoke his voice was oddly detached.

'That's not all Blake Lorrimore said. There was something else. Something that makes me think if Blake isn't going mad then the whole world must be.'

XIV

Brasenose swung back towards me but for a moment said nothing. When he did speak there was a weariness in his voice that I hadn't noticed before.

'It seems Mr Jaszczak is playing a bigger role in all this than we had appreciated. I did wonder why it was Krypton, or Kirilov as we must now think of him, who was bringing the money to the lake. It would surely have been much easier for Flanagan and Sokolowski to take it to the lake themselves. Why would they somehow smuggle it to Kirilov in Kaliningrad for him to then smuggle back into Poland? Now we know. It wasn't Company money, it was Jaszczak's. And as Jaszczak didn't trust Krypton with his money his people only handed it over to him at the last minute, when Kirilov had crossed over from Kaliningrad into Poland.'

'So Jaszczak has people actively involved in the operation in Poland? They were actually in the area at the time.'

'Apparently so. Hoeven insists that Jaszczak's people weren't anywhere near the hut by the lake but they were certainly somewhere in the area. I don't like it. Nobody told us anything about Jaszczak being involved in Operation Coronation let alone him having people on the ground. And another thing Blake told me. It wasn't Father Paszek who was contacted about buying the Crown in Helsinki it was Jaszczak. How did that happen? How did anyone know he was the person to speak to? Apparently a man simply phoned Jaszczak's office in Chicago and said he wanted to sell the Great Crown of Jan Kazimierz.'

'I suppose Jaszczak may be known as a collector of Polish artifacts,' I suggested.

'No wait, it gets worse. Jaszczak agreed a price with the caller but demanded proof that he really had the Crown. This is where the whole thing really starts to stink. You remember the two Americans were supposed to be meeting a peasant called Broniszewski who would bring the Crown to you and Father Paszek. Well this caller claimed that Broniszewski was too frightened to go to the rendezvous on his own and the caller had agreed to go along with him. Once there they met Flanagan and Sokolowski as arranged but had then been jumped by two armed men wearing ski masks. Broniszewski had a hunting rifle and fired a shot, whereupon all hell broke loose. Soldiers appeared, bullets were flying everywhere, Broniszewski was hit but this man claimed he himself had managed to escape with the Crown. So far unlikely but possible. But this is where the fairy story starts.

'While he was running away the caller claims he saw a man in a dinghy. The dinghy had a number on it which he gave Jaszczak. The man in the dinghy would recognise him, so Jaszczak should trace the owner of the dinghy and question him. He could confirm that he had seen someone running past the lake with a black and red bag. Jaszczak of course realised he didn't need to trace anyone, the owner of the dinghy was Krypton. And he had already mentioned a black and red bag. The story fitted together perfectly.'

'Too perfectly,' I said. 'It's utterly preposterous. As you say it's mad. This mysterious man with the Crown is running away from a gunfight but has time to note down the number on a dinghy. And when he suggests trying to track down the dinghy's owner in a remote corner of Poland we just happen to know exactly who he is talking about and amazingly have the dinghy owner sitting in a safe house in Washington. It's ludicrous.'

'Of course it is. Hoeven and Jaszczak believed it because they wanted it to be true. Just like they want the whole nonsense about the Great Crown of Jan Kazimierz to be true. Lorrimore realises that now. But the story does raise some massive questions, the first being: how did this man in Helsinki come up with a fairy tale that matched exactly what Hoeven and Jaszczak could be expected to believe? I could suggest quite a few possible answers to that one but it's what else Blake said that is totally mad.

'Blake gave me two names. Kirilov was one, the other is simply not possible. When she received a call from Helsinki Jaszczak's secretary naturally asked for a name, and the caller gave it.' Brasenose paused for effect.

'Tadeusz Modjeski. The friend Kacper Nowak said he had last seen in the Gdańsk docks with a bullet in the back of his head.'

I was speechless. That simply made no sense at all. It couldn't be. In my mind there were two different boxes, one labelled Operation Coronation and the other labelled Kacper Nowak. Operation Coronation involved two American agents taking Julia and me to the Masurian Lakes and then disappearing. It was about exactly what Brasenose and Lorrimore had been discussing: a legendary Crown which Mark Jaszczak and Father Paszek thought would somehow inspire a revolution. It had nothing to do with Kacper

Nowak, an officer in the Polish navy, being pursued for no obvious reason by a KGB assassin.

The two boxes were completely unrelated apart from the coincidence that both involved Poland. The only thing the two had in common was utter improbability. Magical crowns in the late twentieth century and Russian killers in Cornwall belonged in the pages of bad comic books.

But now it seemed the two boxes were connected. How far did that connection go? Was Modjeski involved in the events at the lake? Did the story about swapping consignments in the Gdańsk docks have something to do with Operation Coronation? Or if Modjeski really had turned up in Helsinki was anything Nowak had told us in Cornwall true?

I tried to remember just what Nowak had said in the pub in Port Gaverne. He had been quite definite that his friend Modjeski had been killed by a Russian. Knowing what I now knew about Nowak's mental state I could believe that the whole story was some sort of delusion, that there was no Modjeski and no Russian. But for Modjeski to turn out to be a real person and what's more to be alive and well and holed up in Helsinki with the Great Crown of Jan Kazimierz was beyond belief.

Something else suddenly struck me. 'Nowak said that his friend Modjeski was SB, security police.'

'I know. If Jaszczak has bought this Crown from the Polish secret police then you're almost certainly walking into a trap. But why would they be so elaborate? Why an exchange in Finland? It would have been far less risky in Poland. And what are we to make of Kacper Nowak's story about his adventure in the Gdańsk docks? We know he was there because that's where he boarded the boat bound for Teesside. So some of his story is true, why make up the stuff about Modjeski being killed?'

'Unless he really is insane.'

'Did he seem that way to you?' Brasenose asked.

'No, not before he was shot at. He seemed scared. Confused. But in control of himself. Having said that he did have a lot to drink. Perhaps he just can't handle alcohol and was repeating something he had seen in a film or read in a cheap thriller. His story was second-hand fiction.'

Brasenose was not convinced. 'So while in a drunken stupor he comes up with the name of Tadeusz Modjeski which by pure coincidence happens to pop up again in Helsinki. That simply won't do. Somewhere behind everything that's happened there is a logic, the more absurd it gets the more I'm sure that someone is trying to lead us where we shouldn't be going.

'We've been told to cooperate with the Americans on this but be careful in Poland. Don't get too close to Jaszczak. As soon as you've introduced him to Father Paszek's intermediary, make yourself scarce. No heroics. Anything smells odd just pull out, walk away. I'll take any flak. It looks like the Americans have already lost two men, we don't want that happening to you and that's an order.'

With that cheery instruction I collected my case and headed out to the airport.

I had always found flying exciting, my mind full of whatever was ahead of me. But despite Brasenose's warning this time it was not where I was going that occupied me but what I was leaving behind. Julia was pregnant and I wanted to be with her. It was a new feeling; real love was not about taking pleasure, it was about taking responsibility. By the time I was halfway to Heathrow I had given up all attempts at making sense of my new mission and instead turned my mind to more important matters, like possible names for the new member of our family. I decided on Robert for a boy. What, I wondered, would Julia say to having Bob Dylan as a son? I didn't need to ask. She would not be amused. Let's hope we were having a daughter.

As I checked in I realised that Julia would probably be fine without me around. What she needed was peace and quiet. In the event she had neither.

XV

JULIA'S STORY

I'm not entirely sure why my husband has asked me to contribute this chapter. He says it is because only I can explain what was happening in London after he had gone to Warsaw. I think it more likely that even after all this time he still is not completely convinced that the chain of events I shall describe arose entirely by accident. One coincidence after another can strain credibility. It certainly felt that way at the time.

December 1981 was one of the coldest months on record in England and yet it had started well. On the first of the month we arrived back from Moscow via Poland and our peculiar adventure to find the weather rather pleasant, especially after the bitter cold we had left behind. That certainly changed a week later. Blizzards swept the country. Every day the weather forecasts seemed to warn of new cold fronts approaching from Greenland and there was much talk of the likelihood of a white Christmas.

It was a peculiar period in our lives. What I remember most is that nothing seemed to happen in the way we had expected, especially, of course, the discovery that I was carrying baby Eveline.

Returning to England was inevitably going to require a period of readjustment. A lot had changed while we had been away, not least prices which had risen by more than fifty per cent. Finding that we couldn't live in our own house was the last thing we needed or expected. We had really been looking forward to moving back into our own home, so it was quite upsetting when we found that was impossible. Having said that, the prospect of a new kitchen was exciting.

Leaving Russia should have been a huge relief although, unlike Thomas, I had enjoyed rather more than he the social side of life in Moscow. At first some of the Embassy wives had looked at me with a degree of suspicion; not only did I have a degree, I was also working, which was almost unheard of for 'wives'. I was clearly not a traditional diplomatic wife any more than Thomas was a traditional diplomat. But the way I spoke together with my family connections gave me an advantage Thomas did not have, an irritating reality in those days. And being brought up in a naval family always on the move had certainly prepared me for the peripatetic life that the Foreign Office people also took for granted. I might not have the amazing social skills of my formidable aunt, Lady Grimspound, but I certainly found it easier than Thomas to fit in. Sociable small talk is not his forte. Seriously dull conversations at Embassy cocktail parties invariably gravitated towards Mrs Thatcher's battles with the trade unions until the marriage of Prince Charles and Lady Diana provided a more glamorous focus: on neither subject did Thomas have anything diplomatic to contribute.

The social life of the Embassy was important because Moscow itself was unspeakably dreary. As Thomas was told on our first day: there's opera, ballet and bugger all else. (Not a comment that would have been repeated in front of the ladies.) To my complete surprise I actually became very fond of a couple of the wives who have remained friends to this day.

And I really enjoyed my work. It was an exciting time to be on the Defence Intelligence Staff. The Russian invasion of Afghanistan provided us with a wonderful opportunity not only to observe the Red Army in action but also to learn lessons for any similar operations that the British Army might be called upon to undertake. How sad that when British troops were sent to Afghanistan as part of Operation Veritas in 2001, the reports I had carefully crafted in my Moscow office twenty years earlier clearly remained unread in some Whitehall filing cabinet.

Perhaps I realised even then that although my work interested me, it wasn't as valuable as I had at first imagined. There was never any useful feedback from London, just requests for yet more detail. Frustratingly, although my Russian became passable in order to answer such demands, I had to call on my linguist husband far too often for my pride's sake.

As the end of our tour approached I was looking forward to leaving Moscow and being in our home again. But there was no corresponding desire to return to Whitehall or to take up the RAF career I had once set my heart upon. Thomas wanted to start a family and slowly I was starting to realise that perhaps that's what I wanted as well. Of course it was much easier for him, there was no question of his having to choose between children and career. The term 'house-husband' was then non-existent.

The death of my parents when I was a child had not been quite as traumatic as most people assumed it must have been. My parents had been living in Singapore and sent me

175

to prep school in England. They had deliberately chosen the one attended by my cousin Susan. My beloved Aunt Anne, when she was not herself following Uncle Gordon around the world, was the one who attended all my school events and scooped me up in the holidays when flights home were a problem. Oddly enough it was the assassination of General Demirkan in Yaroslavl that made me realise how much I had missed when my parents died.

I travelled to Ankara with the murdered man's widow, Shanar Demirkan. We didn't talk much but I observed her quiet dignity. The funeral was organised by the general's colleagues and it seemed to me that metaphorically speaking, and indeed at times quite literally, Shanar was relegated to a back seat. The comfort she found came from her family, her three daughters and her own ageing parents. Her father, grey haired but still upright, although I imagine well into his eighties. Her Kurdish mother, bent over a little now but still fiercely protective. Her daughters all starting families of their own. They stood apart, three generations held together by the most natural of all bonds, bonds that I wanted to feel myself. A feeling perhaps strengthened by our realisation that starting a family was not as easy as we had thought.

All I wanted to do when the test finally proved positive was to share the news with everyone I met. We decided it was too early to do that. Nevertheless almost all my thoughts turned to our future as a family. Looking back, even the events in Cornwall seemed to me merely a sideshow. Neither of us could have been closer to the attempted murder of Kacper Nowak and to the collapse of Operation Coronation in Poland but it all now seemed unreal, part of a very different world. The most direct impact of it all for me had been the sudden departure of Richard Mendale and General Fearmont from the DIS. Nominally Fearmont remained DG until his replacement arrived but he disappeared from the office, leaving the whole organisation in a state of suspended animation.

When I asked my direct superior what I should be doing I was simply told to continue with 'police liaison' until the situation was clearer. What that actually meant was left to me to determine.

In truth when Thomas set off for Warsaw my real priority was sorting out the refurbishment of our house, paying a newfound attention to the spare bedroom, which I was already thinking of as the nursery. I managed to comfortably combine my shopping expeditions with my work. I set up meetings with the Metropolitan Police at New Scotland Yard, in those days situated on Victoria Street, conveniently close to the Army & Navy Store, now also long gone.

Most of the information relating to the man who had tried to kill Kacper Nowak was held by the Devon & Cornwall and Essex police forces, but a photofit picture had been circulated to other forces in the hope that we might discover more about his time in the UK. A young WPC named Wendy helped me sort through the various reports of possible sightings that had come in. Not a single one of them produced anything genuinely useful. Indeed the only really solid report was from a police sergeant in Kent who reported that he had visited Cornwall for a family wedding and had sat opposite our suspect on the train down. The sergeant had observed that the man's book had a brown paper cover so that its title could not be seen. The sergeant obviously thought that was highly suspicious but he had first noticed the man for another reason: the stranger didn't seem to know where he was going. At each station he put the book into his travel case and stood up as if to get off. But once the train had come to a halt he looked out of the window and sat down again. He eventually left the train at Bodmin.

We quickly established that it was the train I knew had been taken by General Fearmont. The man really didn't know where he was going, rather he was waiting for the general to disembark.

'But why cover his book?' Wendy asked. 'Do you think it was pornography?'

'No, I think it more likely that it wasn't English. He wouldn't want anyone knowing what language he was reading.'

By now we knew the bird had flown the country and there didn't seem much point in hanging around in the office. Wendy insisted we go for a cup of tea before I left. The weather outside was awful, there had been heavy snowfalls right across southern England. In the canteen she proudly showed me her newly acquired, and very stylish, Art Deco diamond engagement ring.

She held her hand out for me to examine.

'It's beautiful,' I enthused. 'I love step cut diamonds. So unusual these days. Is it a family piece?'

'It belonged to my boyfriend's grandmother.' She quickly corrected herself. 'My fiancé's grandmother.'

Wendy was clearly delighted by my enthusiasm. 'You obviously know a lot about jewellery.'

'Not really. Crowns seem to be my speciality these days.'

It was a flippant remark unprofessionally made; my mind really was elsewhere. Wendy looked at me quizzically but I was not about to discuss Operation Coronation with a WPC I had only just met.

'Somebody important lost a crown and we were asked to look for it,' I lied. 'It all blew over.'

'Did they find it?'

'I don't know. We dropped the investigation. It turned out it wasn't particularly valuable: pearls not diamonds.'

And that was it. One casual conversation. Forgotten before I had even crossed Victoria Street. I had more important things to think about.

My Aunt Anne had bought a very expensive Silver Cross pram for her daughter but now that Susan no longer needed it I suspected it was destined for me. I had to find a tactful way to say no; I had no intention of pushing a heavy pram around the streets of London. As an RAF officer I knew Owen Finlay Maclaren as the designer of the Spitfire's undercarriage but now I appreciated him far more for his invention of the collapsible baby buggy: I had to buy one of those before the next conversation with my aunt.

Wendy phoned me at the Bayswater flat the next afternoon. I can't remember now why I had given her my number but I do remember being surprised that she was working on a Saturday. She must have felt it odd to phone me at home because she explained at some length that she had called now because she was off duty on Monday and would be at Hendon for the rest of the week. She had phoned to say that my remark about crowns had triggered a memory. At first I had no idea what she was talking about. It was only when she mentioned a crown with pearls that I remembered the conversation in the canteen.

'It's really peculiar,' she said. 'It was the pearls that made me remember. The crown with pearls you said, not diamonds. There was a report about exactly that. A crown with pearls. Nearly three months ago. It came in from the police in Camden. We just filed it. We get lots of strange reports. Somebody sees something that they don't understand and they tell Scotland Yard. What are we supposed to do about it, my sergeant asks. Like I say, we just file them. That's what we did with the Camden report. It didn't mean anything to us. But now you come along and I thought perhaps you should see it.'

'But what does the report say?' I asked.

'Oh yes, of course. It's about a jeweller somewhere near Hatton Garden. He reported that a man had asked him to make a crown. It was to be a copy of an old crown. With real gold and real pearls. It cost a lot of money. The jeweller made it but he was worried there was some sort of fraud going on. He was told the crown was for a play but you wouldn't use real gold for a stage prop. And the man paid for it in cash. That's really strange, don't you think? Who carries that much cash around?'

'I don't suppose there's a name and address for the customer.'

'Yes, there is, but it's fake. The address he gave was in Soho somewhere. Yes, here it is: 69 Poland Street. I've checked, there's never been a man called David Prince living there.'

'David Prince!'

'Yes, that's the name the man gave. Do you know him?'

'No, I don't think so.'

'That's a shame. I thought perhaps you did. I'll send you a copy of the report.'

I was thoroughly alarmed. Thomas was in Warsaw pursuing an identical crown and Wendy's report was far too much of a coincidence, especially with David Prince already under suspicion. I needed to act swiftly.

'No, I'll come over. I'm coming that way and I can pop in again.'

And that's what I did. The report was short and basically repeated what Wendy had told me. The man Wendy had called a jeweller was actually a goldsmith making gold jewellery, usually to his own designs. He had been approached by a potential customer who had a black and white photo of a medieval crown which he wanted copied. It was to be used in a play and the man wanted it to appear as authentic as possible. He paid a significant deposit in cash and collected the crown three weeks later. Again he paid in cash. As Wendy had said, the customer gave his name as David Prince.

The report gave the goldsmith's name, business address and phone number. I tried the number but there was no answer.

'You think this really is connected to your old investigation?' Wendy asked.

'It could be, but that would be a really long shot.'

'Why don't you call Camden? Perhaps they'll remember something that's not in their report.'

I did as Wendy suggested and struck lucky. The PC who had filed the report was on duty and actually in the station. PC Henderson couldn't tell me anything more about the crown or its purchaser but he could tell me how to contact the goldsmith.

'Chap called Rothenberg,' he told me. 'Been around for ages, never had any trouble. I remember it all well. He wanted me to check out his new security and while I was there he mentioned this crown thing. Said it really smelled. This bloke comes in with a photo of what he says is an ancient crown. But Rothenberg says he's never seen a crown like that. And it has to be an exact copy, using only materials that would have been available in the old days. Claims it's going to be in a play on television, it might be in close-ups and critics will notice if anything's wrong. Very odd. And then everything was cash. The chap made a joke about keeping the tax man out of it, which is just the sort of thing you shouldn't say to a man like Rothenberg.'

'I tried to phone Rothenberg earlier,' I said. 'No answer.'

'No, there wouldn't be. Sabbath and all that. If you can't wait until Monday try tomorrow. I have his home number on file.'

I was extremely grateful, though I tried to hide my increasing sense of foreboding. I stopped by the office to pick up the photos of the crown Blake Lorrimore had helpfully given us and made my way back to Bayswater.

Next morning I awoke to discover that the news on the radio was still dominated by the weather. It had been the coldest night recorded in England since 1879. I flicked the radio off angrily. I wasn't concerned with the weather in London, I was concerned with what Thomas was planning to do in Warsaw. I tried phoning him but couldn't get through. I called the Duty Officer at the DIS in the hope he could contact the Embassy but apparently they were having the same problem. Although I knew it was unacceptably early in the day to call Rothenberg I had to do something; it was already eight o'clock in Warsaw and Thomas had told me he would soon be setting off to hand over the supposedly ancient Great Crown of Jan Kazimierz.

The phone was answered almost immediately by an alert-sounding Mrs Rothenberg, who didn't seem at all put out by a strange woman asking to speak to her husband at seven o'clock in the morning.

It was some minutes before Mr Rothenberg came on the line. I apologised for troubling him at such an hour and then went straight to the point.

'Mr Rothenberg, I'm calling from the Ministry of Defence. PC Henderson has given me your number. I need to speak to you urgently about a gold crown you told him you had recently made. I have some photos I would like you to look at.'

'Of the crown?'

'That's what I need you to tell me. Can I bring you the photos right now?'

'You mean to my home? Now?'

'Yes please, precisely that if at all possible. To your home or to your nearest police station. I can't tell you why at the moment but I can assure you it is a matter of the utmost importance.'

I thought I sounded faintly ridiculous but fortunately Mr Rothenberg took me seriously. Less than half an hour later a taxi was dropping me outside his house. The grey hair and gentle smile of the man who opened the front door gave him the appearance of a favourite uncle. I had put on my RAF uniform to make myself seem more official but it had not been necessary.

'Come into the sitting room.'

He led me into a room in which every surface was covered by photos of what I took to be his children and grandchildren. I passed him my own photos.

'That's my work,' he exclaimed without hesitation, pointing at the colour photos Lorrimore had given us. 'And that's the photo I was given to copy.' He indicated the black and white photo Lorrimore told us had come from pre-war Lviv.

'How sure are you?'

'Absolutely certain. It's a very odd crown. The circlet is just plain gold, a real medieval crown would have had jewels all round the head.'

'And you made the crown for a man named David Prince?'

'That's right. I asked him about the plain circlet and he said putting jewels on the circlet would be far too expensive. That seemed crazy if the idea was to make it look authentic.'

I wanted to ask a lot more about Mr Prince, not least what he looked like, but there was absolutely no time to lose. I had to find a way to contact Thomas as my absolute priority, descriptions could be taken later.

'Thank you, Mr Rothenberg. That is extremely helpful. My superiors will need to speak to you again, quite possibly today. Hopefully they will be able to tell you more than I'm authorised to disclose.'

Refusing Mrs Rothenberg's offer of tea or coffee as graciously as I could I almost flew out of the house to where the taxi was waiting for me. It was 8.45 London time when I was dropped outside the Ministry of Defence. I wasn't sure what to do next but when I reached my desk there was a note from the Duty Officer. Contact had been established with our Embassy in Poland. I sent a top priority message to the DIS man there, Major Brampford, and prayed I was in time to stop Thomas from doing whatever he was about to do.

XVI

It had been well below zero centigrade when I arrived in Warsaw and hovered around zero all the next day. I spent the morning with our man on the spot, Paul Rembury. Barely thirty, Rembury exuded a calm self-confidence that would carry him a long way. He had certainly not been idle. There was a lot to tell me. Rembury had actually written himself a list of points to make sure he would not forget anything.

'First,' he said, 'the names London sent me. Kacper Nowak we had already been looking into. We've found nothing at all. Nowak is a common name. But there's no mention of any kind of search for a navy lieutenant with that name.

'Second, his friend Tadeusz Modjeski. Prince has a source in the SB secret police.'

'Firefox?'

'Yes. As you probably know, Firefox is relatively junior and based here in Warsaw so I wasn't expecting him to be able to find out anything about SB operations in Gdańsk. But Modjeski is big news. He disappeared and the SB don't like one of their own vanishing. There have been all sorts of bulletins about him, nationwide bulletins.'

'When did he disappear?'

'Round about the day Kacper Nowak must have boarded that ship. The odd thing is that the first bulletin wasn't issued right away, it was issued the day after your little adventure in the Masurian Lakes. It's as if nobody noticed he was missing until then. But Firefox says there is something even more peculiar. Any sightings of Modjeski are to be reported to the Wspólny Zespół Badawczy, the Joint Research Team, here in Warsaw.'

'And who are they?'

'That's simple. KGB. It's a Russian team embedded in SB headquarters.'

'So the KGB are looking for Nowak's friend, which means that whatever Modjeski has been doing in Helsinki it wasn't part of an SB operation. He's gone freelance.'

'It looks like it. And the Russians are after him.'

Rembury wasn't finished. 'There's another name I was given. Broniszewski. I gather he was the peasant the Americans were planning to buy the Crown from. He's dead. Hunting accident according to the local paper, on the day you were due to meet him. It doesn't say where but no doubt it was where you heard the shots.'

'Looks like it. And it ties in with what Jaszczak claims happened there. Broniszewski had brought the Crown to sell and was then jumped.'

'Perhaps, but what may be interesting is that Broniszewski wasn't really a simple peasant. There was a glowing obituary for him, full of praise for his leading role in the Party in Olsztyn province. He seems to have been a lifelong Communist, spent the war in Russia. He was Party chairman in a little place called Bartoszyce, right up near the frontier with Kaliningrad.'

'And yet he was happy to sell the Crown to a man like Father Paszek.'

'That doesn't make sense, unless he was being offered an awful lot of money.'

'Which it now seems he was. But it still doesn't make sense. Why would a die-hard Communist insist on having me at the exchange? Remember all that stuff about me having to be there because his brother had flown with the RAF. He doesn't sound like someone with an overpowering sentimental attachment to the British.'

'There's one more thing I should mention,' Rembury said. 'Things are hotting up here, not the weather, of course, but there's something in the air. There are all sorts of odd opposition groups springing up. An outfit called the Army of Fighting Poland, Polska Walcząca, has been calling for an armed uprising and issuing communiques that only foreign journalists ever read. Polska Walcząca was a name used by the Polish Resistance during the war but these guys have nothing to do with that. They're probably a black op set up by the SB to justify a crackdown. The problem for most of these dissident groups is that they have no recognisable voice. Solidarity has Lech Walesa but the only other group with any authority is the Catholic Church and their problem is too many voices: some radical priests are in bed with Solidarity, the likes of Father Paszek want to turn the clock back fifty years and Archbishop Glemp tries to sit in the middle.

'The SB high command are getting jumpy. Leave has been cancelled. Apparently an arms cache was discovered in a factory near Torun. Firefox doesn't know any details except that it was pure chance that the weapons were found. That's a really new development, Solidarity has been entirely peaceful until now. Firefox thinks the Russians could roll in at any time.'

'But,' I commented, 'our station in Moscow is still reporting no signs of activity on the border.'

We knew that the Soviets had developed plans for an invasion the previous year, the Company had got hold of them and President Carter then made them public. The Century House view seemed to be that Yuri Andropov and the KGB were calling the shots and were now arguing that the Soviet Union had so many problems of its own that even a Solidarity government in Poland would be better than another military adventure.

'Perhaps Jaruzelski will go it alone,' suggested Rembury, referring to the Polish general who had been the country's Prime Minister since February. Just two months ago Jaruzelski had been appointed leader of the Communist Party and thus effectively the head of state.

'I can't see that happening,' I replied confidently. 'There's no way the Polish Army will turn on its own people.'

Rembury said nothing.

We spent the rest of the morning fleshing out the briefings I had received in London. Rembury had been interviewed by Brasenose and others as part of the investigation of David Prince, and was completely dismissive of their efforts. 'They're mad to even suggest David is anything but loyal. He got Radlowski out, recruited Firefox and I'm sure is about to conclusively identify the so-called mole in the Embassy. The whole thing is ridiculous.'

I had arranged to meet Jaszczak at four o'clock the next afternoon at the Hotel Bristol, a half an hour walk from the British Embassy, which in those days was situated in a nineteenth-century palace opposite the Ujazdowski Park. Although it was bitterly cold the walk gave me a chance to clear my head. It would also give Paul Rembury the opportunity to ensure that I wasn't being followed. After things had gone so disastrously wrong in the Masurian Lakes I was determined to have my back guarded this time.

Handsome buildings lined the avenue, which ran parallel to the River Vistula, although too far away to catch any glimpse of the river itself. The avenue evoked both Warsaw's glorious past and the more bitter recent memories. Almost next door to the Embassy was the spot where the Polish resistance assassinated the head of the Warsaw SS in 1944, leading to the execution of 300 hostages in reprisal. Warsaw had been destroyed and rebuilt, the scars of war covered over. It was not so easy to hide the scars on the body politic.

There had been demonstrations throughout Poland for weeks. The Catholic Primate, Józef Glemp, had met Solidarity leaders to try to calm the situation but all the signs were that calm was the last thing on anyone's mind. It seemed to me that there were more troops around than when I was last here just ten days before.

Jaszczak had taken a suite of rooms at the Hotel Bristol, one of the few buildings to survive the war and that only because the Germans had taken it over for their own use. A burly man took my coat and then expertly frisked me. What, I wondered, was he expecting to find? We were, after all, on the same side.

'Wait here,' he instructed, leading me into a small dressing room. I could hear raised voices nearby. They were speaking rapidly in Polish and the only word I could pick out was '*armia*' meaning army, perhaps they too had noticed that there seemed to be more troops on the street.

After five minutes Jaszczak appeared with three other men and quickly ushered them out.

'My business managers,' he explained. 'We've had a problem at one of our plants. Nothing to do with our little project. Everything's set for that. Dragan has the Crown.' He gestured towards the man who had frisked me. Dragan nodded but said nothing.

'I'll show it to you,' Jaszczak continued.

Dragan left the room and returned with what looked like a small hatbox. Inside, the Crown sat snugly on a velvet base.

Although I had seen the photographs, Jan Kazimierz's Crown was disappointing. It was smaller than I had expected. A plain gold band with six pearl-encrusted arches rising from it to what Julia called a 'monde', on top of which was an ornately crafted golden cross. I could see why Anne Grimspound had reservations about it. It was a crown lacking crown jewels.

Jaszczak must have noticed that I was not as impressed as he expected me to be.

'I don't suppose you know the history of Jan Kazimierz's Crown,' he said. 'This isn't the crown that he wore at Lwów in 1656, this is just what remains after the Germans and Russians finished with their pillaging. The original Great Crown was made in 1610 to be worn by the King of Poland when he was crowned as Tsar of Russia. I guess you didn't even know that Poland was far more important than Russia once upon a time. It was the most magnificent crown in the world with more than two hundred and fifty precious jewels: rubies, sapphires, emeralds and pearls. That's the crown that Jan Kazimierz was wearing when he dedicated himself to the glory of Poland in the Oath of Lwów. That's the glory we intend to recapture.'

He paused briefly and then resumed a story I was sure he had told often before. 'When the Prussians invaded at the beginning of the nineteenth century they were determined to wipe Poland from the map for ever. The Prussian king, Frederick William III, seized the Polish royal regalia and had everything melted down, he wanted to destroy every symbol of Poland as a nation. The Prussians looted every last piece from the Polish Treasury except for just one thing: Jan Kazimierz's Crown. They couldn't take that for a very good reason: the Russians had got there first. The Crown had been ripped to pieces. All the jewels were stolen. The most glorious emerald is now in the Kremlin Armoury in Moscow. All that was left were the six half arches with their pearls and the orb and cross. The people of Lwów took those six pieces and melted down their old own gold to make a band on which they could be mounted. This is the result. It symbolises everything about Poland's past and it will come to symbolise everything about its future.'

He carefully put the Crown away again and waited for me to respond.

'I recognise the power symbolic actions can have but do you really think Father Paszek appearing with that Crown will produce a revolution?'

'Of course not,' Jaszczak responded impatiently. 'Everything has to come together. We need the right messenger, Paszek. We need a symbol, the Great Crown. But we need far more. Money. Men. Weapons. Above all, organisation. We need a movement. With that and with the will of God, yes, we can produce a revolution. The country is ready.'

'And the movement will need a leader. Father Paszek.'

'Perhaps. This is a Catholic country. Thirty-five years of Communism haven't changed that. We have a Polish pope remember. The Church is the only force in Poland that the Communists could never control. Pope John Paul represents the soul of the Polish people. But of course the Holy Father in Rome and Cardinal Glemp here in Poland have to be careful. Their first responsibility is to protect the position of the Church. Father Paszek can be more outspoken. He can show that the way forward is the way back. To throw out the Communists is not enough, we must eradicate all traces of their ideology and return to the values that made Poland great: respect for the Church, respect for the family, respect for the nation. That's what Solidarity don't understand. The Communist state is not something to reform, it is something to destroy. Only then will there be true freedom. Father Paszek understands that. He understands that we cannot negotiate with our enemies, they must be eliminated. Already his sermons are read by thousands. His message resonates with all true Poles. We need him and he needs us.'

Who, I thought, is the 'us' that Father Paszek needs? It was a question I decided not to ask.

Instead I turned to a question closer to home. 'What I still don't understand is why you need me? Why the whole business of setting up a meeting with a representative of Father Paszek to hand over the Crown? You're obviously in touch with Paszek yourself. Why not just give him the Crown?'

Jaszczak looked genuinely surprised. 'Tradecraft,' he explained. 'I don't know how you guys in MI6 operate but the Agency prides itself on its tradecraft and so do we. I've never met Father Paszek. Tomorrow will be the first time and then only if his man and my man give the all-clear. We always use cut-outs. The whole operation is on a need-to-know basis. We have sleepers in place to provide the humint we need.'

Jaszczak had used the word humint in London and it had jarred then. He was using terms he didn't really understand. Sleepers by definition are not there to provide intelligence, the whole point is that they are deep cover agents who don't do anything that might arouse suspicion until the time comes for them to be woken up. He seemed to imagine he was some sort of super spymaster. His constant references to 'we' and 'us' made Operation Coronation sound like a private enterprise. He had asserted that the Company prided itself on its tradecraft 'and so do we'. Who did he mean by we? I was supposed to be supporting an agency of an allied nation, not becoming involved in a personal campaign.

Jaszczak was determined to convince me that he was the super-professional and I was the rank amateur.

'Don't trust anybody. That's my motto. This is my money we're dealing with. We tried to pass the Great Crown to Paszek by the lake and somebody screwed up. Well it wasn't us. We had checked everything. Cut-outs every step of the way. My people checked the money when they received it. When it was passed on to Kirilov we had him check it again and then it was sealed. And what's more we watched him all the way across the lake so he couldn't do a runner with my money.'

I interrupted. 'You had men at the lake! They saw what happened!'

'No, they didn't see what happened. We put a radio transmitter in one of the cases and stayed well out of the way.

No need to spook anyone. Kirilov knew that if the tracker suddenly stopped working he would answer to me.'

'But you must know what happened to the money?'

'Well I don't. These trackers only have a range of a few miles. Flanagan was supposed to take over the monitoring when Kirilov got close to the lake.'

So that's what Sokolowski was carrying in his bag. Something to track the transmitter Kirilov was carrying with the cash. I wondered how the Americans would have explained that if we had been stopped on the road to the lake.

'We'll never know if Flanagan picked up Kirilov's signal,' Jaszczak continued. 'But that's not the point. We're not trying to figure out what happened back then. I'm just telling you that whatever went wrong the first time it wasn't down to us and I'm making damn sure nothing will go wrong this time. There's only one weak link, and that's you.'

Without giving me time to respond Jaszczak started outlining his plans for the next morning. I was to be in Castle Square standing in front of Sigismund's Column at precisely ten o'clock.

'We'll be standing not far away, in front of the Royal Castle. Don't come near us.'

'And if you're not there?'

'We will be.'

I would be approached by Father Paszek's representative, Walentowicz, whom I had last seen when he dropped me at the railway station in Elk. We would shake hands. That would be the signal that Walentowicz was happy for the Crown to be passed over. Jaszczak and Dragan would then join us and I would make myself scarce.

'You walk away,' Jaszczak explained. 'The shorter the meeting the better, although there are a few things I need to make clear to Father Paszek.'

'Will he be there?'

'Of course not. I can't be seen with him at this stage. Walentowicz will pass on my message with the Crown.'

'What do you mean at this stage?'

Jaszczak frowned. 'Nothing. Just tradecraft. Nobody must connect Paszek's people and ours. Each cell is kept away from every other one. Secrecy is the name of the game.'

'So we meet at one of the most popular places in Warsaw?'

'That's right.' Jaszczak was irritated now. 'Out in the open where we can all see each other. Where a couple of American tourists won't seem at all out of place. Where people meet every day. There's no better place to start the fight back, you know the Russian cavalry massacred hundreds of civilians right there in 1861. You think we should be meeting in a dark alley wearing false moustaches, carrying a rolled-up newspaper and mumbling some stupid phrase about bluebirds over the white cliffs of wherever? What's the matter with you people? This isn't a game. You're here because Walentowicz knows you, that's the only reason. After he shakes your hand you and your clever Mr Brasenose aren't part of this. Leave it to the grown-ups. We know what we're doing.'

I stood up. 'I'll be there.'

'And don't say a word to anyone. No reporting back to London tonight; like I said, this is strictly need to know.'

I turned to the door. Jaszczak didn't move. Dragan stood up to see me out and as he did so his jacket fell open revealing a holstered pistol. I hoped he wasn't planning to bring that to Castle Square. I put on my coat and went out into the biting cold.

Tradecraft. Need to know. What was Jaszczak talking about? It was melodramatic nonsense. This simply was not the way operations were supposed to be run. Tradecraft was Paul Rembury sitting in the hotel lobby to check that I wasn't being followed. It was making sure that someone knew exactly what I was going to do in case anything went wrong. It wasn't flying into Warsaw on your private jet and then setting up a meet in a place that was bound to be regularly patrolled by the police.

I walked around aimlessly for ten minutes before entering a bar and ordering a beer. Rembury joined me a few minutes later.

'You're clear. How did it go?'

When I told him, his reaction was the same as mine. 'You think he was serious? Don't tell London?'

'I think he was entirely serious. He sees this as his operation. Not the Company's, his. And it feels like it. If this was a normal Company operation there would be detailed plans, contingencies, backups. Why wasn't there anyone from the Company at the hotel? It's all too amateur.'

'There is a possible explanation,' Rembury replied.

'I know, deniability. If this goes wrong the Company can deny all knowledge of Jaszczak. Deny all knowledge of the Crown. And if anyone gets caught it's us not them. It's happened before but I'm not convinced. Operation Coronation is Chuck Hoeven's project, he's lost two agents already and you don't give up after that happens.'

'And you're not giving up? I know Brasenose authorised

you to bale out if you didn't like the smell of things on the ground.'

'That's an exaggeration. Something would have to really stink and so far Jaszczak is pretty well doing what was discussed in London. No, as I told him, I'll be there tomorrow. Just make sure you are as well.'

'I will be. Although,' Rembury added with a smile, 'I won't be armed, of course.' The smile quickly vanished. 'Let's hope that if you're right, and Dragan really does have a gun, he keeps it well out of sight. Something really is going on at the moment, I have a low-level source in Gdańsk who's just let me know that one of the Solidarity leaders was picked up earlier this afternoon. If the authorities have decided to provoke a confrontation with Solidarity that could spell trouble and if there are protests here in Warsaw, the one place they will kick off is Castle Square.'

I went to bed mulling over Rembury's concern. I thought of phoning Julia but decided not to worry her. I didn't know that she was already worried and that next morning she would rush off to see a goldsmith and start to worry even more.

I slept well. When I woke up I discovered the world had changed.

XVII

At six o'clock in the morning the Polish leader, General Jaruzelski, had appeared on television to make an announcement that would be endlessly repeated throughout the day.

The country, he declared, is in crisis. Chaos and demoralisation are everywhere. Strikes and protests have become everyday events, even schoolchildren are taking part. Hatred and political vendettas are causing moral degradation. Violence and threats of violence are spreading across the country. The state is ceasing to function. The economy has collapsed while unscrupulous business sharks amass fortunes. Everything, the general concluded, for which his generation had sacrificed the best years of their life was under threat. For that reason it was his duty to declare that today a Military Council of National Salvation, acting in accordance with the Constitution, was assuming power and imposing martial law. Nobody should think that this meant a military coup or military dictatorship. He was acting only to create the conditions that would allow the necessary restoration of order and discipline.

The one thing we all agreed would not happen had happened. The Polish Army had seized power.

I rushed to the Embassy. There were troops everywhere, army lorries and armoured personnel carriers seemed to be parked on every street. A truck full of ZOMO militia with riot shields passed looking menacing in their military-style camouflage. The ZOMO had a reputation as the best trained militia in Eastern Europe. Recruits had to be at least 5'11" and were usually equipped with far more lethal weapons than riot shields.

Normally on a Sunday the Embassy would be closed and almost empty. Now a police patrol was stationed outside stopping Polish citizens entering the building. When I produced my passport they let me through. Inside there was a degree of confusion. All telephone lines had been cut but some radio contact with London was still possible. It seemed to me obvious that the meeting in Castle Square would not be going ahead. Rembury agreed but I was not sure that Jaszczak would reach the same conclusion.

'I'll go over to Jaszczak's hotel and make sure he's still not trying to go ahead,' I told Rembury. 'You come too but wait outside.'

When I reached the hotel the reception called Jaszczak's room. I was not invited up, instead I was told Mr Jaszczak would be down in a moment. I waited in the lobby for nearly ten minutes before Jaszczak appeared.

'What are you doing here?' he asked belligerently. 'I thought I explained everything yesterday.'

'Haven't you heard,' I said, 'the military have taken over.'

He looked at me as if I was mad. 'Of course I've fucking heard. What do you think we've been doing? This is it. The revolution starts today. The people are going to rise up and we need to make sure we're leading them. We have to get that Crown into play. Now.'

'But Jaruzelski has mobilised police, army, everything. Every inch of Castle Square will be under observation.'

'I doubt that but even if it is, so what? They'll be looking for students, trade unionists. I told you yesterday they won't trouble tourists. What are you so scared of? All you've got to do is identify Walentowicz and shake his hand. That's my signal. Then you can run away. Go back to London and watch the fireworks. God is on our side today. Just be there at ten o'clock, not one minute later.'

Without waiting for a reply he turned round and was off.

I left and looked for Rembury. Next to the hotel was one of Warsaw's most elegant palaces, like the hotel spared by the Germans so that they could use it themselves. Now it was used by the Communist authorities and a throng of soldiers were standing in the courtyard surrounding a statue of a swordsman on horseback.

Rembury was standing nearby. 'Prince Józef Poniatowski,' he said, gesturing towards the statue. 'Nephew of the last king of Poland. He fought for the Austrians, then for the Poles, then turned down the tsar's plea to join the Imperial Russian Army and eventually died a Marshal of France fighting for his friend Napoleon. I wonder what he would think of nationalists like Jaszczak.'

'Jaszczak's planning to go ahead,' I told him. 'He says he wants to get the Crown into play, whatever that might mean.'

'He wants what?'

'Jaszczak thinks the revolution is starting, the masses are just waiting for a sight of that Crown.'

'He's mad. Nobody out there has ever heard of Jan Kazimierz's Crown. I bet they don't even know who Jan Kazimierz was. All that stuff about the Oath of Lwów is just history. And in any case there isn't going to be a revolution, not today anyway. General Jaruzelski has done what nobody thought he would do and it could work. He's caught everyone unprepared. It looks like the entire opposition has been rounded up. If there's anyone who was missed they will be so disorganised they won't be able to do more than wave a few placards. We should go back to the Embassy and try to contact Brasenose.'

'No. We must try to see this through. I don't want our Service being accused of running away. If something goes wrong and I haven't shown up, Jaszczak and Hoeven will have a ready-made scapegoat.'

Rembury reluctantly agreed. We separated and I found somewhere to grab breakfast before I set off along the broad Krakowskie Przedmieście towards Plac Zamkowy, the Castle Square. On top of the column where I was due to meet Walentowicz, King Sigismund stood directly facing me, with his curved sword in one hand and cross in the other. Neither sword nor cross would help me much today.

Jaszczak was right that in normal circumstances Castle Square would be a good place to make an exchange. It was always crowded and a couple of apparent tourists wouldn't stand out. But these weren't normal circumstances. Even as I approached I noticed army snipers under the green cupola at the top of the bell tower of St Anne's Church on my right. Beyond them stood a dozen ZOMO militiamen in full combat gear, lounging beside a balustrade. The ZOMO had driven a BTR-60PA armoured personnel carrier right across the square and parked it at the corner of the Royal Castle nearest St Anne's Church. There was more than a hint of menace about its turret-mounted heavy machine gun. I didn't know then that within days the Russians would be handing over to the ZOMO the even deadlier BTR-60PB, fresh from service in Afghanistan. This, rather than the TV announcement a few hours earlier, was the real face of the military coup.

I reached the square at five to ten and tried to look inconspicuous. The 'square' was more accurately an isosceles triangle with a short base at the end of Krakowskie Przedmieście and two longer sides, at the apex of which I noticed Rembury arriving from the direction of the green-roofed John the Baptist Cathedral. The column stood near the base of the triangle with stone steps at the bottom and a massive four-sided stone support. On three of the four sides were huge brass plaques with long patriotic inscriptions written in Latin, while the fourth side bore an elaborate coat of arms. That's where I was expected to be, I thought, behind the king's back.

Jaszczak and Dragan were standing outside the Royal Castle and had at least had the sense to move to the far corner, away from the ZOMO. As instructed, I didn't approach the two men. Jaszczak was holding a brown cloth bag. I wondered what he was making of the scene in front of him.

Despite the bitter cold the square was thronged with people trying to make sense of what was happening to their country. There was a palpable sense of shock. Some were huddled together in animated conversation, others simply stood silently as if waiting for something to happen. A police patrol moved through the square and was met with silent, bemused stares.

At ten o'clock exactly I walked to the column and stood below the coat of arms. I could see Jaszczak staring directly at me. Someone approached from behind the statue. It was Father Paszek's driver, Walentowicz. We shook hands but he said nothing.

'Everything's arranged,' I told him. He merely nodded.

Looking over towards the Castle I could see that Jaszczak was already moving towards us. Walentowicz followed my glance. 'Those are the Americans?'

'Yes.'

'The famous Mr Jaszczak.' There was a hint of disapproval in his voice which surprised me. 'A powerful man.'

'Money brings power,' I replied.

Walentowicz looked at me sharply but said nothing.

Jaszczak strode towards us, Dragan right behind. Ignoring me, Jaszczak grabbed Walentowicz by the hand which he pumped vigorously and launched into a stream of greetings in fluent Polish. Walentowicz, who was nearly a foot taller, looked startled.

Before he could respond, Dragan took my arm. 'We'll take it from here.'

Over his shoulder Jaszczak added, in English, 'That's right. Introductions made. You can go home.'

I was dismissed. I nodded to Walentowicz and turned to walk away. 'Goodbye my friend,' I heard him say.

I moved off past a group of students towards the small Piwna Street on the side of the square opposite the ZOMO. I was about thirty yards away when I heard someone shout my name.

I turned round. Jaszczak was passing the cloth bag to Walentowicz but stopped when he heard the shout. Off to his right someone was running in my direction.

'Thomas, stop! It's a trap!'

I recognised Julia's DIS colleague from the Warsaw Embassy, Major Brampford, coming from the direction of the Krakowskie Przedmieście. He slowed to a walk and waved when he realised I had seen him. My eyes switched back to the scene by the statue. Walentowicz seemed to be trying to pull the bag from Jaszczak's grasp as they both stared at Brampford. The major by now was only a few yards away from them. He was still waving vigorously in my direction. And then Dragan pulled out a gun. There was a scream. One of the students was pointing at Dragan. The first shot came from the direction of the militiamen. It was followed by more as people threw themselves to the ground. Dragan seemed to have been hit. Jaszczak stood transfixed. Walentowicz made a final lunge for the bag, which ripped apart.

The Great Crown of Jan Kazimierz tumbled out and rolled slowly towards the column. Up above, the statue of Jan Kazimierz's father stared icily down.

XVIII

When the bullets started to fly I hurled myself to the ground like everyone else in the square. Almost immediately the shots stopped and I looked up. The militia were running towards the column where Jaszczak had been standing. At the same time people started pulling themselves to their feet and running in the opposite direction. I grabbed Brampford by the arm and pulled him away. More police were arriving but seemed to have no idea what to do. When we reached the far side I looked back. As if by magic the square had emptied, leaving just a cluster of militia and police surrounding the column.

'Come on,' said Brampford. 'We need to get away from here.'

I didn't need any urging. The streets were emptying rapidly. The only sounds were sirens seemingly approaching from every direction.

We had only gone a few hundred yards when Rembury appeared. 'What the hell happened?' he asked.

I didn't answer, I had a lot of questions of my own. Yet again Operation Coronation was a disaster. First the Masurian Lakes and now this. And in both cases I had no idea what had gone wrong. Undoubtedly the Americans would blame us, or rather blame me. What should I have done? Should I have told Jaszczak it was ludicrous to go ahead with the militia right there? I could have refused to have any part of it. Brasenose had told me I should pull out if I thought my life was at risk. Should I have insisted Dragan leave his gun behind? Would Jaszczak have listened?

'Not here,' I replied to Rembury's question. 'Let's get back to the Embassy.'

However, all the taxis seemed to have disappeared. Bracing ourselves against the bitter wind, we set off to walk the forty minutes to the Ujazdowskie Park.

'Just drop back and check we're not being followed,' I told Rembury.

'You're not,' he replied, but did as I asked. Ten minutes later he caught us up again. 'All clear. Now, what do we think happened?'

That was the question I couldn't answer. I was furious with myself for not finding some way to prevent things from going wrong yet again but I was more dispassionate than I had been a few minutes earlier.

'Everything seemed to be going to plan when Major Brampford here turned up. Let's start with that.'

A black limousine with police outriders raced towards Castle Square, paying no attention to us. We continued walking as Brampford explained that less than an hour ago he had received a message from Julia.

It simply said, 'Urgent for Thomas Dylan. Crown is a fake. Abort mission.'

'What did Julia mean: Crown is a fake?' I asked but Brampford had no more idea than I did.

'I thought you would know. I just knew I had to pass the message on.'

'How did you find me?' I asked.

Brampford glanced towards Paul Rembury.

'I told him,' said Rembury. 'It was ridiculous, Jaszczak expecting you to charge around Warsaw without letting anyone know what was happening. Totally unprofessional. You let me know about your plans so that if something happened to you I could report back to London. I did the same. I went to the Embassy first thing this morning but I couldn't get through to London and with David Prince away there was nobody in our Service I could brief. So I put a note in the DIS box. If something happened to both of us London would know what we had been doing.'

'I found the note when I came in this morning,' said Brampford. 'It said you were meeting the contact in Castle Square at ten o'clock. It didn't say where in the square but the square's not actually very big. As soon as Julia's message was decrypted I got one of the Embassy drivers to drop me nearby and just went looking for you.'

'And he found you,' interrupted Rembury. 'And it was a trap. The ZOMO militia were there.'

'I'm not so sure,' I replied. 'Given what's happening in Poland right now, the ZOMO are likely to be everywhere. If it had been a trap the whole square would have been surrounded. There would have been security police or ZOMO all over it. The militia were on the alert for sure but I don't think they were looking for anything in particular. I think we triggered it all off.'

'We did?' Brampford exclaimed in surprise.

'Yes, inadvertently you did. You couldn't have been more than a few feet away from Jaszczak when you shouted my name and something about it being a trap. That must have spooked him. And more importantly spooked that idiot with him.'

'You mean his bodyguard, Dragan,' said Rembury.

'That's right. The shooting began after Dragan started waving his gun around. One of the militiamen must have seen him and reacted by opening fire.'

Rembury agreed. 'I couldn't believe it when I saw the gun in Dragan's hand. What the hell did he think he was doing? The militia were on to him right away, they paid no attention to anyone else. Bloody cowboy.'

'Perhaps a dead cowboy. Did you see what happened after the shooting?'

'No. Two truckloads of soldiers turned up looking very nervous, they must have been very close when the shooting started. I thought it was more sensible to chase after you.'

We made our way back to the Embassy hoping to learn more there but rapidly realised that nobody had much idea about anything. There was no mention of shots being fired in Castle Square on the radio or TV but that was hardly surprising, the new military censorship was draconian. London clearly knew even less than us. The phones were still not operating properly and the Polish military were trying to jam our radio communications with varying degrees of success.

Brasenose sent a garbled message which, when I finally managed to decrypt it, told me to contact the Company's Station Chief at the American Embassy and give him a full report. When I tried, I discovered that getting to see the Company's Warsaw station chief, Gary Reese, was almost impossible and I didn't want to settle for one of his underlings. It was not until two days later that Reese found time for me.

Brasenose also confirmed that the Great Crown of Jan Kazimierz was a fake but he didn't say how he knew and it wasn't until I got back to London that anyone mentioned that David Prince's name was linked to the forgery. Nor did anyone tell me that Julia had been the one to track down the Crown's maker. Brasenose did, however, end with the comment that he had given retrospective approval to the DIS recommendation to abort the meeting in Castle Square.

From that it appeared that Julia's message to Brampford telling me to abort had not been authorised by him. I later discovered from Julia that it had not been authorised by anyone.

XIX

The military regime's clampdown was total. The news that emerged was only what the new government wanted to emerge. The shooting I had witnessed might as well have happened on another planet. The Embassy's normal news sources dried up and although it was inundated with stories from around the country it struggled to find the truth under mountains of misinformation and rumour. None of the rumours mentioned the Great Crown of Jan Kazimierz or the name of Mark Jaszczak.

I was desperate to find out what had happened in Castle Square but the truth was that nobody knew, nobody here on the ground, nobody in London and, as far as we could tell, nobody in Washington. It was no better the next day.

'I'm going to go down to Castle Square,' I told Rembury, 'to see what's going on.'

'You won't find anything,' he replied. 'You can be more help here.'

'Doing what?'

'Finding Esterka.'

David Prince had mentioned the name Esterka to me back in London but with a military coup in full swing and bullets flying past I had completely blanked it out.

'What's Esterka?' I asked, my mind still on the previous day's events.

'She's a Jewish princess,' replied Rembury with a smile, 'but more importantly it's the name David Prince gave to the source the other side obviously have here in the Embassy. The infamous mole.'

'Esterka? Does it stand for something?'

'No, I told you it's the name of a Jewish princess. I'll explain in a minute. As you know, all the extra security measures we put in place turned up nothing at all, not even a hint. David wondered whether that was because there was no mole, at least not when we were conducting security reviews. He realised that whoever was leaking stuff was doing it pretty erratically. There was a lot of secret material that the other side obviously never found out about. What they did seem to pick up was inside knowledge of special events. There was a trade mission here and quite clearly the Poles knew exactly what our negotiating positions were going to be. Ditto when we had a big Intelligence meeting with the Company and senior people from London. It made him think again about the timing of the leaks. He asked himself the question that should have been obvious right at the beginning. Was there anyone who had access to information only when something important was going on? And that led him to Judith Delavere-Hamilton.'

'Who's she?'

'She's the doyenne of the expat community here. Couldn't be more respectable. Her husband has been here for years and knows everyone. He describes himself as a businessman. He's a fixer, lots of banking connections back home. But that makes him sound sleazy and he's not. He's smooth, charming, will do anything for anyone. A couple of years ago he received the OBE for services to Anglo-Polish relations and the promotion of British exports. The

Delavere-Hamilton parties are famous. And Judith Delavere-Hamilton is just like her husband, always happy to help out. When she and her husband met she was personal assistant to some big noise in the City, flying around the world all the time, sorting things out. Whenever we have something big on here, like the trade negotiations, she pops up. She's happy to take on quite menial stuff. When the Ambassador's secretary got food poisoning she even stepped in to act as his PA for a couple of days.'

'Isn't that pretty irregular?' I asked. 'Has she been vetted?'

'Oh yes. She and her husband went through the whole positive vetting procedure some years ago. She has a full Embassy pass. And Justin Brasenose has put them under the microscope again now. Absolutely nothing there. Her parents met in Riga before the war, her father was Consul General there. Her mother is Polish, which is why she speaks the language like a native. That's what makes her so useful to the Embassy.'

'And you think the pair of them are spies?'

'Not him, no. He's given us lots of help over the years and besides, he's never had access to the detail of what's been leaked. He's just not the type, he's an old school Tory. Before the war he might have been governor of one of the smaller colonies. Now there is no empire to explore he ends up demonstrating British values to the unfortunates behind the Iron Curtain. There's nothing in the least left-wing about him, he doesn't need money and he's clearly deeply in love with his wife. The problem I've had with David's theory is that the wife is just the same. On top of which we've absolutely no evidence that Judith Delavere-Hamilton has ever betrayed anything.'

'So why does David suspect her?'

'I think the truth is because there's no one else to suspect. And also because he pictures her as Esterka.'

'You'd better explain that.'

'As you know, David's obsessed by Polish history. Apparently Esterka was the wife or maybe mistress of a king called Casimir the Great.'

'He of the Great Crown?'

'No this was another, earlier Casimir. Anyway Esterka and Casimir is one of the great love stories in Polish history. And the important point is that Esterka was Jewish, the daughter of a tailor. In those days Christian kings simply didn't even think of marrying Jews. Whether they actually married isn't clear but they had two strapping sons. The boys were baptised as Christians but Esterka never forgot her faith. Casimir the Great's reign was a golden period for Jews in Poland. She's one of David's heroes.'

'So why name a spy after her?'

'It's the motivation. Esterka married the love of her life and enjoyed all the pomp and wealth of a great Christian monarchy, but she remained true to her people. She helped them overcome the obstacles her husband's faith put in their way. David thinks that's what Judith Delavere-Hamilton is doing.'

'She's Jewish?'

'No, not at all. I don't think she's particularly religious. David's point is that she looks English but her soul belongs here.

'In England David really dug into her background. Her father returned home in 1939 with Judith's mother. They were about to get married when he was killed in the

213

early days of the Blitz, leaving his wife-to-be alone and pregnant. Baby Judith and her mother then shuttled around the country. The father's family seemed to have turned their back on them, evidently a Polish nurse was not what they had expected for a daughter-in-law and they never recognised their granddaughter. Judith and her mother became exceptionally close, two lost Polish-speaking souls in the middle of a war. Then in the late fifties the mother died and Judith had to fight for herself. And she did. Until she met the man who became her husband and history looked like repeating itself.'

'In what way?' I asked.

'Well an illegitimate Polish secretary was not what the Delavere-Hamiltons wanted for a daughter-in-law, even though Judith's father had actually been a pukka English gentleman. But they married anyway and Judith persuaded her new husband to find a new life.'

'In Poland.'

'Precisely. In Poland.'

'And I suppose David Prince's theory is that she came here looking for her roots, for a sense of identity, to escape an alien life and was therefore ripe for plucking when the Opposition came calling.'

'Something like that. She's become another of David's obsessions. He's interviewed her three times. He managed to track down her mother's two sisters and discovered one was still alive and living in Torun. He went there under some flimsy excuse but she refused to talk to him. So he found her children, Judith's first cousins once removed, and tried to speak to them. He didn't get very far. So he approached their children, they would be Judith's second cousins. Somehow he established from one of them that he had met an "aunt" who was English but living in Warsaw.'

'Does that get you anywhere?'

'David thought it did. It's the only lie we've ever caught her out on. Delavere-Hamilton had told him she has no family here and had never met any of her mother's family. We now believe that's not true.'

'That's pretty flimsy. You can't accuse someone of spying based just on that.'

'True, especially as her husband is so prominent here and they're personal friends of the Ambassador. She's still very much persona grata in the Embassy. David made himself pretty unpopular just by interviewing her so often. Especially after we discovered from Firefox that the SB had managed to get hold of a report which had been written and sent to London at a time when the Delavere-Hamiltons were on holiday in the south of France. She couldn't have seen it; the only copy was kept in the security safe and she's certainly never had access to that.'

'So doesn't that rule her out?'

'David argued that she must have planted bugs somewhere in the Embassy and we'd missed them. He argued that battery-powered bugs would explain why the leaking seems to have been so irregular; it stopped when the batteries ran out and only started again when Delavere-Hamilton had an excuse to come into the Embassy and could renew the batteries.'

'But we'd swept the Embassy more than once. We can't have missed something like that.'

'I know,' Rembury replied. 'We've had constant radio monitoring in place, if bugs were transmitting to someone outside the Embassy that would have been picked up.'

'How do you think I can help?' I asked.

'Well obviously there was a lot of pressure on the Embassy yesterday, and even though the Consular section is closed on Sundays the switchboard was jammed. When the doors opened this morning we were immediately swamped. You'd be amazed how many Brits there are in Poland and they all seem to think we will be able to tell them when flights will be resumed, when the telephone lines will be back on and how strict the 10 p.m. curfew will be. We've been asked to send the most ridiculous messages back home, all apparently urgent. I wouldn't be surprised if some idiot comes in asking us to get in touch with his wife and remind her to put the dustbins out. But it's all got to be treated seriously and courteously. And on top of that we're trying to do our real job and find out what the hell's happening. Who's actually been arrested, for example. Judith Delavere-Hamilton has already offered to help. She's downstairs right now. The Ambassador wants her to help on reception and try to deal with stuff that just needs good local knowledge.'

'And you think I should interview her? Why should I be any more successful than you and Prince?'

'Precisely because you're not David Prince.'

Rembury, I thought, was being hopelessly optimistic. Delavere-Hamilton wasn't going to suddenly give herself away because someone new turned up. If she hadn't admitted anything incriminating to Prince she wouldn't do so to me. What's more, she would realise that I wasn't the low-grade foreign office official I was supposed to be; I didn't want the other side to know that. But I had another idea. As Rembury had just said, the Embassy was swamped at the moment. Many of the staff had been away from Warsaw for the weekend and hadn't been able to get back. It was all hands on the deck, and that could include me.

'I'll work alongside her,' I suggested. 'I can handle simple queries and I know enough to be able to point anyone else in the right direction. That way I can keep her under observation and make a note of everywhere she goes.'

Rembury was as unimpressed with my idea as I had been with his. 'You think she'll do something stupid when you're sitting right there? She's hardly likely to prowl around opening filing cabinets while you're at her side.'

Of course he was right, but it maintained my cover. 'If she has put bugs somewhere in the Embassy and if our monitoring hasn't picked up any transmissions then they weren't transmitting conversations, they were just recording them. And those recordings must be being collected and somehow taken out of the building. And, with everything else going on, today would be the perfect time for her to sneak off and do that. That's what I can try to find.'

It wasn't why I was sent to Warsaw but as long as the airport remained closed there was not much else for me to do. And I was intrigued to meet the mysterious Mata Hari who Rembury was describing.

When I went downstairs she was already seated behind a desk with a large selection of forms and leaflets in front of her. I was introduced by one of the Consular staff.

Judith Delavere-Hamilton bore less of a resemblance to Mata Hari than she did to the mother of a former girlfriend, the formidable Lady Captain at the local golf club. Charming, engaging and apparently open but just a little condescending. The sort of woman who would talk to everyone at a cocktail party but none but a select few for very long. Mrs Delavere-

Hamilton, I was sure, would brook no opposition and take no prisoners.

'No time to waste,' she insisted when we had shaken hands.

As far as she knew I was a career diplomat with four years' experience at the Embassy in Moscow but somehow she still managed to convey to our 'customers' that she was the authority they had come to consult. And I had to admit that most of them went away satisfied. By lunchtime the pressure had eased.

'Do you know where the canteen is?' she asked and then led the way without waiting for an answer.

Sitting down, Delavere-Hamilton switched on the charm but again with the tinge of condescension I had observed in her during the morning. I would enjoy Poland she assured me. The people were so friendly and the effort put into rebuilding the country since the war was quite incredible, although of course the current situation was terribly sad. She would not be drawn further on this morning's coup.

'I'm sure all politicians do what they believe is best for their people. Who are we to judge? Politics can be so unutterably tedious.'

'Tedious' was not a word I would have used. It was becoming clear that in the last twelve hours thousands, perhaps tens of thousands, of men and women had been arrested.

My companion preferred to talk about the Embassy. 'Such a beautiful building,' she said. 'Built in 1875 and designed by Jozef Huss who was famous for his eclectic style. It used to belong to the Wielopolski family. Although of course not as grand as their famous palace in Kraków.'

'It's not something I know anything about. I was supposed to receive a briefing from someone who had just come back from the Embassy here but it didn't happen. Apparently he resigned from the Service quite suddenly.'

'Really. Who was that?'

'A man called Prince. Did you know him?'

'Everybody here knew David. A rather unpleasant fellow in some ways.'

'Yes. The gossip is that he was recalled suddenly. Upset the Americans apparently.'

Disappointingly, Mrs Delavere-Hamilton made no comment, other than remarking that she never listened to gossip.

By mid-afternoon the stream of visitors at the Embassy had lessened and the Consular staff no longer needed our support. Mrs Delavere-Hamilton gathered up her collection of forms.

'I'll put them back in the storeroom,' she said.

'Good idea, you can show me where that is.'

'Of course,' she replied without enthusiasm.

I watched her put her stationery away on shelves at the back of the storeroom; nothing at all suspicious there.

The whole exercise had been a complete waste of time. I had seen nothing to suggest that the woman was a spy and as we had spent the entire time doing nothing worth spying upon that was hardly surprising.

'I must just pop in and see the Ambassador,' she said as we left the storeroom. 'I have to cancel this week's tennis with his wife. I'm sure we will meet again soon, Mr Dylan.' She marched off towards the stairs leading back to the Ambassador's office.

I should have followed her, although that would have been a bit obvious. I don't know what made me stay behind instead. Something in her tone of voice perhaps when I suggested accompanying her to the storeroom. Or perhaps it was the oddity that the bundle of leaflets she had presumably picked up from the storeroom this morning, and had just put away again, seemed to consist mainly of flyers for the new London Docklands Development Corporation: how could anyone possibly expect them to have been useful today?

I walked away from the stairs. Some way along a corridor running in the direction of India House at the back of the building I found an alcove looking out on to the side street, Aleja Roz. From there I could just about observe the staircase. This part of the building was largely unused at the weekends and after more than ten minutes in complete silence I had begun to think I should have found an excuse to walk with her towards the Ambassador's suite.

Then I heard her. Ducking back into the alcove I caught sight of her shoes descending the stairs. There was nothing furtive about her actions. She strode straight to the storeroom and went inside. I gave her a moment or two and then moved quietly after her.

She was standing with her back to me behind a row of shelves. Although I could not see clearly what she was doing she seemed to have opened a cupboard on the far wall and was now closing it again. There was something in her hand and as I watched she dropped it on the floor and then appeared to stamp on it. She then bent over, picked up whatever she had stood on and walked a few yards to the side, where she dropped it into a rubbish bin. I stepped back quickly as she started to turn round.

'Can I help you?' asked a female voice behind me.

My attention had been focussed entirely on Delavere-Hamilton and I had missed the sound of someone coming down the stairs behind me. It was one of the secretaries I had met briefly the day before. I seemed to remember she was called Anne. Her memory was much better.

'Oh, Mr Dylan, I didn't recognise you, sorry. You're Mr Prince's replacement aren't you?'

I heard an exclamation behind me.

A startled expression on Delavere-Hamilton's face transformed almost instantly into her practised smile.

'Mr Dylan, you should have said you needed something in the storeroom, I could have found it for you.'

With that she was off, leaving me with Anne, who informed me that her department was 'clean out of treasury tags'. When that was rectified I was left alone again.

There was an internal phone in the corner of the room and I called Rembury. 'Our target is off home,' I told him. 'You'd better make sure she leaves the building, then meet me in the storeroom in the basement.'

Ten minutes later Rembury arrived.

'She's left the building. I had Security search her, nothing.'

'No you wouldn't find anything. It's here.'

'What is?'

'This.'

I showed him what I had found in the bin: a microcassette of some type, probably from a dictation machine. The plastic case was smashed and the tape hung loosely in my hand.

'And there was another one at the bottom.'

I tipped the half-full bin on to the floor. Amongst the various bits of packaging was another broken microcassette.

'I think she came in here first thing this morning pretending to collect stationery, retrieved the first cassette from somewhere, smashed it and dropped it in the bin. Then before leaving she did the same thing again. I saw her take the cassette out of this cupboard. I presume the contents of the bin are emptied each day and the contents taken away with the rest of the rubbish. Somehow her employers find a way to search through it once it's outside the Embassy and retrieve the tapes.'

Rembury opened the cupboard to reveal two boxes of microcassettes still in their packaging and half a dozen dictation machines along with various headsets, microphones and assorted cables. An old reel-to-reel tape recorder sat gathering dust on the floor.

'We'll need to get all this checked,' I said.

Rembury was thoughtful. 'The Ambassador is really hot on ensuring that anything even slightly secret is incinerated and doesn't leave the Embassy. The other waste is sent off somewhere but I'm sure we've checked that thoroughly.'

'Not thoroughly enough perhaps.'

'I suppose so. Security don't check all the bins, especially when they have other things going on. And of course Delavere-Hamilton was usually here when there were other things going on.'

'And even if they did inspect the bins, would Security have thought of checking discarded recording tape?' I asked.

'They should have done but if you're pushed for time it's the sort of thing you might have missed.'

'Of course this doesn't help to find out how conversations are being recorded or how she recovers the cassettes.'

'No it doesn't. But if those tapes are what we think they are we've found our mole.'

Rembury smiled, as well he might. As acting head of station this would look very good on his record. 'I'll take it from here,' he said. 'I'll have a camera rigged up in here and a tracker fitted to the bin. We'll probably need to send the tapes to London for analysis, but I'll try listening to them here to see if I can pick anything up.'

I wasn't sure that what he planned would produce anything. Even if Mrs Delavere-Hamilton hadn't taken fright at hearing the secretary refer to me as David Prince's replacement, her employers would surely realise she had been found out when they discovered that the two tapes she had dropped in the bin were missing.

'We could leave the tapes here,' I suggested, 'and see what happens to them.'

'Perhaps,' Rembury replied dubiously.

As he had said, this was now his problem.

My reason for being in Warsaw was Operation Coronation. Uncovering Delavere-Hamilton as a spy had only a slight bearing on that. Proving that she was the mole meant that David Prince was not. If he wasn't then the suggestion that he was, which had originated with the Company's Russian agent Krypton, or Colonel Kirilov as I now had to think of him, was wrong. That could imply that Kirilov was not as well informed as he claimed to be. More dangerously, it could mean that he had deliberately misled us.

The other implication with a bearing on Operation Coronation was one that I missed at the time but became acutely aware of very quickly. The Opposition now almost certainly knew that I was not the minor Consular official that I pretended to be. Now I would be on their radar. Fortunately, I thought, with so much else going on neither the Polish SB nor the Russian KGB would have time to waste on me. Wrong again.

XX

The following day Rembury and I were shown into the office of the CIA's Warsaw head of station after sitting in the Embassy reception for nearly half an hour.

Gary Reese was a big man, with the physique that Americans associate with their college football players. Now in his early fifties he still looked as if he worked out in the Embassy gym every day, with golf or tennis at weekends. He rose to greet us and then returned, unsmiling, to the seat behind his desk. Unsurprisingly he looked exhausted.

Everyone knew that the whole US Intelligence establishment was coming under enormous pressure back in Washington. The lack of any warning that General Jaruzelski was even considering a military coup was already being described as the biggest Intelligence failure since the near-catastrophic Tet Offensive in Vietnam thirteen years earlier.

'Sorry about the wait, we're kinda busy. But then I guess you folks won't be going anywhere until the airport opens again. What did you want to see me about?'

'I understood you were expecting a report from me on your Operation Coronation.'

'I'm expecting lots of reports, Mr Dylan. And there are all sorts of operations going on. You'd better just go ahead. Do you have your report in writing? That would be much easier.'

I had of course written a report for Brasenose but I hadn't

brought that with me. Given the comments I had included on the amateurish nature of Jaszczak's preparations, it was probably wise not to share it with the Americans.

'No, I haven't, I'd rather do that when I get back to London. More secure.'

'Right, worried about your mole I guess. You still think it's David Prince?'

There was of course news on that subject but I wasn't inclined to let Reese be the first to know. 'If there is a mole it could be any one of a number of people,' I replied.

'That's right, it could. I like David. Anyway go ahead. Start from when you arrived in-country.'

I ran succinctly through the whole story, from seeing Jaszczak at his hotel on the day before the exchange until the events in Castle Square. At first Reese looked interested. For example, he asked me to describe the business managers Jaszczak was meeting when I arrived at the hotel. After that he rapidly lost interest. He took no notes at all and by the time I arrived at Sigismund's Column he seemed to have stopped asking questions.

When I finished he did manage two questions.

'What made your colleagues in London decide that the Crown was not genuine?'

'I'm afraid I don't know the answer to that one.'

He nodded. 'Can't say I'm surprised. Magic crowns are kinda rare. Did you see what happened to it when the ZOMO stopped shooting?'

'Sorry, I've no idea.'

He nodded again. 'That's very helpful, Mr Dylan. I'll report back to Langley. If they have any further questions no doubt we'll be in touch.'

It appeared that our meeting was over. 'Mark Jaszczak must have seen what happened to the Crown,' I said. 'You could ask him, unless the police are holding him.'

'Unfortunately I can't ask him. He's dead. The Polish police informed my colleagues this morning that Mark Jaszczak was killed in a car crash near Torun. His body is being flown home today.'

That was a shock. 'And Dragan?'

'We have no information on the whereabouts of Mr Dragan. I understand he has dual nationality.'

Reese must have pressed a buzzer on his desk as his secretary entered the room and we were politely shown out, Reese insisting it was always a pleasure to meet folks from England.

'What do you make of that?' Rembury asked. 'The man's an idiot. You could have told him that Sigismund had come down from his column and put the Crown on his head and Reese would have just nodded. He just wasn't interested.'

'No he wasn't, but why? Not just because of everything else going on surely.'

'You think he had already heard everything before? Perhaps Brasenose briefed Washington yesterday and forgot to tell us.'

'It's possible, but I don't think so. Reese would have told us. I think he knew because he or one of his people were there.'

'In the square?'

'Yes. Why else would Reese ask about the men I saw in Jaszczak's suite but ask nothing about the handover itself? He's not an idiot. Did you notice his ring?'

'No. What ring?'

'The big chunky ring he was wearing. Phi Beta Kappa.'

Rembury looked perplexed.

'Phi Beta Kappa. It's an American college fraternity for very, very bright kids. I tell you, Reese wasn't nearly as uninterested as he wanted us to think he is, but again why? A high-profile American businessman with powerful Washington connections and an inside track with the CIA is killed in the middle of a military coup and Reese shows no more interest than he would if the Embassy cat had been run over. It doesn't ring true. You checked that I wasn't being followed, what we should have done is check to see if Jaszczak was being followed. And if he was then who by, the Opposition or his own side?'

Gary Reese, I concluded, was not a man to be trusted. I was glad that I hadn't told him we had found our mole.

After that there was really nothing left for me to do in Warsaw. As soon as the airport reopened I wanted to be off, taking with me the two microcassette tapes Mrs Delavere-Hamilton had smashed and then discarded in the storeroom and which were now in Rembury's safe, Rembury having ignored my suggestion that we put them back in the bin and try to track them.

I was staying at the Hotel Victoria, one of the new hotels built by the Polish authorities to entice business travellers and tourists to contribute to the Polish economy.

'The Victoria is what passes for luxury here,' Rembury assured me.

The hotel seemed to have come out of the same mould as the ubiquitous rectangular apartment blocks and offices but it was functional and clean. It was a short walk from there to Jaszczak's hotel, which had been convenient, but a much longer walk back there from the Embassy. The biting wind and the uncertain curfew made me decide to take a taxi back but before doing so I needed to clear my head.

Opposite the Embassy was the Ujazdowskie Park. I crossed the road and entered the park, turning right and walking all around the pond before leaving by the entrance on Aleja Piękna. The park was empty but as I approached Aleja Piękna I became aware of footsteps some distance behind me. A large, white, official-looking building stood opposite the park gate and in front of it a car was parked. As I reached the car the driver's door opened, blocking my way. At the same time two men approached from my right and the steps behind me quickened.

I started to swing round and felt my head being pushed down. 'In the car,' said a voice in English. Within seconds I was sandwiched between two well-built men on the rear seat and the driver was moving off. Behind us another car started up, blue light flashing. I protested loudly to no avail.

We turned left on to Aleje Ujazdowskie and drove past the British Embassy, but there was nothing I could do to attract attention. My arms were released as we passed the Botanical Gardens. At the end of Aleje Ujazdowskie we just carried straight on and I knew where we were going: Mokotów. It was a surprisingly short journey from the centre of Warsaw to Mokotów Prison, a journey that for many had been one-way. I was not feeling encouraged.

The prison had been built when Warsaw was part of the Russian Empire and the Okhrana, the tsar's secret police, wanted somewhere whose solid walls would block out the cries of their victims. More recently it had been used by the Nazis and then the Communists for torturing and executing all who stood in their way. The worst days of Stalinist brutality had passed but the Polish secret police still found the facilities of the prison useful.

We pulled into a courtyard thronged with police, army and militia. A truck in front of us disgorged half a dozen men in naval uniforms dragging four handcuffed women behind them. One of the women had a blood-stained bandage around her head while another limped painfully. They were hurried into the building. Our car was directed around to the back, passing through two checkpoints in high security fences on the way. We were clearly expected and I was whisked quickly in through a metal gateway and down some steps into the building. A desk with three armed men in civilian clothes blocked our way but again I was whisked past and pushed unceremoniously into a cell with a single tiny bed. The cell was otherwise empty.

I had only been in the cell for five minutes when two uniformed police entered, clanging the heavy metal door shut behind them. They pulled me to my feet and the three of us stood staring at the door. From somewhere down the corridor came a piercing scream which left the two guards unmoved, it was obviously a common occurrence. Eventually the flap on the door dropped down and I was looking straight at a pair of eyes and the top of someone's head. The head nodded and turned away.

Someone had been asked to identify me. As the flap closed again I heard a voice asking, 'Are you sure?' The question didn't startle me, but the language of the question did. Russian.

I had seen enough of the face looking in at me to be sure it was male, but not much more. It had been a small man, much smaller than the two guards standing beside me, and perhaps there was a flash of short greying hair as he turned away. I thought for a moment there was something familiar about the eyes, but I was surely imagining that.

The guards left the cell but stood chatting outside with the door closed but not locked. Twenty minutes later the door opened again and I was led along a dimly lit corridor and then upstairs along a better lit but institutionally grey corridor lined with numbered doors. At room 204 the guards stopped and knocked.

We entered a large but windowless room with an enormous table in the middle and half a dozen chairs. Two men sat at the table, one tall and thin, the other broad shouldered and broad faced, neither in uniform. In front of them were bottles of mineral water, glasses and a brown cardboard box. A vase of flowers had been placed incongruously near the centre of the table and a pair of ornate gilded mirrors hung on two of the walls.

'Sit down,' the tall man told me in English, pointing at one of the empty chairs opposite him. He pushed a bottle of water and glass in my direction.

'Why have I been arrested?' I asked before either man could say anything more.

The tall man smiled. 'You have not been arrested, Mr Dylan. We do not arrest foreign diplomats engaged in their lawful business. You have been invited here for what I believe you call a chat. An opportunity to discuss matters of common interest.'

'And who am I chatting with?'

'Our names are not important, just two humble policemen.'

Without waiting for me to respond he continued in the same level voice. 'We of course have the advantage that we know who you are. You are a member of your country's Secret Intelligence Service and following more than three years in Moscow you have now arrived in Warsaw.'

I started to protest but he waved my objection away. 'Our conversation will be much better if we do not play games. You are here to replace Mr David Prince as one of your country's spies in Poland. You arrived here with your wife on twenty-fifth November, travelled to the UK on December the first and returned here on the tenth. Is that correct?'

'You know it is. There is nothing secret about my travel plans, but I'm certainly not a spy.'

'Indeed. Your travel to and from this country may not be secret but I wonder what you can tell us about your travel inside Poland.'

He looked down at the papers in front of him. 'For example, on thirtieth of November you travelled with your wife and two Americans named Sokolowski and Flanagan to meet a man named Konstantin Kirilov. Mr Kirilov, I regret to say, is a Soviet citizen who dreams only of being very rich. It appears he believed that you would pay him an enormous sum of money to betray his country. But he was wrong. You didn't bring the money you had promised, just worthless paper. Perhaps you realised Kirilov had nothing of value to sell. Only you know what happened. Were you armed, Mr Dylan?'

I wasn't falling for that. 'I have no idea what you're talking about.'

'That is unfortunate because you see, Mr Dylan, we are in reality on the same side, you and I. We should be cooperating.

Kirilov is a traitor and we want him back to stand trial. You should want him sent back as well, to stand trial for killing your two American colleagues.'

I said nothing, but the tall man may have seen the involuntary widening of my eyes.

'That's right, Mr Dylan, Kirilov is a killer. You seem surprised. Let me tell you what happened up there in the lakes. On the day you and the Americans went to meet him there happened to be some army conscripts exercising nearby. They heard shots, three shots followed by three more and of course went to investigate. The bodies of your American companions were found inside a small hut beside a lake, along with the body of a local man. Each man had been shot twice; the killer clearly wanted to make sure no one would be left alive. They appear to have been unarmed. I believe Kirilov killed them.' He paused briefly. 'Unless perhaps you did.'

Again I kept silent.

The tall man smiled and continued. 'Let us assume you did not, and that Kirilov for some reason let you go, you and your wife. Perhaps he had a soft spot for a beautiful lady. You flew to England the next day. But then you return to Poland again, why? Is it to meet Kirilov again? No, I don't think so. This time you are here for something entirely different. You are here with the absurd intention of provoking an armed insurrection.'

This time I could not hide my surprise. 'Nonsense, you're imagining things.'

'No, Mr Dylan. I am not the one imagining things. It is you and your friend Marek Jaszczak and his absurd so-called Army. A handful of fascists who will do anything for the sake of American dollars.'

233

I shook my head. 'I have absolutely no idea what you are talking about.'

'Really? You've never heard of the Army of Fighting Poland, Polska Walcząca? Perhaps not. It's what I think is called a fantasy. It exists only in the mind of your friends Jaszczak and Dragan and a handful of terrorist renegades in Torun. How could these fools ever imagine anyone would follow them? It needs more than a few smuggled guns to start a revolution. Did they believe in magic? Do you believe in magic, Mr Dylan?'

He paused, glancing quickly at the man next to him, who as yet had said nothing. His companion remained silent and the tall man resumed.

'Do you know Castle Square?'

'Every visitor to Warsaw knows Castle Square.'

'And have you been there?'

'Of course, I visited Castle Square with my wife. Like I say, every tourist goes to the square at one point or another. What's this all about?'

'It's about why you are here in Warsaw. What were you doing with Jaszczak and Dragan in Castle Square?'

It was another question I had no intention of answering.

'You admit you were in the square, I understand that, but not every visitor brings a gift.' He leaned forward and pulled the cardboard box towards him, dramatically removing the lid. Then he reached inside and passed me the Great Crown of Jan Kazimierz.

'What is this?' he asked. 'Why did you bring this with you?'

'I've never seen it before. What is it?' I handed the Crown back to him.

'But you have seen it before, Mr Dylan, in London. And you know very well that Jaszczak brought it to this country in his private plane. Jaszczak told us he had the crown made in London, by a Jew who makes such things.'

Now I really didn't know what he was talking about. Where was this leading? I needed time to digest what I was being told but underlying everything was a simple question. Why was I here? Why had I been hauled off the street and then treated as if I had merely dropped by for a cup of tea? The best way to find out, I decided, was to ask.

'What do you want? You didn't drag me here just to ask me questions I can't possibly answer.'

At last the tall man's voice hardened. 'We invited you here to give you two simple messages, for you and for the Americans. First: you are not welcome here. If you play with this so-called Army of Fighting Poland, Mr Dylan, you play with fire. Smuggling weapons to terrorists is the act of a hostile nation. It seems that two young Polish officers were killed in the Gdańsk docks by Jaszczak's fascists. We will not allow such things to go unpunished. Marek Jaszczak has had a tragic accident, these are dangerous times.'

It was the first time I had heard anything about the deaths of two Polish officers and the mention of Gdańsk startled me. Surely he could not be referring to Kacper Nowak and his friend Tadeusz Modjeski? Nowak was in MI5 custody in England, he was still alive. And so quite possibly was Modjeski, if Jaszczak had indeed bought the Crown from him in Helsinki. Could this man imagine that they had been murdered in the Gdańsk docks, murdered by Jaszczak? He didn't give me time to consider the implications of what he was saying.

'Our second message for you is just as simple: we want Konstantin Kirilov and we will have him. He couldn't hide in Sweden and he can't hide in America. Tell your American friends that.'

This time he sat silent, willing me to say something. When he saw that I was not going to his tone became conversational again.

'Did you know that a representative of the US Embassy in Warsaw came to see me last week? Mr Reese asked for me personally, a very well-informed man is Mr Reese. He knew my name. He requested my help in finding two of his compatriots who have disappeared while vacationing in the Masurian Lakes. A very odd time of year to vacation in the north of Poland but let us ignore that. The families of these two men want to know what happened to them. If they have met some unfortunate accident and perhaps are dead their families want them brought home to be buried in America. All very reasonable. But I too am a well-informed man. I know very well that Mr Reese is the CIA resident here, what they call the chief of station. And he knows that I know, why else would he ask for me? He thinks we are playing games but you have seen what is happening in Poland today, we are not playing games.'

I silently registered the fact that only a couple of hours ago Reese had been telling me that he knew nothing about Operation Coronation. Now it seems he had in fact been negotiating with the authorities for the return of his agents' bodies. That would be a difficult negotiation. He could hardly say 'We'd like the bodies of our agents back so that we can inspect the bullet holes.' The Poles were not going to allow that.

As if he was reading my mind the tall man spoke again. 'If the relevant authorities are holding the bodies of Sokolowski and Flanagan it is only because we have not caught their killer. The case is not closed.'

The silent civilian spoke for the first time. 'The case cannot be closed while Konstantin Kirilov is alive. Tell your American friends that.'

I turned to look at him and realised that I had heard that voice before, outside my cell. Then it had been speaking in Russian.

'You will leave now,' the tall man said. 'There is an aircraft waiting for you.' He got up and knocked on the door. One of the guards entered.

'I thought the airport was closed,' I said.

'There are always exceptions.'

There were no farewells. I followed the guards back the way I had come and was bundled into a car and driven off. My experience of Mokotów Prison had lasted less than an hour, surely some sort of record.

What had it all been about? The tall man had asked questions he knew I wouldn't answer and there had been no real attempt to make me. The tone had been more interview than interrogation.

The streets seemed eerily quiet although the curfew had not yet begun. It had started to rain and the flashing blue light on our car reflected off pools of water. Police and army patrols were everywhere, ghostly figures in an unreal world.

We took the main road towards Gdańsk but soon turned off to the military airfield at Modlin. Perhaps this is where the real interrogation was about to start. But the driver was directed to the far side of the airport where a Cessna Citation jet was parked well away from any other aircraft. Then we waited.

It seemed that I really was being sent home. I wondered how Julia would react if I walked in through the door in the middle of the night. Was it really only two weeks ago that we had passed through Modlin on our way to the lakeside rendezvous?

There seemed to be a lot of activity around the control tower and hangars but we were too far away to see what was happening. Two Mi-8 helicopters clattered in from the north-west and then another, this one with Russian markings, took off and disappeared to the east.

Eventually two vehicles appeared behind us. One was a hearse. Four men unloaded what was clearly a coffin and carried it to the waiting aircraft and loaded it into the hold. Only then was I allowed out of the car. The suitcase I had left at my hotel was passed to me and I was hurried up the steps and into the plane where I was greeted by a larger than life Texan who introduced himself simply as Blue. He explained that he was Mark Jaszczak's pilot.

'Didn't expect to be taking Mr Jaszczak home this way,' he said, pointing towards the hearse that was now driving away. 'He was an OK guy.'

I was the only passenger.

'Just you, me and Tonto,' said Blue.

'Tonto?'

'Yeah. There is a Polish Air Force guy upfront with me, he's there to do all the talking until we're out of Polish airspace.'

With that Blue returned to the cockpit. He showed no interest at all in me. It occurred to me that his lack of curiosity may well have been why Jaszczak had hired him. In no time at all we were airborne.

The flight gave me plenty of time to think. There were still questions in my mind about what had happened in Castle Square and about what the Americans were really up to but right now I was trying to understand what the Russians were up to. Although the tall man who had questioned me in Mokotów Prison was undoubtedly Polish, the man beside him, the man who I was convinced was pulling the strings, was Russian.

What had they hoped to learn from me? The answer had to be: nothing. They were not asking, they were telling. I was there to receive not give.

Ostensibly they wanted me to deliver two messages. The first was to stop 'playing' with the Army of Fighting Poland. There were two problems with that: as far as I knew we weren't playing with the supposed 'army' and it was in any case obvious that the Polish authorities wouldn't want us to. There was no need to pull me in to say that. The second message was that they wanted Kirilov. And what's more would be willing to do a swap for the bodies of the two Americans apparently now confirmed as killed in the lakeside shootout. But again why tell me? They had already talked to Reese. It was nothing to do with British Intelligence.

These were not the real messages they wanted me to deliver. There had to be something else. They might have just been letting us know that they knew what we were up to. They knew why I was here, why Flanagan and Sokolowski had been here, what Jaszczak was up to. But by now none of that was really secret. It had to be something more specific. I listed in my mind everything I had been told. Was there a lie that they wanted to make us believe?

First there was the story of what had happened at the lake. In the tall man's version Kirilov was a Russian spying for America. That was something everyone agreed on. What the Pole had gone on to say was that we had promised to bring money to the meeting but hadn't brought it and that Kirilov had therefore killed the Americans. That didn't make sense at all. If there was no money why kill anyone? And in any case, it wasn't the Americans bringing the dollars it was Kirilov. Jaszczak's people had already given him the money so he didn't need to kill anyone to get hold of it.

So if he did kill them did he do so for some other reason? I had no idea what the tall man had meant when he said that we had brought no money, just 'papers', but it did seem to imply that the Polish soldiers had not found any dollars. Where had they gone? Flanagan and Sokolowski certainly expected there to be enough money at the hut to make someone 'very, very rich'.

I simply didn't believe the story I had been told, that Kirilov had killed the two Americans and 'a local man'. It was far more likely that the killers arrived in the army trucks Julia saw. The tall man had said they were army conscripts who just happened to be exercising in the area. That was ridiculously unlikely and certainly wouldn't explain the presence of a military vehicle with Russian plates. Was the 'chat' at Mokotów Prison simply trying to persuade us that the KGB had no hand in killing the two Company agents? They could surely not expect anybody to believe that.

The second thing the tall man clearly wanted me to know was that the Army of Fighting Poland, which Rembury thought was imaginary, something cooked up by the Polish secret police as a pretence for a crackdown, was not only real but had been financed and organised by Mark Jaszczak. That had the ring of truth about it. If it wasn't true why bother arranging a car accident for Jaszczak? I remembered the men I had seen leaving Jaszczak's hotel suite. The one word I had overheard in their conversation was 'army'. And Jaszczak had mentioned problems with his business in Torun which tied in with Rembury telling me that an arms cache had been discovered in the town. I had to admit that the tall Pole might have been telling the truth. It could be that Jaszczak was smuggling arms into Poland in order to foment, as he thought, some kind of revolution. He would have been well placed to do so, concealing arms in the machinery and supplies he was bringing in through Gdańsk and sending to his factories elsewhere.

Would he have had official American approval? Did Lorrimore and Hoeven know what he was doing and the risks he was taking? I knew my Service would have been horrified at the thought of an operation with so little chance of success and with potentially disastrous consequences if discovered. The Americans, however, were different. Poland was part of what President Reagan would two years later describe as the 'evil empire' and evil was something that had to be fought. It was quite possible that Jaszczak's supposed army had been officially sanctioned.

The more I thought about it the likelier it seemed that somebody in the CIA knew exactly what Jaszczak had been trying to do in Poland. Earlier in the year, President Reagan's Cabinet had been bitterly divided over the building of a pipeline across Russia to deliver Siberian natural gas to

Western Europe. Alexander Haig and the State Department urged caution, they knew how much the project meant to European allies, including Margaret Thatcher, who was desperate that the contracts won by British engineering companies should not be jeopardised. However, the Defense Secretary Caspar Weinberger, with the strong support of Bill Casey and the CIA, had been determined to kill the project off and to hell with what the Germans and British thought about it.

When the situation in Poland started to unravel, the same tensions would no doubt have surfaced in Washington again. Casey would have cast caution aside and demanded action from his team. Poland had been hitting the headlines in the USA for a long time and President Reagan had vigorously condemned the military coup. Everyone in the Embassy had heard about the President going on television to light a candle in the White House in solidarity with the people of Poland. He had called on all Americans to do the same. The President would soon be dining in the White House with the leader of the recent Turkish coup but there was no chance of there ever being a similar welcome for General Jaruzelski. Men like Chuck Hoeven might well believe they had the green light to foment an armed uprising.

Thinking about Jaszczak's arms smuggling led on to the apparently casual reference the tall man had made to Jaszczak's people killing two men in Gdańsk. I tried to remember exactly what he had said. He talked about two officers being killed. He didn't say army officers or naval or police, just two officers. That description would certainly fit Kacper Nowak and Tadeusz Modjeski, a naval officer and an SB officer. But that was surely clutching at straws. On the other hand the tall man had mentioned the docks, which exactly fitted with Nowak's story. He seemed to imply that the two young officers had somehow discovered what Jaszczak's group was doing and the group had then killed them. I suppose that once the Polish authorities realised that the two men were missing they might well have concluded that they had been killed. But why did they link that with Jaszczak and how did it all relate to the story Nowak had been telling consistently since he turned up in Middlesbrough?

Since arriving back in Poland my mind had been fully occupied with what was happening around me – the coup, the events in Castle Square, Esterka, the encounter in Mokotów Prison – but in the background my subconscious had been puzzling over Nowak's story. He had insisted that it was a Russian who had killed his friend. He said that they had crossed the border from Kaliningrad and driven to Gdańsk just as the Russian asked but still the man pulled a gun, shot Modjeski and tried to shoot Nowak himself. Could that Russian be Kirilov? Kirilov had been in charge of the KGB in Kaliningrad and one of the key KGB units under his command would have been the KGB Border Guards. Who better to get Nowak and Modjeski past those Border Guards than the man at their head? And who was more likely to be able to similarly outwit the authorities on the Polish side of the frontier?

Suddenly it all came together. Jaszczak and Hoeven were smuggling weapons into Poland. That was not as easy as it sounds but Hoeven had an asset ideally placed to help: Kirilov. Somehow Modjeski discovered what Jaszczak was doing, just as the tall man had told me, but rather than Jaszczak's people killing him, Jaszczak used Kirilov. Kirilov

243

lured the two Polish officers to the docks in Gdańsk and tried to shoot them both but Nowak escaped. Kirilov was not merely spying for the Americans, he was working for Jaszczak and his Army of Fighting Poland.

Jaszczak had used an odd expression when talking about putting a radio transmitter in with the money at the lake. He'd said, 'Kirilov knew that if the tracker suddenly stopped working he would answer to me.'

The implication surely was that it was Jaszczak who was telling Kirilov what to do. I was straying into pure speculation but it made sense of the tall man's belief that Jaszczak was behind the murder of the two officers in Gdańsk.

Another unexpected assertion from the tall man was that the Crown had been made for Jaszczak in London. Since Julia's curt message telling me to abort my mission I had been curious about how we had discovered the Crown was a fake. Because of the coup normal communication with London was impossible and Brasenose was insistent that our radio messages appear as innocent as possible. As the Cessna flew steadily west I simply had no idea what to make of the Pole's claim. It was not until I returned to England that I discovered Julia's part in the story. Nor did I know that the goldsmith whom she had discovered was Jewish.

By the time Blue told me to fasten the seat belt for landing all I knew is that whatever the tall man had told me had been said for a reason. I had also realised that whatever he had not said was also for a reason. He knew Julia and I had been at the lake with the two Americans but there had been no mention at all of anyone else being there. Had they really been able to identify Julia and me but not Father Paszek and his driver? What about the peasant who was supposed to have delivered the Crown? Rembury had found a newspaper report saying he had died in a hunting accident but the tall man's assertion that a local man had been killed alongside the two Americans certainly seemed more likely.

As we landed at RAF Northolt I had one last thought, a sudden spark of recognition. I knew the name of the man whose face I had briefly glimpsed at the prison. It was Father Paszek. The flap on the cell door had been lifted and Father Paszek had looked in like a startled rabbit, turning away as he caught my eye. I was suddenly quite certain. And I was equally sure of something else: Father Paszek had not been brought to Mokotów just to identify me, there had been fear in his eyes.

XXI

Justin Brasenose was waiting for me in a meeting room at Northolt. He was alone.

'Tell me everything. Starting from the moment you arrived in Warsaw.'

For the second time in a few hours I sat down at a table bearing glasses and water but this time no flowers. This was not to be a chat or even an interview, this was an interrogation. For well over two hours Brasenose went through every minute of my time in the Polish capital but even then he was not satisfied.

'All right, let me play that back. Tell me what I've missed.'

It was after three o'clock in the morning when he finally flipped his notebook closed.

'That will do for now. I have a phone call to make. We'll continue in my office in the morning, nine thirty. There's a car waiting for you.'

I wondered who he was calling at three o'clock in the morning.

I phoned Julia from the office where the Service driver was patiently waiting. Nobody had told her that I was back in the country. I was not surprised; Brasenose had not told me anything either. It occurred to me that my whole interrogation had been one-way. It wasn't until I got home that Julia filled in some of the blanks, starting with how she had discovered that the Great Crown of Jan Kazimierz was a fake.

'Clever girl,' I whispered patronisingly as we lay in each other's arms. 'But did Jaszczak commission it? Do we have any name to go with the crown?'

'Yes,' Julia replied, 'David Prince.'

She must have sensed my shock. No wonder London hadn't communicated that piece of information to Rembury and me in Warsaw.

'But that can't be. He is above suspicion now that we've caught the mole in the Embassy.'

Julia could not comment. Since she had sent me the message to abort my mission she had been told absolutely nothing. The Defence Intelligence Staff were now completely out of the loop. Her only further communication with my Service had been an unexpected and uncharacteristic phone call from Brasenose shortly after she had taken it upon herself to cancel my mission. At that time she had no way of knowing what was happening in Poland and whether she had been right to act as she did.

'I wanted to thank you,' Brasenose had said. 'You did the right thing. Your message reached your husband in time.'

At Northolt Brasenose had been totally professional, focussed entirely on gathering information, determined not to let the smallest detail escape. He was like a machine hoovering up facts that could be sifted and sorted later. But the phone call to Julia illustrated a different side of him, it had been a thoughtful gesture that he hadn't needed to make. When I arrived at his office the next morning yet another part of his character was on display. He couldn't have had more than a few hours' sleep but he looked completely fresh, his suit and shirt without a crease out of place. He had filtered, compared and analysed my story and was now in a reflective mood.

'Sit down, Thomas. Let me tell you what I think about all this. I'll start with the Great Crown. Who had it made and why?'

'David Prince.'

'Yes, that's what Rothenberg said.'

'Rothenberg?'

'The goldsmith who made the crown. He told your wife that it had been commissioned by David Prince. But is it true?'

'You mean Rothenberg might have been making it all up?'

'No, nothing like that. We've interviewed him and crawled all over his background. He is completely above board. No, what he told your wife was perfectly true, the man who commissioned the Crown gave his name as David Prince. But it wasn't David Prince. That was easy to establish by simply taking David to see Rothenberg.'

'So somebody wanted us to think that Prince commissioned the Crown.'

'Perhaps. But with respect to your wife, her finding Rothenberg was a complete fluke. Rothenberg happens to mention the crown to a policeman, the policeman happens to file a report, the report happens to be seen by someone else who happens to mention it to your wife. Nobody could have anticipated that. If someone had wanted us to discover that David Prince had commissioned a fake Crown from a London goldsmith they would have made it much easier for us.'

I was still confused but one thing seemed clear. 'So you are confident Prince is on our side.'

Brasenose smiled. 'I always have been and you proved it. We were able to speak to Rembury in Warsaw late last night. On my instructions he asked the Americans for help with those tapes you found. The Company has a Signals Intelligence team at their Warsaw Embassy. What they found was a shock to everyone. It seems that the Opposition, we think the Russians rather than the Poles themselves, had somehow managed to bug most of the dictation machines used in the Embassy. They had put miniature transmitters in them; whenever they were switched on, anything said nearby was transmitted to a battery-powered receiver hidden inside an old reel-to-reel tape recorder stored away in a cupboard somewhere. The receiver recorded everything on microcassettes. The cassettes filled up in a week or two but as you worked out, whenever Delavere-Hamilton visited theEmbassy she replaced the old cassettes, made it look as though they had fallen to pieces and dropped them into a bin. They were then taken out with the rubbish and somehow intercepted.'

I was astonished not only that such a thing was technically possible but that the Russians had been able to get the equipment into the Embassy in the first place. In those days the Soviets were way ahead of us in such matters. I remember that as a result of our discovery we issued a security alert to our Embassies around the world. Nowhere else did we find anything as sophisticated but not long after, the Americans discovered that sixteen IBM electric typewriters in the US Embassy in Moscow had been doctored, every key that was struck was transmitted to receivers the KGB had positioned outside the building.

'David Prince was right about the spy he called Esterka,' Brasenose continued, 'and everyone else, including me, was wrong.'

'What will happen to Mrs Delavere-Hamilton?' I asked.

'Nothing of course. She won't come back to this country knowing she would be arrested. The Ambassador will take her name off his garden party list and that will be it.'

Brasenose was right. The Warsaw Embassy mole was yesterday's news.

'Let's stand back,' said Brasenose. 'We're in a drama with just two principals but we are constantly distracted by a host of bit players: that sailor Kacper Nowak and his supposedly dead friend Modjeski, Jaszczak and his sidekick Dragan, Delavere-Hamilton, David Prince. Then there's Father Paszek, who seems to have been picked up as part of the purge that's going on in Poland and who you may have seen in Mokotów Prison. Not to forget the mysterious scarfaced assassin. They all played their part but behind them are those pulling the strings in Washington and Moscow. Hoeven, Lorrimore and their opposite numbers.'

'There's another bit player you didn't list,' I suggested. 'Krypton, alias Karacek, alias Colonel Konstantin Kirilov.'

Brasenose smiled again. 'Kirilov. Now is he a bit player or is he a principal? To mix metaphors at the moment we should think of him as the wildcard. We'll come back to Colonel Kirilov. It's the principals we have to understand, the Americans and the Russians, about one of whom we know too much and the other too little.

'Washington is in turmoil. General Jaruzelski's coup is the most traumatic shock to US Intelligence that I've seen in my lifetime. They didn't see it coming, they don't know why it happened and they can't agree what to do about it. They have politicians of every colour screaming at them. One thing we know for certain is that inside the Company the knives are out. When all this blows over there will be the most massive inquest, Congressional hearings galore and heads will undoubtedly roll. The Polish vote in America can't be ignored and the media are having a field day. Putting candles in windows is not going to convince anyone that the administration is on top of things.

'There are two schools of thought in the Company. People like Lorrimore think that the objective of Intelligence is to provide information to policymakers, to make sure that the White House has the best possible factual evidence available to it in every circumstance. Hoeven, on the other hand, thinks the Company is there to act, to change events not merely to report on them. The agents in the field are caught between the two, they either take sides like Jacobs in Moscow or try to keep their heads down like Reese in Warsaw.

'When Carter was President, Lorrimore's side had the upper hand. Carter was instinctively cautious. When he tried to be an action-man by authorising the helicopter rescue of the American hostages in Tehran it went wrong. Overthrowing governments was off the table and people like Hoeven were out in the cold. Then Reagan arrived and as you know appointed his campaign manager, Bill Casey, to head the Company. Everything changed and covert operations were flavour of the month. Jaszczak appeared with a deluge of dollars that weren't subject to any sort of Congressional oversight and Hoeven was back in business. They cooked up this Fighting Army nonsense and started running arms into Poland, imagining that they just needed to light a spark and the whole country would rally to them. Father Paszek had established a reputation as an ultra-nationalist and they decided he would be the figurehead.'

'And he needed a symbol,' I interrupted. 'That's where the Crown comes in.'

'Perhaps. I spoke to Lorrimore when you left last night, or rather when you left earlier this morning. He hadn't realised quite what Hoeven and Jaszczak were up to with their Operation Coronation and is furious with them. It's one thing for Hoeven and his cowboys to train the Mujahidin in Afghanistan or the Grey Wolves in Turkey, it's another thing entirely to encourage guerrilla groups so close to home. If the Russians can prove the Company had been supporting terrorists inside Poland it will cause enormous damage. It undermines everything we've been saying about the coup. Operation Coronation may well have been approved by Casey but Lorrimore doubts if anyone else in the Company hierarchy was kept informed. Interestingly, Lorrimore still doesn't know where the Crown fits it. Apparently Hoeven continues to insist he thought it was genuine.'

'So who did commission the Crown?'

'Well we didn't and I think we can take it the Americans didn't.'

'Jaszczak?'

'That's what you were told. But if he did, why would Jaszczak tell the other side?'

'Torture?'

'I don't think so. They didn't hold him for long. For the Reds Jaszczak was an embarrassment they didn't need. I doubt if he could tell them anything they didn't already know so they organised a quick accident and sent his body home as soon as possible.'

'But if Jaszczak didn't tell them the Crown had been made in London, who did?'

Before Brasenose could say anything I answered my own question. 'Nobody. They had it made themselves. But that's crazy. Why would they want a fake Crown in the hands of people like Jaszczak and Father Paszek?'

'You're right,' Brasenose agreed. 'It doesn't make sense. It would mean the whole exchange by the lake business was a charade. But either Jaszczak or the Russians had that Crown produced. We've shown that goldsmith photos of every Russian and Polish diplomat and sympathiser in London. He hasn't recognised anyone but we'll keep on trying.'

Brasenose seemed to be collecting his thoughts and I stayed silent.

'Let's just think,' he said eventually. 'We know what the Americans are up to. What we don't know is what game the Russians are playing. Leave aside the possibility that the Russians and the Poles are playing different games. The Pole at Mokotów Prison may have been asking the questions but as you rightly said the other man, the Russian, was writing the script. This isn't about what General Jaruzelski has just done. Whoever had that Crown made has been working on this operation for months. I'll tell you my theory, and at the moment it's only a theory.

'Go back a few months. The politicians in the Kremlin are alarmed at developments in Poland. Their instinct is to send in the troops as they have before. But the head of the KGB, Andropov, is urging caution. The Red Army are nervous. They're bogged down in Afghanistan. There are rumblings in the Caucasus.

'Remember hundreds of people died when Russian tanks went into East Berlin in 1953, into Hungary in 1956 and Czechoslovakia in 1968. Then the world stood by. But this time the resistance could be far stronger and it could spread. What would happen if a group of Polish refugees crossed into East Germany and tried to reach the Americans in Berlin? The foreign policy establishment in Moscow know that Poland is far more sensitive in the US than Hungary or Czechoslovakia. President Reagan is unpredictable. The upshot is that Brezhnev and the gerontocracy in the Kremlin tell the KGB to do whatever they can to defuse the situation inside Poland. Attack Solidarity not by force but by stealth. Destroy the Opposition's credibility. Show that far from being Polish patriots they are just pawns of Western imperialists.

'So what I think happened is that some clever brain in an office in the Lubyanka dreamed up their version of Operation Coronation.

'They would invent a fairy tale about a legendary crown and feed it to the Americans, complete with a fake Crown. They co-opted Broniszewski, who was not the illiterate Polish peasant we thought but a lifelong Communist, to help out. They must have discovered that Kirilov was working for the Americans. Perhaps they turned him or perhaps they just fed him their fiction. The plan was that if the Company bought the story and set up a meeting with the American stooge Father Paszek the Polish cavalry would arrive and arrest everyone. There would be a massive show trial in Warsaw. You can imagine the media circus. American spies, British spies, Polish fascists. And no doubt in the middle of it the Great Crown of Jan Kazimierz would be produced and a friendly Western journalist would be helped to discover that it had been made in London.'

'And made by us,' I interjected. 'By David Prince.'

'Exactly. That would be a welcome bonus for the Russians. David was getting close to their mole in the Embassy. This would take him out of circulation. You remember the peasant who was supposedly selling the Crown insisted there be one of us there. Some ridiculous story about him only trusting the Brits because his brother had flown with us in the war. Now that we know his name we've established that there was no Pole of that name connected in any way with the RAF in the war. They wanted a Brit at the lake because they thought it would be David Prince but they had been too clever. They had already used Kirilov to discredit Prince with the Americans. That's why you were there.'

'So what went wrong?' I asked. 'Why didn't the Polish cavalry arrive at the lake and whisk me off to Mokotów for a real interrogation?'

Brasenose smiled ruefully. 'That is where my theory does rather fall down. The only thing I can imagine is that Jaszczak's people were somehow involved. Lorrimore told me they delivered the money to Kirilov somewhere near the lake and then disappeared. Perhaps they didn't disappear. Why put a radio tracker in with the money and then not stick around to track it?'

Brasenose's theory was clever but it seemed to me that it left a lot unexplained.

'Who were the men with masks who Kirilov says stole the Crown and somehow got it to Helsinki? And how does the whole business with Kacper Nowak and Tadeusz Modjeski fit in? What were they smuggling into Poland from Kaliningrad? Who was the man who tried to shoot Nowak in Cornwall?'

'That I don't know. But I doubt there were any masked men at that lake. I think Kirilov made that up.'

'You mean Kirilov himself stole the Crown and sold it to Jaszczak in Helsinki?'

'No. Kirilov was in the US when Jaszczak went to Finland. But I'm still convinced that everything leads back to our wildcard, Krypton, Colonel Konstantin Kirilov.'

'Then we need to talk to him.'

'Blake Lorrimore is going to do that. I've outlined my theory to him and he is inclined to agree. The problem is that Kirilov is Hoeven's man and you know how tribal they are inside the Company. Blake needs to follow procedure. Apparently Hoeven is in Europe somewhere and not easy to speak to. Nevertheless, Blake is confident he can get access to Kirilov this morning, this afternoon our time. But I'm not sure he will get anywhere. If Kirilov knew the whole operation was a Russian sting he's not going to say so. My suspicion is that the Russians discovered Kirilov had been working for the Americans and turned him. But he got nervous and somehow escaped to Sweden. He may not even have been at the lake. When Blake Lorrimore presents him with evidence that the Crown is a fake, he will probably just stick to his story and claim that's all he knows.'

'So there's nothing more we can do.'

'Just business as usual. We'll keep showing Rothenberg photos of every Russian and Pole who's been in London in the last six months. Our friends across the river will attempt to interview Kacper Nowak again. I've sent someone to help our man in Helsinki try to find out what Jaszczak was really doing when he said he bought the Crown from Nowak's apparently dead friend Tadeusz Modjeski. And we'll keep digging into the Swedish alias, Karacek, that the Americans created for Kirilov.'

Our discussion seemed to be over and I started to stand up. Brasenose stopped me.

'There is one other thing that intrigues me,' he said, looking right at me. 'Why are you here?'

XXII

'Why am I here?'

'Why aren't you stuck in Warsaw? There's a massive military operation going on in Poland. Thousands have been arrested. The country is completely sealed off but they make an exception for the private jet of a dead American. And then they put you on it.'

'They must have wanted me out of the way as they thought I was on to Delavere-Hamilton.'

'No I don't think so. They knew you'd removed the broken tapes from the bin she had dropped them in. Once we had them it was just a matter of time until we worked out how the bugs were working. Getting rid of you wouldn't gain them anything. No, they didn't want you out of Poland quickly, they wanted you here quickly. They wanted their message delivered right away. Why? What did they expect us to do and have we done it?'

Brasenose left me with that thought but I didn't have long to ponder it. Just before five o'clock I was summoned back to his office. To my surprise Julia was there.

'Things are hotting up,' he said as soon as I arrived. 'You and your wife are going on holiday, a few days in Italy.'

Given the weather outside, wet and miserable in London and with much of the country still covered in snow, the

258

prospect of a holiday was obviously attractive but Brasenose saw my look of surprise.

'Let me explain. An hour ago the editor of one of our more responsible papers was in touch. He's planning to run a story tomorrow that he thought we might like to discuss. It seems that a keen young journalist named Lenny Milne had approached them with a story which they had at first dismissed as fiction. But they had introduced Milne to one of their old timers and the two of them have produced something which, in the editor's words, 'had legs'. It seems young Lenny did indeed have an amazing scoop. In parenthesis I might add that this young man is well known to our colleagues across the river. His father is a hardline Communist who writes for the *Morning Star*, the Party rag. Lenny says he's uncovered a plan by British and American intelligence to destabilise Poland with a fantasy about a magical crown. And Lenny has been very diligent. He's not only discovered that the Crown was made in London but he's discovered who made it. What's more, he claims he's spoken to a source in Hatton Garden who tells him that the Crown was made for a Mr David Prince.

'Of course it didn't take long for Lenny to establish that David Prince had until recently been on the Embassy staff in Warsaw and is now back in London but doesn't seem to appear on any official list. We all know what that means. On top of that they've managed to get photos of everyone entering Rothenberg's premises this morning and claim to have identified one of our people, which is quite possible. We sent over a new load of photos for Rothenberg to look at.'

'Can't we stop publication?' Julia asked. 'Official Secrets Act and all that.'

'We can stop the photo of our man being published and we can stop them quoting David's name but that would just add credibility to the story. The story is just too good to suppress entirely. Lenny's even managed to introduce a femme fatale into the story. Apparently one of Rothenberg's neighbours has told them that a glamorous young woman in RAF uniform was recently seen rushing out of the Rothenbergs' house at some unearthly hour of the morning.'

'Me!' Julia exclaimed.

'Of course. The Poles will play this for all it's worth. They will claim it justifies everything that is happening over there. Lenny Milne is linking the whole affair to the Army of Fighting Poland and here's the part I didn't understand at first, he's linking it to Father Paszek. And now I know why. Half an hour ago the Polish Interior Minister Czesław Kiszczak called a press conference. You'll remember that until recently Kiszczak was head of Polish Military Intelligence. Alongside him sat Father Paszek.'

It was my turn to be surprised. 'Paszek? I thought he was in prison. I'm fairly sure he was the man I saw peering into my prison cell at Mokotów.'

'And I think you were right. My guess is that he was given a choice: support the coup or rot in prison nursing a body full of broken bones. It would have been an easy decision. The man is close to being a fascist. He hates Lech Walesa and Solidarity, to him they spell anarchy, atheism and the end of civilisation.'

'But he also hates the Russians,' I objected.

Brasenose has thought of that. 'He's probably persuaded himself that Jaruzelski was acting to pre-empt a Russian invasion. Whatever the motive, he claimed that Jaszczak and David Prince had approached him with a story about Jaszczak finding the Great Crown of Jan Kazimierz in America and wanting to restore it to the Polish people. Paszek had at first welcomed the offer. But then he discovered that Jaszczak expected him to support the Fighting Poland terrorist group, part of a plot for Jaszczak to seize control of the Polish economy. As a patriotic Pole Paszek refused and immediately contacted the authorities. A trap was prepared. Jaszczak agreed to hand over the Crown in Castle Square but he didn't turn up. Instead the terrorists sent a courier, an American called Dragan. When the police moved to arrest him he pulled a gun and was shot dead.'

'Very neat.'

'Wait. I haven't finished. Here comes the really clever bit. It seems Dragan was not alone. He had an accomplice who was subsequently arrested. The Poles have released a sixty-second film clip of the man admitting his involvement.'

'You mean they filmed Jaszczak before he was killed?'

'No,' said Brasenose turning to look directly at me. 'Not Jaszczak. You. Sitting calmly at a table with flowers and bottles of mineral water in front of you admitting you were in Castle Square and with the Crown in your hands. It will be all over the television news tonight.'

I cursed myself. One or both of the mirrors in the room at Mokotów Prison had concealed cameras. Not terribly sophisticated but then they hadn't needed to be. I simply walked into the trap. I tried to remember what I had said. The tall man had asked me about Castle Square and I replied that like most tourists I had been there. It was easy to see how judicious editing would remove any reference to tourists. And I had indeed handled the Crown, it had been passed to me. Reversing that piece of film would show me giving rather than receiving it. In fact they didn't need to do that, I had handed the Crown back. They had only been able to cobble together sixty seconds of apparently incriminating film but it was enough.

'So you want Julia and me to lay low until everything blows over?'

'It would be wise if both of you were out of sight for a while but things aren't as bad as you may suppose. We've managed to spike the other side's guns. This morning Rothenberg identified the man who commissioned the Crown and he's Russian. An employee of their airline Aeroflot. And stupidly he wasn't pulled out as soon as he collected the Crown. They left him in London. We have him under arrest.'

'But what can we charge him with?' Julia asked. 'It's not illegal to buy an imitation crown.'

'At the moment we're just holding him on suspicion of espionage. We'll keep him in Paddington Green for a couple of days and then I expect we will just expel him. The Home Secretary is holding a press conference at this very minute. He will maintain that this was all a mad Russian plot that they cooked up to justify the coup.'

'Will that work?'

'Most of our press will lap it up and that will keep the politicians off our back. The real damage will be overseas. I can't imagine Polish TV will even mention our version.'

Brasenose was right: the Service's relationship with most Fleet Street editors was good but this was a story that would not die quickly. Julia and I needed to be out of the way for a while.

'We had better be off and pack,' Julia said. 'We have a

friend in Sicily who could hide us. Nobody goes there at this time of year.'

I knew the friend Julia was thinking about and had no great desire to stay with him. 'Rome might be better. I know it well enough from my student days to keep us out of sight. Even in December it's a beautiful city.'

'Don't get too enthusiastic,' Brasenose replied. 'You're not going to Sicily or Rome.'

Julia gave him a quizzical glance and I knew just what she was thinking. Like me she understood why we needed to be out of London but Brasenose was not her boss and she would not be happy that he was trying to decide exactly where we were going to hide. In truth she probably wanted to retreat to Cornwall again. Brasenose must have sensed her reaction.

'This media palaver is not the only development today. There's another reason I want your husband on a plane. I've had another call from Blake Lorrimore. Our wildcard has really gone wild. Colonel Kirilov has disappeared. The Company have lost him.'

'How?' Julia and I responded in unison.

'It seems that they had put him in a house in Fairfax County, Virginia. The area is full of military bases and for some reason Hoeven thought this would make it more secure. Kirilov had an armed Company man with him at all times, supposedly for his protection but I suspect really to keep an eye on him. Three days ago Kirilov claimed he'd seen people watching the house and he was sure they were Russian. The Company had installed cameras but they had picked up nothing. Nevertheless Hoeven's people went into a panic. They had police patrols crawling all over the area. They found nothing.

'The next day Kirilov and his minder went off to breakfast at McDonald's. Dreadful thought, I know, but apparently Kirilov loved it. Just as they were finishing a leisurely breakfast, if you can imagine such a thing in a McDonald's, two men drew into the car park. Kirilov jumped up, insisted the two men were Russians and disappeared to the gents at the back. Instead of going with him the minder went outside to take a look. The car had red diplomatic plates with the letters SX on them. Apparently SX is like the numbers 250 on a diplomatic plate in London, it means Soviet Union. The agent rushed back to find Kirilov but our man had disappeared, along with the minder's car.'

'Surely he can't have got very far.'

'You wouldn't think so,' Brasenose agreed. 'But Hoeven seems to have assumed Kirilov would go back to the house or make contact in some other way. He put out a police alert for the car and waited. Only when the car was found parked in a shopping mall not far away did he consider the possibility that Kirilov was not planning to get in touch. Even then he seems to have been reluctant to issue an all-ports bulletin, an APB. News was still coming in about the coup in Poland and people were already asking how it could have happened without any warning. Hoeven didn't know what had happened to Jaszczak and his merry band. The last thing he wanted was something blowing up right on his doorstep.

'By the time he issued an APB Kirilov was in the air. He'd used the American papers the Company had given him to fly to Mexico City. Those papers were in the name of King and when Hoeven found out where Kirilov had gone he had the Mexican authorities put out an alert in that name. But Kirilov also had the papers the Americans had given him in Sweden, papers in the name of Karacek. Hoeven forgot about those.'

'You're joking!'

'No I'm not. Blake Lorrimore is incandescent. He hadn't been told Kirilov had gone AWOL. He even hinted that Hoeven and Kirilov might have cooked the whole thing up between them.'

'That's not very likely,' pointed out Julia. 'Not if the men at McDonald's really were Russians.'

'Oh they were certainly Russians, they've been identified. They went into the place and sat there for over an hour, as if waiting for someone. And it's too much of a coincidence to think that they just turned up by chance.

'The Americans hadn't been watching Kirilov's every move. He was their guest, not their prisoner. My theory is that at some point he managed to contact the Embassy and set up a meeting at the McDonald's. He probably posed as someone with information to sell. I don't think the two Russians had any idea that they were dealing with Kirilov, they were simply following up some sort of contact. Anyway the point is that Kirilov reached Mexico and the Mexicans weren't given the Karacek name. The result is that our man simply changed planes and boarded the first flight to Europe. In no time at all he was airborne again. The Company have now established that he travelled to Vienna via Madrid and then vanished. Hoeven is desperately chasing after him. And I want you to do the same.'

'But you said we were going to Italy not Austria.'

'I did. You see we have an advantage over Chuck Hoeven.' Brasenose paused. He had clearly been building up to this moment. 'I think I know where Kirilov is going.'

XXIII

Julia and I could only sit and wait for Brasenose to explain.

'We've all become so obsessed with fake crowns and Russian plots that we've forgotten that a young Polish naval officer arrived in this country clearly fearing for his life. What was Kacper Nowak afraid of? That's not a difficult question to answer because he told us. A Russian, he said, had shot his friend and tried to shoot him. But first they had smuggled something over the border from the Kaliningrad enclave into Poland and then into the port area in Gdańsk. Supposing that was true the obvious question was: what were they smuggling? Drugs, probably, but it could be weapons or money or something else entirely. But there was a more useful question: where was it being sent? There were quite a few ships in Gdańsk that night, where were they all going? I keep telling people most of our Service's work is just boring routine and this is a good example. We've investigated every single ship we were able to identify as having been in port that day or the following week.'

'But what were you looking for?' Julia asked.

'That's the difficulty: we had no idea. Getting hold of shipping manifests in Eastern Europe is not always easy and those we did find produced nothing. So we started at the other end, at the destinations. We've had our people visiting ports all over the world but we found what we were looking for not far from Gdańsk, just up the Baltic in fact. The day after Nowak says his friend was shot a ship left Gdańsk for Helsinki carrying general cargo. Fortunately our man in Helsinki is rather good. One small item caught his attention: fabric samples.'

'Fabric samples? What's suspicious about that?'

'Nothing at all. It was the consignee who was receiving the samples that rang a bell. K K Karacek.'

'The name Kirilov was using for his bank account in Sweden?'

'Exactly. But Colonel Kirilov didn't collect the consignment. Nobody did. Our man discovered that it had sat in a bonded warehouse for more than two weeks. Then the supposed fabric samples were loaded on to another ship, a Greek tramp. The *Mavri Lefkota* had been chartered to carry machinery from Helsinki and Gdańsk to Marseilles and Trieste. Unfortunately we couldn't establish where the Karacek consignment was destined to be unloaded. The charter for the voyage was arranged through a shipbroker here in London and was perfectly above-board but Karacek's stuff was too small to appear on the manifest. The ship would first travel from Helsinki to Gdańsk, load more machinery, then head south for the Mediterranean. We assumed our samples would be unloaded back in Gdańsk. With everything happening in Poland there's no way we could track them there. But just in case we sent a man to Marseilles to check what the boat was unloading in France. We found nothing suspicious. Then we made enquiries in Trieste and bingo. In addition to the cargo listed in the original voyage charter there was another item arriving from Helsinki, a small container consigned in the name of Karacek.'

'So what happened when the *Mavri Lefkota* arrived in Trieste?' I asked.

Brasenose gave his familiar smile. 'It hasn't arrived. Helsinki to Trieste is well over four thousand miles. The *Mavri Lefkota* docks tomorrow afternoon. I want you there. If my theory is right that ship is carrying something that is so important that Kirilov decided he needed to kill the two men who had helped him smuggle it out of Kaliningrad. We need to find out what that was, we need to see who collects it and what they do with it. I'm betting that Kirilov himself is heading for Trieste.'

Brasenose produced a large-scale map of the northern Adriatic. The frontier between Italy and Yugoslavia ran south from the Austrian border almost to the sea. Just short of the Adriatic the border turned east so that a long thin stretch of land now belonging to Italy ran along the coast to the city of Trieste and a few miles beyond.

Julia's attention was drawn to a small village just west of the city. 'Prosecco.'

Brasenose nodded with a smile. 'Yes that's where Prosecco originated, although most of it is now made elsewhere. But you won't have time to go wine tasting. Trieste has its own attractions. It used to be the fourth city of the Austrian Empire, after Vienna, Budapest and Prague. And what made it that was the port, Austria's window to the sea. That's where you need to focus your attention.'

He broke off to point at the row of old black and white photos of ships on the wall of his office. 'You've probably never noticed the picture on the left, one of my grandfather's old ships. The Cunard liner RMS *Pannonia* on its maiden voyage in 1904 from Trieste to New York. Tens of thousands of what my friend Lorrimore would describe as Europe's huddled masses left Trieste back then for a new life across the Atlantic. The old port is to the west of the town but there are now massive docks to the east, built by the Italians after they annexed the region following the First World War. That's where the *Mavri Lefkota* berths tomorrow. Trieste is still a Free Port so there will be all sorts of customs controls but I'm relying on you to find a way in.'

It was a sign of the urgency Brasenose attached to the operation that he had managed to gain approval from those who controlled the Service's finances to charter a twin-engine Piper to take us to Italy. But before we left he had something more to say.

The Service, he pointed out, lacked what he called *locus standi*. In other words, by rights we should mind our own business. This was an American operation and they had not asked for our assistance. We should not be getting involved.

'But we've discovered where Kirilov may be going,' put in Julia.

'Then we should have told the Company and let them get on with it.'

'So why didn't we?'

Brasenose looked at her for a moment. 'Why indeed? Because Blake Lorrimore asked me to help, unofficially of course, and he is a man I respect. Because the position of Her Majesty's Government is that anything that might encourage Russian military intervention in Poland is to be avoided and my judgement is that providing arms to groups like the Army of Fighting Poland might easily provoke a military response from Moscow. But the main reason why I'm sending you to Trieste is that I will not have the Service treated like half-witted errand boys. The Central Intelligence Agency serves a noble purpose. It is by far our most important partner, although we are of course the junior partner. It therefore behoves us not to interfere in their affairs. But their Operation Coronation has put the life of a member of my team at risk, twice, and I will not let that happen without knowing why.'

I appreciated what he said but it did prompt me to ask the question that was always foremost in the minds of those heading up the Service.

'Have we got political cover? As far as ministers are concerned does everything we do in Trieste need to be deniable?'

'Not entirely. A man with a gun attacked two soldiers outside a military base in Essex. The same man later shot at someone inside a pub in Cornwall. We have reason to believe he may be in Trieste. That's enough to cover our back.'

'But do you think Scarface really is in Trieste?' Julia asked.

'I've no idea. It is not at all clear where so-called Scarface fits in. Who is he? What could the assassination of a Turkish general and the attempted assassination of a low-level Polish naval officer have in common? I'm beginning to think that somehow the link is Kirilov. Think about him for a moment. Suppose the Crown really was at that lakeside and it disappeared before the Russians could grab it. Who could have taken it and transported it to Finland? Not the two Americans, they are dead. So, apparently, is the peasant who supposedly brought the Crown to the meeting. I can't believe one of the soldiers who the Poles allege just happened to turn up stuffed it into his backpack and made off with it. And

I don't believe Kirilov's story about two men in balaclavas popping up out of nowhere, stealing the money and with bullets flying having time to memorise the number on his boat, that's nonsense.'

'What about Jaszczak's people, the ones who brought the money and gave it to Kirilov?'

'No, if they had taken the Crown there would have been no need for Jaszczak to go to Helsinki to buy it back.'

'Unless one of Jaszczak's people saw the chance to get rich by selling it back to him,' Julia suggested. 'That would explain how the man in Helsinki knew that Jaszczak was the right person to phone when it came to selling the Crown.'

'Possible. But it would have been easier just to steal the money when taking it to Kirilov. And how did they then get the Crown out of Poland?'

He was silent for a moment and I drew the obvious conclusion. 'That just leaves Kirilov. We know the Company set up an escape route for him if he ever needed to get out of Russia. That's how he arrived in Sweden. If he had the Crown he could have taken it with him.'

'Exactly. The Crown is much easier to hide under your coat than a million dollars. But if Kirilov took it he couldn't have sold it in Helsinki because he was in the US at the time. At first I wondered if Jaszczak had made up the whole story about buying it in Finland but that's unlikely, we know he was there when he said he was. But in that case Kirilov must have an accomplice.'

'Scarface,' Julia suggested.

'But there's nothing to link Scarface to Kirilov,' I pointed out.

'But there is,' Julia said, thinking aloud. 'We're assuming

Kirilov is heading for Trieste precisely because we now believe Kacper Nowak's story about a Russian trying to kill him and his friend. Think about it. First Kirilov tries to kill him in Gdańsk and then Scarface tries in Cornwall. That can't be a coincidence.'

Brasenose nodded. 'And there's another thing. The man Jaszczak claims to have bought the Crown from was using the papers of Nowak's friend Tadeusz Modjeski. If we are to believe Nowak, Modjeski is dead and probably at the bottom of the harbour. His killer could easily have taken his papers. We know Scarface was using fake Finnish papers when he flew out of Heathrow but the one place where he wouldn't have got away with that is Finland. Unless he was willing to use his real identity he would have needed new papers.'

What Julia and Brasenose were suggesting was improbable but not impossible. And as I thought about it something else struck me. 'You remember that Firefox told us that the Poles were searching high and low for Modjeski when they realised he had disappeared. Well by the time I was interrogated in Mokotów it seems they were convinced that he had been killed. They even claimed the Army of Fighting Poland were responsible. What would have made them change their mind?'

'They must have found Modjeski's body,' answered Julia.

'That's right. There's no other explanation. It can't have been the real Modjeski in Helsinki.'

Brasenose had given us a lot to think about on the flight to Italy.

I was worried about Julia flying at all in her condition but she brushed my fears aside.

'Don't be so old-fashioned,' she told me. 'I'm not an invalid.'

Brasenose had arranged for us to fly not to Trieste or Venice, both of which he thought might be under observation, although whether by the Americans or the Russians he didn't say. Instead we were heading for the small airport at Treviso. It was just within the Piper's maximum range but the pilot insisted on landing to refuel near Milan. As a consequence we didn't reach the hotel until two o'clock in the morning.

The taxi from the airport passed through darkened countryside but as we approached Trieste and the hotel the city's majestic architecture crowded in on us. In another age I could imagine the cream of Austrian society parading along the avenues at night, their jewels dazzling in the gaslight. The hotel was right on the seafront but when we reached our room we closed the curtains without pausing to admire the view.

Five hours later we were woken by a call from Justin Brasenose. Bearing in mind the time differences between Trieste, London and Washington I was astonished when he said he had just been speaking to Blake Lorrimore. Clearly the two men didn't need to sleep.

'Kirilov's been in touch,' Brasenose announced.

'When?'

'Yesterday, but Blake's only just found out. There's obviously some sort of power struggle going on in Washington. Blake tells me he's being kept "out of the loop", which apparently is some new Washington expression meaning nobody's telling him anything. He's been trying to get hold of Chuck Hoeven without success.

'Apparently Kirilov phoned Hoeven's office in Washington at two o'clock in the morning the previous day. Hoeven was halfway across the Atlantic and his people didn't think to call Blake. Rather than put the call through to anyone who could make a decision the idiot on duty just tried to put things off until the morning.

'Kirilov claimed that he fled from the US because his life had been in danger. He said the KGB must have been tipped off by someone who knew all about his movements and about the safe house in Virginia. Someone on the inside. That's why he had been too scared to call Hoeven before. He'd had to get away from Washington. Now, he said, he was in Austria but was sure the Opposition were on his trail. He wanted to come in and asked for details of a safe house in Vienna. Hoeven's man wouldn't give it to him and instead promised he would get the message to Hoeven as soon as possible. Kirilov agreed to phone again but so far he hasn't.'

I didn't try to hide my incredulity. 'Kirilov is playing games. He phoned Hoeven's office at a time when he could be sure Hoeven wouldn't be there so he wouldn't be asked any awkward questions. Then he asked for an address he must have known wouldn't be given out over the phone. He's just trying to persuade Hoeven he's still on side.'

'Exactly. Whatever Kirilov thinks he will find in Trieste one thing is for sure: the Russians will never stop looking for him. They told you that in Poland. If Kirilov wants to enjoy a long life he needs the Americans to protect him. The whole thing stinks.' That was becoming Brasenose's stock reaction to everything about Operation Coronation.

'Blake has a theory,' Brasenose continued. 'He's discovered that Kirilov went on some sort of mission to North Korea a month or so ago. Blake believes that while Kirilov was away one of the security agencies must have found something incriminating, something that made them realise he was working for the US. When he returned from Pyongyang he spent two weeks in Moscow. That's when Blake thinks he was turned. He then popped up in Kaliningrad again with the fairy tales about David Prince being a mole and the magical Great Crown of Jan Kazimierz. Blake could be right.'

'I disagree,' I replied. 'The timings are all wrong. The Crown was commissioned three months ago. The KGB must have been on to Kirilov before that. They planted this supposed peasant on him and then used the peasant to feed Kirilov the story about the Crown. Kirilov would have immediately told Hoeven. Hoeven's not a complete fool. He would have wanted to check the story out before telling someone like Lorrimore who was already sceptical about running guns into Poland. I should think Hoeven tried to do some digging in Lviv. The Russians would have made it easy for him. Perhaps that's where he found that old black and white photo of the Crown. He certainly sent his man Sokolowski to see the niece of the museum curator who had supposedly spirited the Crown away at the end of the war. I expect he told Kirilov that he needed time to do all that. The Russians would have wanted to keep Kirilov on a tight rein without risking him suspecting they were on to him, but they didn't want him carrying on in a sensitive role in Kaliningrad. So they sent him off to Korea and when he came back they gave him some sort of temporary project in Moscow where they could observe any contacts he had with his handlers.'

'That makes sense,' interrupted Brasenose. 'When Jacobs told Kirilov that Operation Coronation was all ready to go, the temporary project in Moscow was shut down and Kirilov sent back to Kaliningrad.'

'Something like that.'

'So you don't think Kirilov was turned at all. He didn't know that he was being used. He thought the Crown was genuine.'

'That's right. We've just said it must have been Kirilov who grabbed the Crown by the lake. If he knew the Crown was a fake why would he do that?'

'Why does Kirilov do anything?' Brasenose asked, speaking as much to himself as to me. 'Why did he shoot Modjeski and try to shoot Nowak? What did he bring over the border from Kaliningrad? Why did he decide to spy for the Americans in the first place? All we really know about him is that he's devious, utterly ruthless and he's a risk taker. The way he got away from Hoeven's people by getting the Russians to turn up at McDonald's was clever, it seems to have convinced Hoeven that Kirilov is still onside, but it was very risky. And now the call to Hoeven's office which he knows Hoeven wouldn't answer but which again demonstrates that he's still their man.'

I agreed. 'He must have realised we would have traced him to Vienna by now so he had nothing to lose by letting us know where he was.'

'Especially if he wasn't planning to be in Vienna for long. Blake tells me that Hoeven's people still believe Kirilov is running scared, has the KGB on his trail and will come back in as soon he's convinced it's safe to do so.'

'But Colin Asperton is back in Washington, hasn't he told Hoeven's office why we think Kirilov's heading for Trieste?'

There was a moment's silence and I thought the line might have gone. When he spoke again I hope Brasenose was having the grace to look embarrassed. 'Colin's primary task as Station Chief in Washington is to ensure that we are kept fully apprised of the thinking of our American cousins. There is no need for him to be distracted by possible developments in Trieste. When we need to keep the Company informed about our thinking I can talk directly to Lorrimore.'

It seemed we were as fractured internally as the Company.

Brasenose sounded genuinely bemused as he finished the call. 'I just can't believe Hoeven still trusts anything Kirilov says.'

I went to sleep thinking about that and woke up with my thinking no further forward.

I discussed it with Julia over breakfast. 'To us it seems obvious Kirilov is either working for the Russians in some way we don't understand or he is purely out for himself. In either event Hoeven has been unbelievably naïve. Kirilov came up with the story about a Polish peasant having come across the Great Crown of Jan Kazimierz and incredibly Hoeven was taken in hook, line and sinker. Then Kirilov set up the meeting by the lake which went horribly wrong but still Hoeven kept believing him. And now Kirilov takes off halfway round the world claiming the KGB are after him and again Hoeven gives him the benefit of the doubt. Why?'

'I don't know,' Julia replied, 'but remember we don't trust Kirilov because we have linked the alias he used in Sweden to the consignment on the *Mavri Lefkota* and we've linked that consignment back to the story Kacper Nowak gave us. As far as we know, Hoeven hasn't made that connection.'

'No he hasn't. But he must have asked himself questions about Kacper Nowak's story. He knew Jaszczak was bringing weapons in through the docks in Gdańsk where Nowak claims someone tried to kill him. And we've told him the Poles are claiming Jaszczak's people shot two Polish officers in Gdańsk. Surely Hoeven would have asked Jaszczak about it. Perhaps Jaszczak said that Kirilov had shot Modjeski because Modjeski was on to them. Jaszczak and Hoeven are both action men. Neither of them would have lost any sleep over the death of a Polish SB officer.'

Julia nodded. 'So there could be one thing that the Americans and Russians agree on, Modjeski discovered the gunrunning and Kirilov killed him.'

'That could be true, and they could both be wrong. What did Nowak actually say he and Modjeski were doing when he was shot?'

Julia was thoughtful. 'He didn't suggest in any way that his friend was investigating some sort of crime. He said they were helping a Russian get two cases across the border into Poland and into the docks at Gdańsk.'

'We think Kirilov was the Russian but why were Nowak and Modjeski helping him?' I asked. 'They may have been bribed or Modjeski may have been a conscientious SB officer who thought they were helping a KGB colonel in the performance of his duties. We may never know. But I'm convinced that, whatever both the Russians and Hoeven may believe, Modjeski wasn't shot because he found out about Jaszczak's gunrunning. He was killed because Kirilov didn't want anyone discovering that he was smuggling something out of Russia via Gdańsk.'

'The Chinese cases?'

'Yes, the two cases that were put in some sort of container, shipped off to Helsinki and are now approaching Trieste.'

'And we still have no idea what's in them. What would anybody want to move from Kaliningrad to Trieste?'

Julia had asked a good question and I mulled it over as I sipped the last of my coffee. There was something else she had just said that triggered something in the back of my mind but there it stayed as we returned to our room.

When the hotel had opened in 1911 it had been lauded as the most luxurious in the whole of the Austro-Hungarian Empire. Now it was looking a little tired but our room on the first floor offered a wonderful view across the bay.

We could just make out the white fairy tale castle of Miramare, built by the twenty-four-year-old Archduke Maximilian before he made the mistake of crossing the Atlantic to become Emperor of Mexico. It occurred to me that Hoeven would have been proud of the way his predecessors had run the guns into Mexico that brought Maximilian down and led to the proud but misguided liberal facing a firing squad at Querétaro.

When we had arrived our room had seemed enormous but now, as I pushed the door open, it didn't appear that way. The presence of three large men rifling through our belongings seemed to make the room shrink. Two of them looked very familiar.

XXIV

Hoeven looked up. 'What the hell are you doing here?' he demanded.

'That's what I should be asking you,' I shot back.

Ethan Jacobs, the Company's Moscow Station Chief, managed a weak grin. The third man, who I didn't recognise, moved around Julia and closed the door behind us.

'Don't try to be funny with me,' Hoeven responded. 'What the hell are you doing in Trieste?'

I didn't answer but Julia did.

'Put my knickers down you pervert,' she shouted. 'Get out.'

Hoeven's startled expression was almost comical. I don't think he realised what he was holding. He dropped the offending garment like the proverbial hot cake but he was not going to be deflected.

Ignoring Julia he looked directly at me. 'We need to talk. Now.' He retreated to the window.

'If you want to talk you start. Why are you here?'

Hoeven glared at me but I wasn't going to be intimidated. There was nothing I could say: he obviously wasn't going to believe we were here on holiday. It was an absurd situation. One of us had to give way.

Finally Jacobs broke the silence.

'We are meeting an asset and we don't need you queering the pitch.'

'Not Kirilov again?'

Hoeven jumped on my question. 'Why would you think that? Why would Kirilov be in Trieste?'

I had to be careful. Brasenose would not thank me for revealing anything he had learned from Lorrimore in confidence.

'Because Jacobs is here, Kirilov's handler. Why else would you bring someone from Moscow with you?'

'I handle lots of assets,' Jacobs started, but he was cut off by Hoeven.

'This is crap. You're here because you knew Kirilov was here. How did you know? Where did you pick him up? Vienna? The Austrians are good, they tracked him to the Brenner Pass for us. Real cooperative we thought. Did they tell you he crossed into Italy?'

I still wasn't saying anything.

Hoeven crossed the room and stood with his face inches from mine. 'That's it isn't it? You traced his hire car, like we did. Now let me tell you something. If you go anywhere near that car, if you make any contact at all with Kirilov, I will personally ram my fist right down your throat. This is our operation. Nothing at all to do with you.'

I smiled at him. 'This isn't your operation: Kirilov's gone rogue. He wants you to believe the Russians are after him and he'll come in when he's lost them but the truth is he's playing with you.'

'To hell with you,' snarled Hoeven. 'Just go home. You don't understand anything about this operation.' Hoeven gestured to the man still standing guard at the door. 'Mitch here will be sticking to you closer than your shadow right up until you take the plane back home. And that better be soon.

Everything you've touched you've fucked up. We've known Kirilov for years. He's produced the goods for us. He's our man, we own him. And now we need to talk to him, and we don't need you idiots getting in the way.'

'Perhaps you owned him once. But now? He persuaded you to buy a crown that turned out to be fake. He gave you dirt on David Prince that turned out to be fake. And now he's telling you he's running from KGB killers.'

'And he is,' put in Jacobs. 'They tried to grab him in the States.'

'And how did they find him?' I asked. 'You don't think that perhaps he arranged that himself to create an excuse to get away from you?'

'You're mad,' said Jacobs. 'Why would Kirilov do that? We are his protection. What possible reason would he have for flying off to Europe? Nobody would come to this asshole of a town unless somebody was chasing them. There's nothing here.'

Hoeven was nodding and I realised that the two of them really did have no idea why Kirilov might have been heading for Trieste. They had simply been following him from Vienna. Julia had been right, Hoeven hadn't found the connection with the *Mavri Lefkota.*

'Let's go,' Hoeven said to his two companions. 'We're wasting time.' He turned to me.

'Remember, Mitch will be in the lobby. Whatever your precious Justin Brasenose has told you to do, don't do it. And tell him he hasn't heard the last of this. If he ever wants anything from the Agency again he can go whistle.'

As he turned to the door Julia had a last question. 'How did you find us?'

Hoeven turned back, he had forgotten she was there.

'We found you because unlike you we're professionals. We're thorough. When we're looking for someone we put the effort in. We're checking every hotel in Trieste. And lo and behold at the first one on the list up pops a familiar name: Thomas Dylan. Your husband didn't even use a cover. You're out of your depth here. Like I said, go home.'

'That was a good question,' I said to Julia when the Americans had gone. 'So they weren't looking for us. They're looking for Kirilov. It seems he hasn't contacted them again as he promised.'

'And the Excelsior is the first hotel on their list so they've only just started. They probably spent all night looking for Kirilov's hire car.'

'It looks like they found the car but no sign of Kirilov. No doubt Hoeven has someone watching the car just in case, but my guess is Kirilov won't go anywhere near it again. We'd better call Brasenose.' I was confident Hoeven had not had time to tap the phone.

Brasenose had nothing new to say other than to report that our man in Helsinki had come up trumps again. He had been trying to establish who Jaszczak had met when he claimed to have bought the Crown in the Finnish capital. He had not been successful in that but he had come up with two new pieces of information.

First he had established that someone using the name of Kacper Nowak's friend Tadeusz Modjeski had been staying in Helsinki at the time. More importantly the man bore a striking resemblance to the photofit we had issued of the Port Gaverne gunman, Scarface. It was the first real confirmation of Brasenose's theory that Kirilov and Scarface were working together, Kirilov stealing the Crown and then passing it to Scarface to sell.

The second item came from Supo, the Finnish Intelligence Service. They confirmed that the day before Jaszczak arrived they had received a visitor at their headquarters in Punavuori. Ethan Jacobs had made clear that it was purely a courtesy visit, he was meeting an old friend for lunch the next day before returning to Moscow. In the peculiar circumstances of Helsinki, where there always seemed to be more spies per square mile than anywhere outside of Berlin, such a courtesy was not unusual. The head of the Company's Moscow Station visiting the country unannounced would have caused far more concern, as we had seen in Sweden.

'What does it mean?' Julia asked when I relayed Brasenose's news.

'Probably nothing. I suspect Jacobs was just keeping an eye on Jaszczak.'

'In which case he might have seen Jaszczak buy the Crown from Scarface, if that's what happened.'

Julia was right, but I wasn't sure what that implied. We were interrupted by Brasenose phoning back. This time it was just to confirm that our target, by which he meant the *Mavri Lefkota*, was on time. That meant that if Kirilov was in Trieste he should be able to collect his consignment some time that evening or more probably next day.

'Which doesn't mean he will,' Julia commented.

'True. Anyway it's time to explore Trieste.'

'What are we going to do about Mitch, the chaperone Hoeven has given us?'

'This morning we'll just play tourist, after lunch we need to lose him. If he's planning to keep us under discreet surveillance from a distance that will be easy. You need a team to do that properly. If on the other hand he is planning to operate close protection style, right on our heels, that might be more difficult.'

'Oh we can deal with that,' said Julia. 'Hoeven can't have a full team here, he's put one man on to watch two people. He's ignored me. We'll go dress shopping. I'll find a nice dress, go off to the changing room and when I do you leave the shop. He'll stay with you and you can lead him round town all afternoon while I get to work. It doesn't need two of us to do a recce at the port.'

I didn't like that idea at all. Julia operating solo was definitely not an option. After all, she was pregnant, I caught myself thinking, and mentally told myself never to make a remark like that to her. But if Brasenose's theory was right, Kirilov had already killed the two American agents Flanagan and Sokolowski and quite probably the Polish peasant delivering the Crown, not to mention Kacper Nowak's friend in Gdańsk. I didn't want Julia coming up against him on her own.

'I'd rather we stayed together. There's a lot to find out. We need to thoroughly scout the port and discover where the consignment is being held and what the procedure is for Kirilov to collect it. In particular try to find out when it will be available for collection. As you said, there is no guarantee it will be collected today or even this week. It was held in Helsinki for weeks before it was put on board the *Mavri Lefkota*. That's the biggest problem we've got. Even if we can find a way into the port area there is no way we can sit watching a cargo shed for a week without Hoeven finding out.'

'You just don't want me getting all the action,' replied

Julia. 'If we split up Mitch will follow you, that's for sure. I can get down to the port without anyone realising I'm even missing.'

Julia was right but there was an even better way to take advantage of the situation.

'I've got another idea. You leave Trieste and go to Venice. Leave everything to me.'

'You can't be serious,' Julia started to object, but then noticed the grin on my face.

'It's seems stupid to you,' I explained, 'but it won't to someone like Hoeven. He'll think you're out of the picture. We go to the train station and buy you a ticket to Venice, I'll kiss you goodbye, you get on the Venice train and I will lead Mitch away for a wild goose chase. You get off the train before it leaves and you'll have time to do far more than just scout out the port. Check us out of the hotel, hire a car and find somewhere to stay outside Trieste that's discrete enough that our friends won't find it in a hurry. Then you can make a few enquiries at the port and pick me up back at the station. I'll find some way to shake off Mitch this afternoon. But be careful.'

We set off. The station was a ten-minute walk away along the waterfront with the Adriatic on our left and example after example of magnificent Habsburg architecture on our right. Occasional glimpses of red roofs on the hillside beyond hinted at the tightly packed medieval streets of the old Venetian city.

We fought against a biting, gusting wind coming down from the north which whipped the sea into white crests.

'The wind can get much worse than this,' said Julia. 'It's the bora, cold air over the mountains rushing down to the

286

sea. It happens when there is high pressure to the north and low pressure over the warmer Adriatic. It's the only katabatic wind in Europe.'

If I had said that I would have been showing off but Julia had a way of making such comments seem perfectly natural.

'I must have missed out on your classical training,' I commented, to show that I at least realised that the word katabatic probably had a Greek origin.

Julia smiled. 'Nothing classical about it, just the staff at Cranwell thinking that all RAF officers would need to understand winds even if they were women and therefore would never be allowed to fly.'

There was no answer to that. I looked behind us. Mitch had adopted a style midway between surveillance and protection, trailing along fifteen or twenty feet behind, making sure we always knew he was there: more intimidation than observation.

The square on which the station stood would not have been out of place in Vienna. The monumental terminus, its walls the Schönbrunn yellow of the Habsburgs, typified the glorious self-confidence of an empire about to die. The high ceiling of the central vestibule, supported by Corinthian columns, had the same dimensions as the walls and floor so that we seemed to be walking into a giant cube decorated with stone wreaths and demonstrating the pride of railway engineers the world over. It had been built in 1878 to replace the more modest building constructed when the magnificent Südbahn Austrian railway crossed the mountains and reached the Adriatic in 1857, effectively linking Trieste at one end of the Austro-Hungarian Empire with Lviv 900 miles away at the other. For a moment I imagined that the consignment on the *Mavri Lefkota* might contain the real Great Crown of Jan Kazimierz on its way back to Lviv, but the fantasy quickly passed.

Crossing the square we passed a small group of schoolchildren being marshalled by an elderly teacher. As they pulled their coats tightly around themselves we heard him explaining that there had once been a statue of Sissi, the Austrian Empress Elisabetta, on this very spot, but now that Italy was free again it had no need for such monuments to the best forgotten past.

I wonder what the teacher would have said had he known that less than twenty years later the statue would be restored to the square in a sign that a more confident Italy no longer needed to rewrite its history.

We bought Julia a ticket to Venice and, after kissing me quickly goodbye, she walked off through a huge decorated arch leading to the platforms, platforms replaced in the twenty-first century when the station was 'modernised' by the addition of the assorted shops and pizza bars that the Habsburg engineers had not realised every railway needs.

Without waiting to see her reach the train I turned and walked quickly from the station. The schoolchildren had crossed the square and were now being told by their teacher that in 1904 the famous English writer James Joyce had arrived here to start a new life. There was something ironic in a teacher so insistent on the purity of his own nationalism describing the Irish-born Joyce as English.

Trieste was as much a symbol of the consequences of unbridled ethnic hatred as Warsaw had been. The Habsburgs had at first been content to rule over a multinational empire but towards the end adopted a policy of Germanisation in their Italian-speaking territories. Only half of Trieste's population had been Italian speakers when Italy annexed the region after the First World War but Slovenian and German speakers had soon been 'cleansed'. Then came the Second World War and the Germans built Italy's only extermination camp in the city, obliterating, amongst others, the city's Jewish population. At the end of the war Tito's Yugoslav partisans and the New Zealand Second Division arrived in Trieste at the same time and for forty days the New Zealanders watched in horror as the partisans murdered thousands of German prisoners of war, Croat fascists and Italian democrats singled out to the partisans by their Italian Communist comrades. Finally the partisans were forced out but the scars remain.

I congratulated myself that the world had come a long way since then. I wasn't to know then that just across the frontier the tensions that had started to boil over with the death of Josip Tito would soon be ripping Yugoslavia apart in an orgy of ethnic bloodletting.

I decided that I should at least try to mend fences with the Company. When I had walked as far as the Grand Canal I turned and approached the American behind me.

'This is ridiculous, Mitch. We're on the same side here. I'm going to the Revoltella Museum and then having lunch. Even if you don't like art let's at least have lunch together.'

The burly American didn't smile. 'Sure, Mr Dylan. And you can explain what you're doing here.'

'I'm on holiday.'

'I don't think my boss wants me to waste time exchanging vacation stories.'

He moved away and stayed behind me all the way round

the museum. When I found a restaurant for lunch he went off to use the phone, presumably to report in, and then sat down at a table as far away from me as possible, as if fearing I might infect him with something, British humour perhaps.

I ordered prawns, *gamberoni burro e aglio*, followed by *fusi fatti in casa con tartufo nero istriano*, pasta with local black truffles. Sitting at a table by the window, I settled down for a leisurely lunch. Mitch looked on disapprovingly when the waiter brought me my wine, a single glass of the local white Vitovska. I felt the same when he ordered Coke to accompany exquisite Italian seafood.

As an exchange student in Rome my friends and I used to spend hours sitting in bars people watching. Italy was starting to recapture the fashion crown stolen by swinging London in the 1960s. Milan had taken over from Florence with new names like Armani and Versace. It was clear that although Trieste had only officially been Italian again for twenty-seven years the Italian sense of style had survived. Even in the cold December wind mini-skirted women in their warmest winter coats held themselves with studied elegance, although some of their male companions had retained the solid, sensible dress of their fathers. Two youngish men meeting each other across the street had none of the natural grace I had envied in Rome.

Just then my food arrived, giant butterfly cut prawns swimming in butter, garlic and lemon juice. Magnificent. Mitch gave no indication that good food was important to him which was fortunate since he had no time to start eating before Ethan Jacobs strode through the restaurant to Mitch's table.

Clearly Jacobs was in a hurry. He scowled in my direction

as Mitch summoned a waiter and then waited impatiently for the bill to arrive. Pushing his meal away Mitch slapped down a handful of 10 000 lire notes and followed Jacobs, who was now shoving past a man trying to enter the restaurant. The man gave up and walked away. It took me a moment to realise that it was one of the men I had seen across the street. I looked out of the window in time to see the other man, who had been staring intently into the window of a shop selling antiques, turn and move off after Jacobs and Mitch.

I could have leaped to my feet and followed after them but by now they were almost out of sight. There was no way I could be sure of catching them.

It was Jacobs, I realised, who was being followed; if one of the men had been watching Mitch there would have been no need to enter the restaurant to see who Jacobs was meeting.

The Company's Moscow Station Chief would be well known to the other side. If I was right that the Russians had been on to Kirilov for at least three months they would undoubtedly have discovered that Jacobs was Kirilov's handler. It was quite possible that when Jacobs had suddenly left Moscow for Vienna someone in the Lubyanka had simply decided to see what he was up to. By then they would have known that Kirilov had left the USA and might well have traced him as far as Vienna. For part of his journey Kirilov had been using the name Karacek and we knew the Russians had discovered that alias in Sweden. It wouldn't have been difficult to follow Jacobs to Trieste, I doubt if he did anything to hide his tracks. I had to tell Brasenose right away.

XXV

The world's first cellular phone system had been introduced in Sweden and Norway two months earlier but it would be a long time before mobile phones reached Italy. I wasn't even sure I could reach London from the restaurant's landline.

'Can you phone England from here?' I asked the waiter.

He assured me I could, he had done it himself. But when I got up to make the call the manager hurried over. I could not use the phone now he explained. Why not? He seemed horrified: surely I understood that it was not possible to reheat my prawns, it would destroy the texture. He would delay the pasta, he suggested, so that I could phone after I had finished my first course. A commendable sense of priorities.

The prawns were delicious and I did not rush to finish them quickly.

The phone was behind the counter in full view of the crowded restaurant. When I reached him Brasenose could hear the background noise and understood why I needed to be guarded in what I said.

'Just thought I should tell you I'm now alone, the stationmaster changed the plans.'

'The stationmaster?'

'From the east.'

'Jacobs?'

'That's right. He's got some friends with him but he doesn't seem to know that.'

'You mean he's under surveillance?'

'Right again.'

'Locals?'

'Almost certainly not. Further east.'

'The Opposition?' I could hear the shock in his voice. 'If they're in Trieste that really changes things. I'll have to call Lorrimore. This isn't the time for faction fighting. You must tell Hoeven, if you can get hold of him. Lorrimore tells me there's complete radio silence from Hoeven and his whole team.'

He ended the call.

The truffles gave my pasta a deliciously earthy, musky scent.

It was all very well Brasenose telling me to contact Hoeven but I had no idea where he was. Hopefully he would find me again.

I decided I had time for an apple strudel, one of Austria's great gifts to the world.

After finishing my meal I spent nearly an hour checking to see if there was anyone on my tail before meeting Julia. She had been busy. She had found us a 'sweet little apartment' near Muggia, less than half an hour east of Trieste, but, she added, we wouldn't be needing it.

'Why not?'

'Because I know when and where Kirilov is planning to collect his fabric samples.'

'How on earth have you discovered that?'

'I went to the port and asked.'

'You did what!'

293

'I found some sort of central administration office. Very nice people, obviously not used to female visitors. Amazingly nobody on the reception spoke much English but they found me a charming young man named Marco who did and he couldn't do enough to help. I explained that I was from Finland and was expecting some fabric samples from Helsinki. I was supposed to collect them from the shipping agent, Signor Karacek, but I had lost his address and couldn't find him in the phonebook. But I knew the name of the ship so I thought I would come down to the port and see if I could meet Signor Karacek there.'

'And Marco believed you?'

'Of course. He wanted to help a damsel in distress. I had come to the wrong place, he said, but no matter he would make some phone calls for me. When Brasenose said that the *Mavri Lefkota* was a Greek tramp I imagined it would be a small freighter carrying all sorts of odd stuff. In fact it's quite a size and has two large shipments from Helsinki and Marseilles that will take hours to unload. But it also has just one small unrelated consignment, the fabric samples. Apparently it's very unusual for such a small item to arrive like that and it can't be processed where the *Mavri Lefkota* is being unloaded. So it will have to go through a different customs process.

'It's all quite complicated here because of course Trieste is a Free Port, all sorts of customs exemptions apply. Marco managed to discover that the samples are being transferred to a small warehouse away from the berthing dock. And that's when we really struck lucky. When he phoned the warehouse he discovered that the samples are being collected by Kirilov at seven o'clock this evening.'

I was surprised. 'My experience of Italian bureaucracy is that nothing works at that speed or with that precision. I know Trieste still has a reputation for Germanic efficiency but I will be amazed if anyone can guarantee that a cargo that is probably still on the high seas right now will be available to be picked up at seven o'clock.'

'Yes, Marco was surprised. But apparently Kirilov, alias Karacek, has made special arrangements. Marco suggests he may have given what he described as "a little envelope" to smooth the way.'

'A little envelope, what they call *bustarella*, a backhander, not so Germanic after all. But what that means is that Kirilov is here, he's already been to the port.'

'Yes and no. Karacek has been to the port.' Julia paused to give emphasis to her next words. 'He was there sometime last week.'

'Last week?'

'Yes, last week, when Colonel Konstantin Kirilov was tucking into breakfast at McDonald's on the other side of the Atlantic.'

So the Karacek who had arranged to collect the consignment today was not the man who had been using that name before, it was not Kirilov. Did that mean that Kirilov, our wildcard, was not acting alone? Had, as Lorrimore had once suspected, Kirilov and Hoeven cooked something up between them? Or was it all part of some elaborate Russian deception? In my own mind the most likely explanation was that the man who had pretended to be Karacek a week ago was a man we called Scarface.

'He's the one player we don't have a handle on,' Julia agreed. 'Our mysterious assassin.'

I explained to Julia that Brasenose wanted us to contact the Americans and alert them to the fact that Jacobs was under surveillance.

'Easier said than done,' she replied. 'Let's go to the port first and see where we are expecting Kirilov to appear. Perhaps Hoeven will be there ahead of us.'

The address Julia had been given was not in the actual port but further back from the sea, beyond the new container terminal and just a few miles from the Yugoslav border. It was a single-storey building which appeared to be a warehouse with an office at the front and a loading bay at the back. There was a parking area at the side, although the employees seemed to park their own cars on the road outside. A wire fence ran between the building and the road but the gate into the parking area was wide open and looked as if it was never closed.

It was surprisingly quiet. Julia parked near the loading bay and I walked back to the office entrance. It was shut and a sign informed me that office hours were 8 a.m. to 1 p.m. and 4 p.m. to 7 p.m. I looked at my watch: 3.50. I could see someone inside but he paid me no attention. There were a couple of vans parked nearby with the drivers chatting to each other.

I returned to Julia. 'Let's see what happens at four o'clock,' I suggested.

'OK, but we are very visible here.'

Julia drove back to the main road. Cars were parked along one side of the road but we easily found a space about 100 yards away from the warehouse. There was a reasonable view of the loading bay and the parking area nearby. Just before four o'clock the doors to the office were unlocked and a few members of staff arrived, but there was no sudden surge of activity. A car drove around to the back of the building, dropped someone off and drove out again. The man ambled slowly around the loading bay and let himself in through a door at the side.

We stayed there for half an hour and the only thing of interest was the setting of the winter sun. In that time half a dozen lorries and vans collected small consignments from the back of the building and as we were leaving a large container arrived for unloading. The building was clearly a storage facility for small low-value shipments that had cleared customs inside the port and were now awaiting collection. Security did not seem to be a priority.

Julia and I spent the next couple of hours driving or walking around Trieste trying to find the Americans. We failed. We later learned that Hoeven, Jacobs and Mitch had been watching a blue Fiat 132 which they had discovered had been hired that morning by someone using a Virginia driving licence in the name of King, a licence the Company itself had manufactured for Konstantin Kirilov. No attempt had been made to hide the car: Jacobs discovered it parked near the university. Kirilov must have been confident that he had lost any pursuers in Vienna.

We returned to the warehouse at 6.30, by which time the sun had long since set. We managed to park a little closer than before. There were two vans loading at the back of the building and another waiting in the parking area nearby. There was a lot of traffic on the road but very little of it turned into our warehouse. We settled back to see what would develop.

'Not long now,' said Julia. 'Perhaps we will finally find out what was in those Chinese cases.'

'Brasenose is sure they weren't Chinese,' I reminded her.

'There was Chinese writing on them,' she insisted. 'Kacper told us that and I believe him.'

I started to argue but thought better of it. Julia had called them Chinese cases at breakfast and something had jarred. We had been asking ourselves what anyone would want to ship from Kaliningrad to Trieste. And suddenly I knew. The answer was nothing. Nothing was being smuggled out of Kaliningrad via Poland to Italy. We had been looking through the wrong end of the telescope. Kirilov's Chinese cases had never been on that ship and I was right, they weren't Chinese.

'We've got it all wrong,' I said. 'All of us. We've been asking the wrong questions. Think right back to the beginning in Olsztyn. We were in the back of that tiny car and Flanagan explained what Operation Coronation was all about. We were going to buy the fabled Great Crown of Jan Kazimierz for a lot of money, money the agent Krypton would be bringing to the meeting. Now why would Krypton be bringing it?'

'Because it was too dangerous for Flanagan and Sokolowski to carry that sort of money around.'

'That's right, although it seems to me the same could be said of Krypton. But consider the practicalities: where would Krypton get that sort of money? He can't just go into a bank and ask for it.'

'From Jaszczak.'

'Yes, we know that now, but the same question arises. Where did Jaszczak's people find hundreds of thousands of dollars in cash? Even if you've got a successful business you can't just draw that sort of money out, especially in a country like Poland, and especially in a foreign currency.'

'Jaszczak must have brought it in from the US.'

'Smuggled it in, you mean. There is no legitimate reason to bring that amount into Poland in cash. And how does he smuggle it in?'

'Through Gdańsk.' Julia was starting to see where I was heading. 'He brought in the dollars in the same way as he brought guns in. By then the routines were probably well established.'

'Yes,' I agreed. 'Established in part by Kirilov. That's what Kirilov was doing at the port with Nowak and Modjeski. He was using them to steal the money that Jaszczak had sent to buy the Crown. Nowak told us they brought the Chinese cases in from Kaliningrad and put them in a container, swapping them for similar sized cases that were there already. We assumed it was that container which was then shipped out and is now here. But the Chinese cases weren't shipped out, they were put in the container that had just arrived. It was the cases that had originally been in that container that were transferred somewhere else and then shipped out, and those cases contained the money Jaszczak was smuggling into Poland to buy the Crown. Kirilov must have known when the money was arriving and he swapped it for the cases he had brought from Kaliningrad. Then he had the money put into a consignment of fabric samples and shipped off to Helsinki and onwards to Trieste. A million dollars is not that heavy, say fifty kilograms in twenty-dollar bills, much less in hundreds. That's what's on the *Mavri Lefkota*: the money that we were supposed to see handed over to a peasant in a hut in the Masurian Lakes.'

'But hold on, Thomas. That won't work. Jaszczak's people would have arrived at the docks the next day, collected the cases and discovered that the money had gone. Jaszczak was definite: his men checked the money before they handed it over to Kirilov. They would have found whatever Kirilov had in those Chinese cases.'

'I wonder. Would they really have checked? Did they know what they were checking? And you keep saying Chinese cases, but the writing wasn't Chinese. It just looked Chinese.'

Julia was perplexed. 'You mean it was Japanese. What difference does that make?'

'Not Japanese. Korean. Those cases originated in North Korea. And what do we know has been coming out of North Korea in great quantities?'

Julia's face lit up. 'Counterfeit dollars.'

'Exactly. Ethan Jacobs even mentioned back in Moscow that the Opposition were planning on dumping large quantities of counterfeit dollars in Western Europe. They're already flooding the Far East. Somehow Kirilov got hold of some. When he was in Korea probably, or perhaps through old contacts in Vladivostok or even when he was back in Moscow. However he did it he managed to get counterfeit dollars shipped to Kaliningrad. I doubt if he had anything like a million dollars but Jaszczak's people wouldn't have counted it. He may have put some real dollars on top, then the fakes and padded it out with paper. The North Korean forgeries aren't very good but they're good enough to fool a Polish factory worker who has probably never seen a dollar before. Like I was told in my little chat at Mokotów Prison we didn't take any money to the lake, just papers.'

I was now sure I understood what had happened. 'Brasenose described Kirilov as the wildcard and he was right. We haven't paid enough attention to what motivates him.'

'Money?' Julia suggested.

'Exactly. Money, purely and simply. Kirilov has always been in this for the money. The Americans have never suggested he was driven by a love of freedom and democracy. They put a lot of money into his Swedish bank account. But Kirilov wanted more. When the Russians fed him the story about someone finding a medieval crown he told Hoeven. And Hoeven did just what the KGB wanted him to do, he dreamed up Operation Coronation. Kirilov saw his chance to hit the big time. He was supposed to take Jaszczak's cash to the lake and exchange it for the Crown. At first he probably thought about simply stealing it and then disappearing. But somehow he got hold of fake North Korean dollars and decided he could steal Jaszczak's cash from the docks without anybody realising it had gone. He transferred the real dollars on to another ship and left the fake dollars there for Jaszczak's men to collect.'

'But why didn't he just steal the money in Gdańsk and disappear? Why risk going to the meeting at the lake?'

'He wanted the Crown.'

'To sell to Jaszczak in Helsinki?'

'Perhaps, but I doubt if he thought that far ahead. With the real dollars he becomes a rich man but he has the Russians on his tail for the rest of his life. The KGB never forgive one of their own who turns against them. He will always be a traitor, the American spy who got away. Except that they will never let him get away. Kirilov will always need protection, a foolproof new identity and somewhere to go to spend his money. And the only person he can turn to for that sort of protection is Hoeven. He has to keep Hoeven trusting him. But if the Americans realise the money has been stolen they are bound to suspect him.'

'Unless he produces the Crown.' Julia completed my thoughts. 'That's why he had to shoot the two Americans and the man bringing the Crown, Broniszewski.'

'Precisely. I think he intended to report back to Hoeven and Jaszczak that they had been jumped at the lake by mysterious armed men and only he had been able to get away, but fortunately he had managed to grab the Crown. So Operation Coronation could carry on.'

'But then the Polish Army turned up.'

'That's right. Kirilov doesn't need to invent any mysterious armed men. Now the Americans have their villains. They won't suspect him of anything. He doesn't need to give them the Crown. Instead he can try to sell it, like you suggested.'

Julia nodded but I could see she wasn't completely convinced. 'You could be right but it's all terribly elaborate. Surely Hoeven must have some doubts about Kirilov. How come Kirilov is the only one to get away when the shooting started? Would he really flee a safe house in Virginia to wander around Europe with the KGB chasing him? Why doesn't he just walk into the US Embassy in Vienna if he really wants protection? I keep coming back to the same question: why does Hoeven still trust him? It's almost as if Kirilov is bribing him.'

Julia could be right. In fact, I realised Kirilov and Hoeven could be in this together. 'Perhaps they cooked up the whole Operation Coronation business between them,' I suggested. 'Jaszczak appeared with a raft of crazy ideas but lots of money. Hoeven saw the opportunity to get rich and invented the fairy tale about a symbolic crown. I bet he had the Crown made in London himself. It wouldn't be the first time a longstanding Company agent has set up a rogue operation that funnels hundreds of thousands of dollars into his own bank account.'

Julia smiled, she knew the case I was talking about, but she wasn't convinced. 'Good try, Thomas, but that part of your theory just won't work. The Crown was commissioned by the Russians, not Hoeven. We've identified the man who ordered it.'

'But just because that man worked for a Russian airline doesn't mean he was acting for the KGB. Hoeven could've paid him to commission it.'

'Then how were the Russians able to invent the story they spun you in Warsaw about Jaszczak commissioning it from a Jewish goldsmith in London? They even knew his name, Rothenberg, they gave the name to that journalist.'

'Hoeven told them. By that stage he and Kirilov had sold the Crown to Jaszczak in Helsinki so they told the Russians about Rothenberg to throw us off the scent.'

Julia's smile widened. 'No, Thomas, stop. I buy Kirilov stealing the real dollars and replacing them with fakes but now you're clutching at straws. Something is keeping Hoeven and Kirilov together but you're making it far too complicated. Unless Kirilov has some sort of hold over Hoeven it must be that Hoeven still has a use for Kirilov. Perhaps he's planning to use him somehow in an internal battle with Lorrimore.'

That seemed fanciful to me but at the same time the final part of my theory was the weakest. I didn't like Hoeven but that didn't make him corrupt. And even if Hoeven was as corrupt as I suggested, I wasn't sure he had the sort of imagination needed to latch on to an obscure medieval legend from Central Europe and turn it into something as fanciful as Operation Coronation. Kirilov was in this for the money but Hoeven wasn't. Hoeven was genuine, a lifetime Company man. Julia was right, something else was binding him and Kirilov together.

Julia interrupted my thoughts. 'Look over there.'

A blue Fiat had arrived and trundled to the parking area, which by now was nearly empty, a solitary brown van waiting in one corner. As the Fiat passed under the bright electric lights that now illuminated the area we could see the car had a solitary occupant.

The Fiat parked well away from the waiting van and a man got out, took a coat from the back seat and started to button himself up against the freezing wind. It was Kirilov.

XXVI

'Is that him?' asked Julia.

'Yes, I'm certain.'

The Company hadn't given us any pictures of their agent but the ones taken by our man in Ystad were enough.

Kirilov hadn't finished buttoning his heavy winter coat when a black Mercedes swung into the car park and shuddered to a stop just in front of him. Hoeven and Jacobs jumped out. We couldn't hear what they said but Kirilov clearly wasn't expecting them. He started to get back into his car but Jacobs pushed him roughly on to the bonnet of the Mercedes.

'Come on,' I said. 'We need to talk to Hoeven.'

We started to walk towards Kirilov and the Americans. Mitch, who had been driving the Mercedes, appeared to have Kirilov in an armlock. As we drew closer I could hear Hoeven shouting at the Russian. 'I don't believe you, Ethan saw him in Finland.'

Kirilov tried to break away from Mitch's grip but then stopped and looked directly in our direction. I thought he was looking at me until I heard the sound of vehicles behind us. A large black van rocketed past and screeched to a halt behind the Americans' Mercedes. Five men jumped out as the three Americans spun round with startled expressions on their faces. Only Kirilov seemed to realise what was happening.

I stopped moving but felt a prod in my back.

'I told you Kirilov was ours,' said a voice behind me. I turned to find the Russian I had last seen across the table at the prison in Mokotów. Behind him was another black Mercedes, its driver now standing looking at me with a Russian PSM semi-automatic pistol in his hand. In the eight years since the PSM's introduction it had become a KGB favourite, there was no need to guess who had arrived.

'Please join your American colleagues,' said the Russian. In case I didn't understand, his companion gestured with the gun.

Hoeven was looking incredulously at the men who had jumped out of the van. I recognised two of them as the men I had seen following Jacobs earlier. Each of the Russians held a small black pistol. The three-inch long barrels made the weapons look toy-like but they were not toys, the PSMs had proved capable of penetrating the new Kevlar vests the Service had been trialling.

Without warning one of the men span round and delivered a blow to Kirilov's neck. It was a perfect chop to the carotid sinus and Kirilov collapsed to the floor. He was lifted effortlessly into the back of the van before Hoeven could even start to protest.

'You can't do that,' Hoeven shouted; not the most sensible comment to make as the Russians had just shown that they could do exactly that.

'You can't get away, the police will be on to you the moment you leave.'

Even Hoeven must have realised how lame that sounded.

'I think not,' replied my friend from Mokotów. 'By the time the Italian police are waking up we will be out of Italy, you must realise how close we are to the frontier. Just in case you have other ideas we will take Mr Jacobs with us. We can exchange stories of Moscow Nights until we reach the border. And I warn you, if you try to stop us Mr Jacobs may find himself lying in the middle of a very busy road, like your friend Mr Jaszczak.'

And that was it. Less than two minutes after they had arrived the Russians had left. Their whole operation had been clinically precise. Almost before we realised what was happening they were gone, taking Kirilov and Jacobs with them.

Hoeven was furious and needed someone to vent his fury on. 'You brought the fucking Russians here,' he shouted at me. 'What the hell are you thinking of? I'll crucify you and your poxy agency.'

'We didn't bring them, Jacobs did. They've been following him around Trieste. We tried to warn you but you haven't been answering Lorrimore's messages.'

'Lorrimore? You've been working with Lorrimore. I'll crucify him too. We've just lost Krypton, one of the most valuable assets we've ever had. I promise you there will be hell to pay.'

'Rubbish. Kirilov hasn't been your asset for a very long time. He's just after the money.'

'Money? What money?'

'The money in that warehouse. The money you expected him to use to buy the Crown.'

'That's balls.'

I tried explaining it to him but he wouldn't listen. 'Are you trying to tell me that on that lake Kirilov just rowed off with two heavy cases full of dollars and nobody noticed?'

'He didn't need to; he'd already stolen the money. It never reached the lake.'

'Crap. Jaszczak's people never let the money out of their sight from the moment it left the docks until they passed it over to Kirilov in that stupid dinghy of his.'

Unless Hoeven was a very good actor, and he wasn't, he still did not understand what was going on. How could I have imagined that he himself was capable of cooking up something as complicated as all this?

'The money never left the docks. Kirilov swapped it. That's when he shot Tadeusz Modjeski.'

'What the hell are you talking about? Modjeski was SB, secret police.'

'I know. Kirilov was using him to steal the money Jaszczak had sent over to buy the Crown.'

'You're mad. Modjeski found out about the supplies we were smuggling in and tried to intercept them. If Kirilov hadn't been armed he might have got away with it. Luckily it was Modjeski who got the bullet. Unfortunately this Nowak guy was with him and managed to escape. When Nowak turned up in England Kirilov explained all that to Jacobs and we believe him. He's our man.'

'You're the one who's crazy,' I insisted. 'Why are you still protecting him? Can't you see that Operation Coronation was never your operation, it was Moscow's. They had the Crown made. It was their man Broniszewski, the peasant who turned out to be a lifelong Party man, who told Kirilov about the Crown in the first place. When your agents arranged to meet Broniszewski to buy the Crown the Russians had the hut staked out. They probably had it bugged but they didn't dare get too close in case Flanagan and Sokolowski searched the area first. But I bet they were close enough to Kirilov to see him collecting the money from Jaszczak's men. Those men weren't from Jaszczak's cell in Torun were they? From the factory where the authorities found an arms dump a few days later, supposedly by chance?'

Hoeven didn't reply. I pressed on. 'I bet they were. The Russians, like you, thought Kirilov was bringing sackfuls of cash to the meeting. But they discovered he wasn't. They told me in Mokotów. Kirilov had intercepted the dollars in the docks and sent them here to Trieste.'

Hoeven stared at me. 'What do you mean sent them here? Kirilov's only here because he's desperate to jump on a ship out of Europe. He's just told us that. The Reds have been on his tail since Vienna, since before, since Virginia. I told Lorrimore that and I've been proved right. Now they have him.'

'Jaszczak's money is here,' I repeated. 'It's in the warehouse behind us. We've been following it from the Baltic, that's why we came to Trieste. Kirilov had it loaded on to a ship called the *Mavri Lefkota* which arrived here today.'

For once Hoeven looked deflated but he wasn't about to give up. 'But that's not possible. You've got it all wrong.'

Neither of us spoke. Julia's calm voice broke the silence. 'No, we didn't get it wrong, and you know we didn't. That's why you were screaming at Kirilov just now. We heard you. You shouted that Jacobs had seen someone in Finland. He must have seen the man who handed over the Crown in Helsinki. You realised then that Kirilov had gone rogue, how else could you explain Scarface appearing in Helsinki with the Crown?'

'Scarface?'

'The man who tried to shoot Nowak in Cornwall. The man so much of this has been about. The man who killed General Demirkan in Yaroslavl.'

Julia paused, as if she needed time to work out what she was going to say. When she spoke I don't know who was more shocked, Hoeven or me. 'Demirkan wasn't killed by the Russians. He was killed by you.'

Hoeven started to protest but Julia was not going to be interrupted. 'Turkey protects Europe's backdoor and stands between the Soviets and the oil in the Gulf. It provides essential bases for your spy planes. And Turkey has been in chaos. The government might have fallen at any moment and who knows who would have come out on top. It needed strong government, it needed, you decided, a military government. But the generals weren't united. And one general in particular stood in your way. Demirkan would have no truck with the hardliners, the ultra-nationalists like the Grey Wolves. His mother-in-law is Kurdish. He knew what a coup would mean to families like hers; today Kurds aren't even allowed to speak their own language in private!

'In your eyes Samet Demirkan needed to go, but President Carter had given a very specific ruling, Executive Order 12036, no involvement in assassinations, even indirect involvement. If Demirkan was to be killed it had to be by someone with no connections to the Company. But how to find someone like that in Russia? You can't just put an advert in the paper: assassin wanted. The only people who might know where to find a killer for hire were the police, especially the secret police. And you had a man right there. Kirilov. It was Kirilov who found Scarface for you, he set it all up. Kirilov was the cut-off; nobody would ever be able to link

Scarface back to you and Jacobs. But that gave him a hold over you, it meant you had to believe in him even when you knew in your heart he was lying.

'When he announced he'd found the Great Crown of Jan Kazimierz you must have had your doubts. But I expect he pleaded for you to trust him, pointed to all the solid intelligence he'd given you in the past. And he may well have believed he'd found the real thing. But by then the Soviets were on to him, they fed him a fairy tale and you swallowed it because you wanted to believe the man who had delivered you Demirkan. And you had to protect Scarface for the same reason, even when you knew he was running around England with a gun. Even when you knew he had tried to kill Nowak in Cornwall.'

I thought Hoeven was going to object but he didn't. His tone changed, his voice was suddenly calm, even boastful.

'Nowak was a loose cannon. We couldn't figure him out. Then Kirilov showed us his record: the guy was nuts. Unpredictable. At any moment he might have gone back home, told the commies everything he knew. When Fearmont told me he was going down to this place in Cornwall to interview Nowak, of course I told Kirilov to take him out. Anyway, what's important is that the world is now a safer place. Turkey is ours again. We've stabilised things. Demirkan was a Communist, but people listened to him. He would have ruined everything. And you're right, I couldn't have Kirilov blabbing to someone like Lorrimore. We've got Bill Casey running the Agency now, a man who understands that you can't defend liberty by sitting on your hands, but even he can't protect anyone who disobeys an Executive Order from the President of the United States. The

Democrats in Congress would have a field day if they knew that we had had any involvement in removing Demirkan. But now they won't know.'

Hoeven motioned Mitch to get into the car and start the engine. Turning to Julia he smiled, 'You've been a very clever young lady but you forget one thing. Kirilov was a threat, but he isn't now. We won't be seeing him again. You said he had a hold over us, perhaps that's true, but he hasn't any more.'

'No he hasn't,' I said, 'but the Russians have. One way or another Kirilov will tell them everything he knows.'

'But who will believe them?'

'That rather depends on what they can extract from Ethan Jacobs. Who knows where and when he'll turn up?'

Hoeven obviously hadn't thought of that possibility. 'They'll let him go at the frontier,' he said, 'they'll have to.' He slammed the door angrily and Mitch drove off.

Julia and I walked back to our car. There was nothing more we could do.

'We'll let the Italian authorities deal with Kirilov's fabric samples,' I said. 'I don't suppose the Company will try claiming the money back. You and I should take a break, perhaps we could use that sweet little apartment you found.'

Julia didn't reply. She was staring over my shoulder at a brown van that had just pulled away from the loading bay. The driver pulled out into the traffic and sped off. The fabric samples had gone. The lights of the oncoming cars caught the vertical black marks on the driver's face that could easily have been mistaken for scars.

AFTERWORD

The political background surrounding the declaration of martial law in Poland and the shock this occasioned to the White House have been depicted as accurately as possible. The CIA was widely criticised for what seemed to be a monumental intelligence failure. The truth, however, may be more complicated than my portrayal suggests. It is now known that the CIA had detailed knowledge of the plans General Jaruzelski had made. A member of the Polish General Staff, Colonel Ryszard Kuklinski, had been a long-term American agent and was spirited out of Poland with his wife and children just days before martial law was declared. The Agency also had accurate information on the preparedness of Russian forces which made clear that a Russian intervention was not imminent.

The intelligence failure was not in intelligence gathering but in its analysis. Put crudely, senior Agency and State Department officials simply did not believe Jaruzelski had the will to implement his plans. They were wrong.

Jaruzelski proved he had the will to crush Solidarity but he lacked the ability. Despite mass arrests and sometimes violent confrontations Solidarity continued to gather support. Communism eventually fell in 1989 and in 1990 Jaruzelski was succeeded as president by the Solidarity leader Lech Walesa. Since then there have been a series of democratically elected governments. However, the twin issues of nationalism and anti-Semitism remain hugely controversial in contemporary Poland.

I have based two episodes on real KGB operations. As suggested in the text the fictional bugging of equipment in the British Embassy in Warsaw reflects the known bugging of typewriters in the US Embassy in Moscow. The KGB's use of North Korean counterfeit dollars is also well known and was confirmed when US authorities in Dublin tried to extradite Sean Garland, a leading member of the Official IRA, who had travelled to Moscow for one such operation. I have, however, taken liberties with timing: in both cases the dates of the real operations were somewhat later than my fictional episodes.

Exodus of Spies

Brian Landers

EXTRACT FROM EXODUS OF SPIES

The killing of Adam Joseff stunned his friends and former colleagues.

Even after all these years I can still remember the shock and disbelief when my wife Julia phoned.

'Adam's dead. He's been shot. In Antigua.'

He had been killed by two shots to the back of the head, fired at close range. There were signs of a struggle but his wallet had been found untouched. The house itself had not been ransacked and nothing appeared to be missing. To many of us that made the initial police assumption of a bungled robbery seem very wide of the mark. Adam had been around long enough to know that if someone is pointing a gun at you the only sensible response is to put your hands up. Adam Joseff had been executed.

Because he had been a pillar of the Intelligence Establishment for so long there were inevitably calls for the Security Services to use their resources to investigate his death. But the reality was that he had retired nearly eight years ago and his death seemed to have no current security implications. My own Service could not get involved.

Why, we all asked ourselves, would anyone want to kill Adam? Collecting early postage stamps, rather than anything in his no doubt murky past, was what obsessed him now. And what was he doing in Antigua? Adam's only known connection with the Caribbean had been a best-forgotten operation in Trinidad many years ago.

The local police did ask for assistance and two Metropolitan Police detectives flew out to the Caribbean. They spent a week in Antigua but nothing new emerged. I was told they had produced a voluminous report but it was not until later that I had a chance to read it. The case remained unsolved. Back in London interest waned.

Adam's death would have remained one more mystery to be filed away and then forgotten but for the discovery of the second body.

That's when we started to realise that the killing of Adam Joseff had *everything* to do with the Security Services. His death, it became clear, was the result of a long chain of apparently unconnected events that went right back to a commando raid in Angola nearly three years earlier, Operation Argon.

***

Salvador da Silva Pinheiro, head of the Angolan Security Police, had been expecting the raid that the South Africans designated Operation Argon. He cursed only that he had received the details too late to do more than send a warning to the army commander in Cabinda on the very evening that Captain Du Toit and his men were going ashore. His mood was not improved when he heard that most of the South African raiding party had escaped.

'Have you heard the news from Cabinda?' demanded the Russian colonel who barged into Pinheiro's office the next morning.

Pinheiro turned. 'Please knock before you enter.'

The Russian merely nodded to acknowledge he had heard the reprimand. He wasn't about to apologise.

'The South Africans have attacked the oil storage tanks in Cabinda,' the Russian continued.

'Tried to attack. They were intercepted. Our forces captured one and killed two.'

'And the rest escaped.'

'The rest? You think there were more?'

'Of course. They will be back inside Zaire by now.'

Pinheiro said nothing. Why should he tell this arrogant pig that he knew for a fact that the raiding party had indeed been larger and that some did unfortunately seem to have escaped? And if the Russian wanted to believe they had crossed the frontier from Zaire let him. There was no point in telling him that he was wrong. The commandos had come by sea all the way from Saldanha Bay in South Africa's Cape Province.

The Angolan turned away. The Russians seemed to think that he should gratefully accept the crumbs of information that they were willing to pass him. But he no longer needed to rely on them. Now he had his own man in the enemy camp and he was not about to share him with anyone: not with his subordinates, not with the Russians, not even with his party comrades here in Luanda. Only one other person needed to know, and she could be trusted.

ABOUT THE AUTHOR

After giving up on an academic career, and deciding not to join the government spy agency GCHQ, Brian Landers helped a former Director General of Defence Intelligence and a motley collection of ex-spooks set up a political intelligence unit in the City of London. Out of that experience sprang the character of Thomas Dylan, a novice who over the years progresses through the labyrinthine world of British Intelligence.

Brian Landers has lived in various parts of North and South America and Europe. He has worked in every corner of the globe from Beirut to Bali, Cape Town to Warsaw and points in between, and in industries as varied as insurance, family planning, retailing, manufacturing and management consultancy. He saw the inside of more prisons than most during three years as a director of HM Prison Service. He has a Politics Degree from the University of Exeter and an MBA from London Business School. In his spare time he helped set up the Financial Ombudsman Service, served on the boards of Amnesty UK and the Royal Armouries, and was Chairman of Companies House.

Landers subsidised his university bar bills by writing a column for the local paper and since then has written articles for various journals, newspapers and websites. As a director of Waterstones and later Penguin his passion for writing was rekindled. His first book, *Empires Apart*, published in the UK, US and India, was a history of the Russian and American Empires. His next book was going to be *Trump, Putin and the Lessons of History* but the subject was so depressing that he turned to fiction.

In 2018 Brian Landers was awarded an OBE in the Queen's Birthday Honours.

brianlanders.co.uk

Find out more about RedDoor Press and sign up to our newsletter to hear about our **latest releases, author events,** exciting **competitions** and more at

reddoorpress.co.uk

YOU CAN ALSO FOLLOW US:

 @RedDoorBooks

 Facebook.com/RedDoorPress

 @RedDoorBooks